Keeping You

Book two in the Trilogy of Light and Dark

S.E DYMEK

ISBN: 979-8-9906015-1-2

Printed in the United States

First edition January 2026

Editor: B. Mauldin with Split in Two Editing

This book is a work of fiction

First Printing, 2026

Dedication

To Aaralyn, Ivy, and Caiden. My biggest inspirations for everything I do. To my husband, Aaron, who is my biggest support.

Acknowledgements

I'd like to thank my parents, close family, and all my inner, dearest friends who listened to me babble about ideas and were willing to read them. I love you all. Thank you to all my readers!

About the Author

S.E Dymek is an upcoming author who has published **The Alpha's War Series:** Including Between the Alpha's War, Breaking the Alpha Council, and The Beta's Betrayal. **The Star Saga** as well as **The Trilogy of Light and Dark** available with Barnes and Noble, Amazon, Kindle, and other book selling sites. She is also published on several ebook platforms. She has a passion for writing romance novels including paranormal romance novels and fantasy. All of her works include twists and turns, keeping her readers on their toes. She is a mother of three and loving wife. When she is not writing; she is working as a veterinary technician. Born and raised in Rhode Island, she has found her second home in Texas.

Follow her on social media:
Facebook: S.E Dymek
Instagram: sedymek
Tik Tok: @sedymek

Website: www.Sedymek.com

Key:

Silas: Death

Ryan: Guardian of the In-Between

In-Between: The place between Earth, Heaven and Hell

Kere: Goddess of night

Balor: Demon

Name Pronunciation

Note: There are several old world gods, goddesses, and demons in this novel, feel free to give them nicknames (as a reader myself, this is what I do) or if you would like below is a list of pronunciations..

Kere: K- EE- r- ess
Balor: Bay-Lor
Charon: Kare-ON
Rhadamanthus: Rhad-uh-man-thus
Minos: My-noss
Aeacus: Ee-uh-sus
Pavel: PAH-vehl
Mal'akh: mah-LAHKH
Nyx: nicks

…"Sunflower… why do you keep calling me that?" Jo smiled as she tried to suppress the tremor he was causing in her.

"I think you are the light in the dark that I have been looking for," Malcolm said as he wrapped his arms around her and his mouth moved to hers.…

Chapter One

     "No, no…no! Damn it!" Jo screamed as she slammed her fist into the steering wheel as the car rolled to a stop.

     "Shit, shit. Shit!" she yelled. Her hand throbbed from the blows she gave the car.

She felt pressure build up in her chest, like at any second her chest would crack and break. She pressed her head forward. Jo couldn't contain the long, painful scream that erupted from her. Anger and defeat washed over her as she tried to calm herself down.

     "This can't be happening!" she groaned out in frustration.

     "I'm not far enough," she whispered.

     She sank further into the leather steering wheel. She felt the weight of the world as it crushed her. Why did she think she could get away? He always found her. She felt a warm tear run down her bruised cheek. Her hands shook as she gently brushed the tear away. Everything still hurts so much from their last encounter. She straightened slowly in the seat, resting her head back. The headlights dimmed and faded out as the car lost power completely. She squeezed her eyes shut as she fought back the overwhelming need to curl in a ball and give up.

     "Ok," she said as she let out a long breath.

     "Ok. Jo, you have this. You can do this. We can figure this out," she told herself as she tried to come up with a plan.

The headlights flickered back on, and the beam of light hit a sign. Jo squinted to read it before the lights went back out. All she managed to catch was "five miles." She could walk five miles. She reached into the back seat and grabbed her backpack. With one quick jolt, she yanked it into the front seat. Her hand found the zipper and opened the front pocket. She pulled out the last bit of cash she had and counted it slowly.

"Fuck," she mumbled. Forty dollars was all she had left.

It would have been one more tank of gas and another three hundred miles, but now it was nothing. She had no car, no way of fixing it, and she was stranded.

"Fuck it," she muttered as she felt her stomach twist.

"One thing at a time." She shoved the cash back into the front pocket, zipped it and looped the bag over her shoulders.

She couldn't stay here. Jo would do anything to make sure she never went back. She hesitated as she got out of the car. It was so dark; she bit her lower lip nervously as she paused. She needed a weapon. Her eyes found the screwdriver in her car door pocket. She grabbed it, and she felt a little better. She opened the car door and stepped out onto the pavement. Her ankle wanted to give out with the slight pressure. She could still feel the burn marks from the iron cuff. Jo shook it off and slammed the car door in frustration. She tried to position the backpack so it wouldn't put too much pressure on her back and began walking.

She never intended it to get this far. It didn't happen overnight. How did she let this all happen? It was her fault, wasn't it? No, she never made him do any of those things. He chose that. Anger bubbled in her stomach and pushed her to walk faster. She focused on the anger and the rage. She needed it to keep going. The light blue walls riddled with cracks from where he pushed and threw her into them. The fist size holes that speckled the same walls, holes meant for her. Images of the small room popped into her head. There was nothing in the room. He had taken everything out but the mattress. The room had no windows, no sunlight, and no way out. She would sometimes be trapped there for days. Days that felt like years. She remembered the first night he had thrown her in there. Jo had thought that was it. She was never coming out. She would die there. Then one day he let her out. He said it was because she was good. She had to be good for him.

She was lost in the horrible thoughts that plagued her mind as she walked as fast as she could. Headlights came up behind her and pulled her from her thoughts. She heard the tires roll to a stop on the side and then the window began to roll down. She tightened her jaw, almost scared to look. Her eyes frantically looked to the side of the road. Could she run? Was it him? Did he find her? She tightened her grip on her bag, and her other hand lingered on her back pocket, where the screwdriver was tucked beneath her shirt.

"Hey, miss. Do you need some help? Need a ride?" he called through his rolled down window.

"I… um." She looked down the long dark road. It could take her hours to get to the next town on foot.

The longer she took, the closer he got to her. Her stomach twisted as she struggled with what decision to make.

"Ma'am?" He called to her again and leaned closer to the window to see if she was ok.

"Do you think you could give me a ride to town?" she asked him. Her voice showed all of her uncertainty.

"Sure, hop in. I am heading that way." He smiled as he pressed the button to unlock the car.

Jo started towards the car. She slowly pulled the screwdriver out of her back pocket and then slipped it into her hoodie pocket. She tucked her hand inside her pocket and gripped the screwdriver as tightly as she could. Her mind flashed with images of stabbing the man if he tried anything. Her jaw twitched as she grabbed the door handle with her free hand and opened it. She looked inside, and he smiled at her again. Jo paused for a second and reminded herself that she had to keep going. She got into the car and closed the door. She looked him over carefully as she adjusted herself in the seat.

"Do you need the heat on? It's a little chilly outside," the man said as he pulled back onto the road.

"It's ok…unless you want to, then…" Jo spoke awkwardly, unsure what to say.

She had been conditioned for so long to think that her needs didn't matter. She was never supposed to want or need anything. Not even things she needed to live.

"Ma'am, you're the one who was walking outside. If you're cold, then we turn on the heat." The

man laughed as he reached over and turned the knob on the dashboard.

Jo was silent but thankful for the warm air. Her toes throbbed from the cold. She leaned towards the vent.

"Knew you were cold." He laughed as he watched her lean forward.

"I'm Danny." He smiled as he glanced from her to the road again.

"Hi…thank you again," Jo whispered.

"You're welcome. It's actually Daniel, but I prefer Danny," Danny said, bringing up the name again.

Jo's mind was panicking. She knew why he had said his name again. He wanted to know hers. She couldn't say her real name. She couldn't leave any pieces of herself behind. Evan would find her.

"Iris," she blurted, as she asked herself who the hell Iris was, but it just fell out of her mouth, and it would work.

"That's pretty. Nice to meet you, Iris." Danny smiled big.

"Thanks," Jo said quietly.

"Was that your car back there? Broke down?" Danny asked with a nod of his head.

"Yeah," Jo answered simply.

"Gas or something else?" Danny asked. His eyes flicked from her to the road.

"I wish. Gas would be easy." Jo frowned.

"Well, maybe it's the battery. That would be easy, too," Danny said with reassurance.

Easy for you, Jo thought. The forty dollars she had left wouldn't cover a battery. She shut her eyes. She hadn't even thought about owing Danny for the ride.

"Danny, I…I don't have any money to give you-" Jo started to stutter out, but Danny stopped her.

"No need to. I'm going into town; I would be using this gas with or without you," he said with a smile.

Jo felt a rush of relief, and part of her was unsure if what he said was true. Were people this nice? Jo kept silent the rest of the drive. She was exhausted, and her body felt weighed down. She hadn't slept a full night in a long time. Her eyelids were heavy, and her head began to nod. She leaned her head against the window. She fought against the sleep that tugged at her but the car rocked on the old country road, and the slight bumps lulled her to sleep.

Malcolm

"I don't know why you hang around in this town. Nothing happens here. No fun, no excitement. Come to Vegas with me. There's so much….sin there. It's invigorating. It will make your bones vibrate." He grinned as he cupped the glass mug in his hand.

"I don't have any interest in Las Vegas," the man sitting next to him mumbled.

"When did you lose all your fun, Malcolm?" the man scoffed.

"Why do you continue to come back and pester me, Leo?" Malcolm snapped.

14

"I miss the old you. The adventures we had. Remember the brothels in Italy?" Leo continued as he swirled the alcohol in his cup.

"I don't want excitement. I just want to be left alone," Malcolm growled.

"Well, you picked a brilliant spot," Leo huffed.

"No one asked you to visit me," Malcolm said as he tapped his glass with his finger.

A young brunette came by and poured more amber colored liquid into his cup. They didn't exchange words; it was all part of a routine. A routine that had been going on for sometime now.

"So, the great Malcolm is just going to waste away in a bar..." Leo snuffed as he pushed his glass forward.

"You can see yourself out whenever you like, Leo," Malcolm mumbled.

"Vegas. Vegas..." Leo grumbled at him as he stood, shook his fist and turned to the door.

As Leo walked towards the door, he bumped into someone.

"Sorry, sir," the person mumbled with a nod of his head.

Leo rolled his eyes as he ducked out the door. Malcolm watched the man go to the bar. There was something about the way he hurried in that caught his eye.

"Hey, Danny." The brunette smiled brightly at him as she set the pitcher of beer she was holding down.

"Hey, Violet... I got a favor to ask," Danny said as he placed his hand on the bar, shifting his weight.

"Ooh favors… if I help you, does that mean you owe me one?" Violet grinned widely.

"Well, that's usually what it means when someone asks for a favor." Danny smirked.

"For you, Danny boy, anything." Violet laughed with a wink.

"Is that room upstairs still open?" Danny asked. He looked up at the ceiling and then back to Violet.

"Umm, yeah… they were going to offer it as a package. Tend the bar, get the room type thing..why? What's wrong? Are you ok?" Violet asked as she leaned forward in concern.

"I'm fine, Violet. There's a girl. She's asleep in my truck. I don't know what she's been through, but I think she needs help," Danny whispered.

"Help, as in?" Violet's eyebrows pulled together as she looked at him.

"I don't know. She's got marks on her that she's trying to hide. She was scared. She's trying to act like nothing's wrong," Danny explained.

"Ok, so what do we do?" Violet asked as she nodded her head.

"Can we let her stay up in the spare room?" Danny asked.

"Of course," Violet said with a smile across her face.

"What about Mick? Would he be ok with it?" Danny asked cautiously.

"You let me worry about Mick. Go bring the girl in. I'll see if there's anything left over in the kitchen for her to eat," Violet said as she shooed Danny out the door.

Malcolm listened to the exchange, and his curiosity piqued. He had been coming to this bar for a few weeks now, and he liked that Violet left him alone. She tried the whole chit-chat thing when he first started coming here but quickly stopped once she figured out he 'wasn't a talker' as she had put it. He watched the door, waiting to see the girl Danny was talking about.

"Hey, Iris." Danny tapped on the glass of the passenger side window.

"Iris," he called louder.

She didn't answer. He pulled his lower lip into his mouth and squinted as he slowly popped the door open. Jo jumped up, and a small yelp escaped her mouth as she covered her head with her hands.

"Hey, it's ok. It's me, Danny. We reached town." Danny backed up to give her space.

"Danny?" Jo asked as she sat up confused.

"Yeah, Danny." Danny chuckled.

"Danny," Jo whispered, and he watched relief rush over her.

"Hey." Danny smiled.

"I'm sorry. I fell asleep. I was really tired," Jo said with an embarrassed smile on her face.

"That's ok. So listen, I figured since your car broke down and no shops are open right now, you'll need a place to crash for the night. My friend Violet bartends here and there's a spare room. You're welcome to it and in the morning we'll figure out your car." Danny smiled brightly at her. He didn't know why, but he needed to help her.

"Danny, I can't. I-" Jo started to say.

"So you have some place to stay tonight?" Danny asked her as he raised his eyebrow at her.

"No," Jo said, and Danny cut her off again.

"Ok, well you do now. Come on," Danny said as he made his way to the bar.

Jo stood there and watched him. She gritted her teeth. A warm bed sounded amazing. To sleep and not worry about if she would open her eyes and he would be standing over her. He wouldn't look for her in a bar, nevermind a room above a bar. Danny held open the door and waited for her. His eyes told her to come on. Jo took a deep breath and went after him.

Jo squeezed her hand around the strap of her backpack as she walked into the bar. The dim lights made her feel better. It was like she could hide in the darkness of the small bar.

"Iris, this is Violet. That's kind of cool. You both have flower names. Violet... Iris," Danny said as his hand tapped the bar for Jo to come over.

'Iris..I'm Iris. You're Iris,' Jo repeated in her head as she cautiously walked to the bar.

"Hey, sugar. So the room is fifty a night. There's a microwave, fridge, and tv up there." Violet started to say as she wiped off the bar top.

"I...thank you, but I can't. I, um..." Jo began to stutter as she tried to say she didn't have money.

"No money?" Violet asked as she stopped and looked at her.

Jo's lips pressed together in a thin line, and she nodded reluctantly. Violet sighed and looked at her for a long second. She ignored the silent plea that Danny was staring her down with.

"Fine. The room's yours, but you need to tend the bar. You can pour drinks? Take orders?" Violet asked. Her voice implied she was annoyed, but her face was still happy. It confused Jo.

"Yeah, your basics. I don't know how to make anything fancy," Jo said as she watched her.

"That's fine. We don't have anyone fancy coming in here. Plus, there's an old book down there with instructions on drinks, and there's the internet. How long are you staying?" Violet asked as she picked up a glass.

"I... I'm not sure," Jo said quietly; she needed to leave as soon as she could.

"Car's broke?" Violet asked as if she could read her mind.

"Yeah," Jo answered quietly.

"Well, then you're staying 'til you earn enough to fix your car. You can shadow me for a few days, and then I have a family event I need to go to, so you'll be on your own. Friday, Saturday and Sunday. I will be back on Monday," Violet said quickly as she slid a drink to another patron.

"Danny, send your uncle to get her car, bring it to the shop, find out what's wrong with it and we can work out fixing it." Violet started to move down the bar.

"Is she serious?" Jo asked. Her face was blank as she glanced at Danny.

"Yup. If you want to, that is. No one's gonna make you." Danny smiled.

"Really?" Jo's lips slowly spread into a small smile.

"Yeah." Danny laughed as he shook his head.

Jo couldn't help but grab Danny's arm and squeeze it.

"Thank you so much," Jo whispered as she held back tears. This was the first time in a long time she thought she might actually get out.

"Hey, no problem. We all fall on tough times." Danny put his hand over the top of hers.

Jo suddenly realized she was touching him and dropped her hand away awkwardly. She smiled as she tried to cover up the panic that she knew spread across her face.

"Here. Show her the room," Violet yelled from the end of the bar and then slid a key down it.

Danny caught it as the key skidded to a stop in front of him. He held up the key to Jo.

"Want to see the room?" Danny asked her.

"Yes, thank you," Jo said again to Danny and then glanced at Violet.

"Thank you," Jo said to her. Violet didn't respond but nodded her head.

Malcolm

Malcolm watched her walk into the bar. The shimmer of her honey blond hair caught his eye. Her movements captivated his whole body. Who was she? He watched her intensely. She was nervous. She was upset. What was wrong with her? He shifted in his seat as he watched her. His whole body inched closer as if it was pulled towards her. The boy grabbed the key the

bartender slid across the table and led her to the room upstairs. He felt a twinge of anger creep up on him. Where were they going? He needed to know. He was so wrapped up in the girl's presence that he didn't hear the conversation.

"Violet," Malcolm called the bartender.

"Well, shit, you know my name." Violet laughed as she walked to his side of the bar.

"What was all that?" Malcolm asked as he ignored her comment.

"Just helping a girl out," Violet said dismissively.

"Helping?" Malcolm pushed the issue further as he glanced upstairs.

"Yeah, you know. When someone needs help, you help. Why are you so nosey?" Violet smirked.

Malcolm let out a grunt. He grabbed his glass and downed the rest of his drink. His eyes narrowed at her as he pressed the glass onto the bar. He stood with his eyes still locked on hers.

"Tell Mick, Malcolm asked for him." Malcolm's voice went cold as he spoke.

"I'll pass it along," Violet said as she tried to ignore the goosebumps that spread across her skin.

Malcolm walked to the door, annoyed, opened it and slammed it on the way out. He didn't know why he was so aggravated. He glanced up at the roof of the bar. A single light was on in the far right window. He clenched his jaw. What were they doing up there? He shook his head sharply. What was wrong with him? He clenched his fists before he shut his eyes. He needed to leave now. Malcolm couldn't control the anger that rushed through him when he thought about the girl

upstairs in the room with that boy. He let out a small breath and felt himself start to drift away. His body vibrated as the phase took him over. In seconds he was gone, and the parking lot was empty.

Chapter Two

She felt her breath hitch in her throat as Danny shut the door. Her body immediately went rigid. Her eyes searched the room as panic set in. She looked for a way out as Danny stood between her and the door. They were alone, and he blocked the only way out. She didn't know what his intentions were.

"Hey," Danny said as his hand moved to touch her arm.

Jo flinched and ducked away from Danny as if she expected him to hurt her. Danny dropped his hand away and took a step back.

"Iris, I'm not going to hurt you." He held his hands up defensively.

"Danny, I don't know what you want for helping me but-" Jo started to say as she stepped further away from him.

"Iris. I don't know what you've been through, but I don't want anything from you. I just wanted to help. No strings attached," Danny said in a soft voice.

She watched him intently. Her eyes pierced through him as she waited for a sign of doubt. She bit her lip nervously. The fear and panic still did not subside.

"Is there a window in here?" Jo's voice shook slightly as she asked.

"Umm, yeah," Danny said, his eyebrows drawn together as he looked at her.

He watched her try to control the fear that rushed through her. He curled his lower lip inwards and

walked over the far side of the room. Thoughts of what could possibly make her respond like that rushed through his head. He couldn't figure it out, but he knew in the pit of his stomach that someone had hurt her. He pulled open the dark brown curtains and revealed a floor length window with a sliding door.

"There's even a balcony." Danny smiled as he tried to reassure her.

As the moonlight trickled in from the open curtain, he watched her take a deep breath in. Her chest rose and fell slower. He slid the door open, and he watched her relax.

"Don't like closed spaces?" Danny asked quietly.

Jo just shook her head no. She watched Danny cautiously as she walked to the window. She took another deep breath in and felt the stress fade away. 'He wasn't going to hurt her. She was not trapped. This was not a room without windows,' she repeated in her head. She then began to think about things she needed. If she were going to stay here, she would need to change her appearance. Even if it was only for a little. Evan was on his way, she felt it in her gut.

"Iris… you ok?" Danny asked as he shifted behind her.

'Iris,' she had to remember, that's who she was now. She turned slowly and nodded.

"Sorry, claustrophobic. Is there a store where I could pick up a few things?" Jo asked him as she fidgeted with her fingers.

"Yeah, it's right down the road. It's closing soon. What do you need? I'll grab it for you on my way to tow your car back." Danny smiled.

"Brown hair dye, something to eat, some scissors." Jo's voice dropped even lower as she said what she needed.

"Got it. You get settled and I'll be back. Here's the key," Danny said, holding it out to her.

"You know about hair dye?" Jo asked as she took the key from him.

"I've got sisters." Danny grinned with a nod.

"Ok." Jo laughed as Danny headed to the door and was gone before she could even say bye.

Evan

He groaned as he held head in his hands. What had happened? A clink noise caught his ear as he felt cold metal around his wrist. Evan gritted his teeth, and anger rushed through him as he realized what had happened.

"Jo!!" he screamed at the top of his lungs. His voice vibrated off the walls of the empty room.

"Jo!" he screamed again; this time he pulled on the chain link that kept him attached to the bed.

The door to the blue room was left open. He waited a minute, expecting to see her timid self make her way to the doorway. Evan could see her now, standing there twisting her fingers as her eyes begged him not to be mad. He was more than mad. She would never leave this room ever again.

"Jo…I'm not mad. I'm actually proud of how strong you are. Come here. I promise I'm not mad. I

know I've been mean lately. I'm just stressed from work," Evan said gently.

No answer came. How dare she make him wait so long! Who did she think she was? He became enraged. His mind began to rapidly process what had led to this moment. He had let her out. Let her cook for him. He knew from the pounding headache and how his body shook that she had drugged him. He had medication in the cabinet; he had even used it on her from time to time to get her back into the room. It was less of a fight. Less noise. She used his own medicine on him. He knew the soup tasted funny, but she was acting like her old self. The girl who was so in love and amazed by him that he didn't want to comment about the soup. Didn't want to hurt her feelings. That bitch.

"Jo, if you do not come let me out, I will get out and it will be so much worse. Get your fucking ass back in here and unlock these damn cuffs! I will put you in a box! In a cage! I will lock you away forever!" Evan screamed.

He waited, but there was no noise. The apartment was completely silent. His stomach sank as his blood ran cold. She was gone. She left. How did she ever find the strength to leave him? He shook with rage as he looked down at the single metal cuff attached to his wrist. He gritted his teeth as he stared at the newest hole he had put in the wall. She had told him no. 'No.' The corner of his lip twitched as he replayed the word coming out of her mouth. His free hand grasped his thumb of the hand that was cuffed. 'No.' Her pouted, chapped, and bloody lips had said to him. Her blue eyes had narrowed, and she tried to stand tall. 'No.' Who did

she think she was? She was his. His complete mind, body, and soul. There was no one else for her. He went too far that night. He used a cord to hit her back repeatedly. Evan tried to control his rage; he hit the wall first, but she squared off with him and he lost control. He slapped her so hard across the face he felt the bones in his own hand ache. When she passed out, he had dragged her to the bed and ripped the remaining clothes from her body. His hand unfastened his belt as he was going to have his way with her no matter what. The blood that seeped out onto the white tile floor behind her stopped him. There was more than usual. He hadn't realized how badly he had beaten her.

"Jo." His voice had cracked as he spoke her name.

He immediately pressed his ear to her chest. Her heart was still beating; it was faint, but it was still there. He got up and raced to his medicine kit. Evan grabbed the black duffle bag in his hand and rushed back into the room. He pulled out an EpiPen and slammed it into her upper thigh. Her eyes shot open as the medicine flooded her bloodstream. She let out a loud cry as pain overtook her. He was gentle with her, took care of her wounds. Let her out of the blue room. She then wanted to make it up to him. Make him dinner. Bitch.

Snap. He yanked hard and fast on his thumb. He let out a deep guttural growl as he dislocated his thumb. Evan carefully slid the cuff off. He stood as the world spun around him. The medicine she had given him was still in his system. He fumbled through the doorway until he got his footing. He didn't know what day it was. She couldn't have gotten far. She had no family or friends.

He made sure she had no one. Evan was supposed to be her world. He would find her.

Malcolm

The floor boards of his home creaked as he paced the entranceway of his house. His hands opened and closed as he made fists with them, as he tried to get the frustration out. His house was old and secluded. Surrounded by woods and made of stone. It was large and had everything he could ever want. It was empty. He had grown accustomed to being alone in this world. He would outlive everything and everyone so it never mattered. No one had sparked his interest until now. He stopped in the middle of his next step as an image of her came to his mind. She was broken. He could sense that when she walked into the bar. Beautiful and broken. She had this light that was hidden beneath all the muck she presented to the world. The timid steps, the cautious body movement. He had only seen her for minutes, but he couldn't get her out of his thoughts. He let out a loud groan as he turned towards the iron framed mirror on the wall. His eyes looked back at him, the whites of his eyes turned black as he watched them. He clenched his jaw and squeezed the iron frame of the mirror.

"Fuck it," he mumbled and then shut his eyes; he gave into the need.

He felt his body go weightless and his bones vibrated. He slowly turned into nothing in front of the mirror. In the next second he was in front of the bar

again, his eyes focused on the room above. The sliding glass door to the room was open, and the balcony called his name. In seconds he reappeared on the balcony. He felt himself take a deep breath in as he carefully stepped into the room. His eyes found her immediately. The darkness in the room seemed to give way to her as if a light was shining from her. Her golden hair was wrapped around her like a shield, and her knees were tucked into her chest. Her arms hugged her knees as she trembled. Malcolm tilted his head as he tried to understand; there was no way she was asleep like that. He watched her twitch a few more times. He stood over the bed as he watched her.

"No." The word was soft and escaped her mouth as she winced.

"Stop. Please. Stop." The words were cracked and broken as they left her mouth.

"I didn't mean it. I won't do it again." She twisted in her sleep, with each word spoken another flinch followed.

Malcolm filled with rage. Who was she dreaming about? Who had hurt her? He reached down and touched her arm. As soon as his hand touched her flesh, her body stopped shaking. Malcolm looked down at his hand as warmth rushed into his body. He never felt like this before. He moved his hand from her arm, and she began to whimper again. Without thinking, he placed it back on her. His touch instantly calmed her. He pulled his lip into his mouth, and a pressed frown appeared on his face. What had just happened? He stared down at his hand in disbelief. How could the hand that thousands were scared of, the hand that has

caused death, trauma, and horrible things bring any type of comfort? She rolled to her side, and he watched as her eyes began to move. Malcolm clenched his jaw; panic twisted in his stomach. He had to move quickly; he watched her go stiff and start to sit up. He shut his eyes and felt his body morph.

"Hello?" Jo called out as she rubbed her eyes. She felt like someone had been there.

She stretched slightly and rubbed her eyes. She glanced at the small island that separated the bedroom from the kitchen. Danny had left some bags. She placed her feet on the ground and went to stand.

"Holy shit," Jo yelled when she locked eyes with a blackbird perched on her nightstand.

"Hey there." Jo laughed as she looked at the bird.

"Cold outside?" Jo smirked as the bird tilted its head at her.

She watched the bird and held her finger out sideways as if it was a tree branch and moved slowly towards the bird. The bird looked at her finger and squawked at her. He moved back, and as she got close, he took off. He flew to the window and out of it.

"Well then," Jo whispered as she shook her head.

She got up and walked over to the counter. She looked through the bags. There was warm chocolate brown hair dye in the bag with a pair of sharp scissors. There were chips and a small personal pizza to pop in the microwave, along with cookies and a candy bar. She smiled at the gesture. She moved to the next bag, and

she found body wash, deodorant, shampoo, and conditioner.

"I hope this helps." was scribbled on a small piece of paper left inside the bag.

She grabbed the body wash and flipped the top of the cap off. She squeezed the bottle and inhaled the warm scent. It was a mixture of brown sugar and vanilla. She smiled softly, now excited to shower. Jo grabbed the bag and the box of brown hair dye and walked into the small bathroom. She looked down at the box of hair dye in hand and then to the mirror. She locked eyes with herself as she touched her golden hair.

"Goodbye." She laughed slightly and then narrowed her eyes at herself.

"Goodbye, Jo. Goodbye, Evan… Hello, Iris," she said firmly and turned from the mirror.

Chapter Three

Jo stood in the small living room, her hand held the scissors. She stared down at them as if they could talk to her. Her hand shook lightly as she felt fear rush through her. She had no clue how to do this. Jo gritted her teeth, shoulder-length brown hair would make her unrecognizable, right? She let out a small breath as she tried to calm her nerves. Three small taps came from the door. She changed her grip on the scissors and now held them tightly in her hand, ready to use them if needed. She cautiously walked towards the door. Every horrible thought came to the forefront as she reached the door. The doom washed over her, and she felt sick instantly.

"Girl, it's me, Violet." The voice called through the door as another tap came through the door.

Jo chewed on her lip nervously, her hand tightening around the scissors as she pulled the door open.

"Hi," Jo said quietly as she found Violet by herself outside the door.

Jo's stomach immediately settled. She had expected to see Evan standing there with Violet when she opened the door. Even though she felt relief, she still wondered what Violet wanted.

"Um…what are you doing with the scissors? And I like the brown." Violet asked, her eyes squinted at the scissors.

"Cutting my hair," Jo said with a defeated sigh.

"Do you want help?" Violet laughed.

"You can cut hair?" Jo asked suspiciously.

"Um yeah. Small town, not a lot of beauty shops. Here, let me see," Violet said as she held her hand out for the scissors.

"Ok." Jo gave in and let Violet take the scissors.

Violet walked past her and into the room. She grabbed the chair from the small island and pulled it away and tapped it.

"Come sit." Violet smiled brightly at Jo.

"Why are you helping me?" Jo asked as she sat down in the chair.

"Because I want to," Violet said as if it meant nothing at all.

"How short are we thinking?" Violet said as she pulled Jo's long hair forward.

"I don't know." Jo touched her long locks.

"Are we wanting a trim, upper arm length, shoulder length? A bob? Pixie?" Violet asked as she touched Jo's arm, then shoulder and lastly chin.

"I don't know. I just need to not look like me," Jo said frustratedly, and her stomach dropped as the words accidentally slipped out.

"Listen, you're not some type of criminal, are you? I can't have cops and stuff all up in here. Mick will throw a fit," Violet said sharply.

"No! No, I'm not a criminal or anything like that." Jo spoke quickly and stood up to face Violet.

"Are you in trouble?" Violet asked, her voice softened as she watched Jo's worried expression.

"I... I just need not to be me," Jo said as she tried to come up with some answer.

"You're running from someone or something." Violet's eyes moved back and forth as she watched Jo's face.

"Someone hurt you," Violet murmured and then patted the chair.

"Violet, I don't want to-" Jo started to say, but Violet held up her hand.

"Sit," Violet demanded as she motioned to the chair once more.

"We will give you the best haircut, and just so you know, there's a 12 gauge behind the bar. Should you ever need it," Violet said as she brushed Jo's hair into place.

"Why are you helping me?" Jo whispered again as she felt tears sting her eyes.

"We all need a little help from time to time. My meme always said, help those to help yourself. Now how short do we want it?" Violet smiled.

"Short, I need to be unrecognizable." Jo said as a small feeling of loss crept up her throat. She had always had long flowing hair.

"Ok." Violet took the scissors in her hand and cut a piece of Jo's hair.

Jo watched the strands of her hair fall to the ground. She thought this would be another crushing blow, but instead of pain, she felt relief as each one fell. Jo felt a weight lift off of her. She would make it this time. She wouldn't go back.

He found himself in his darkroom. He vanished as quickly as he could from the girl's room. Dread and loss seemed to overwhelm him. Malcolm looked down at his hand in disbelief. He still could not fathom that he actually could provide comfort. He could still feel the warmth that radiated off her skin in his palm. Malcolm longed to touch her again. However, his stomach twisted inside of him. He had felt none of this before. Demons don't feel anything,he reminded himself sharply. Malcolm gritted his jaw as he turned into his room. He needed no one. He wanted nothing. Malcolm curled his hand into a fist as he walked out of his room.

"Malcolm." A voice said behind him. He stopped as he rolled his eyes.

"I thought you were headed to Vegas?" Malcolm asked with his voice flat.

"Eh, I wanted to check in." Leo smirked as he watched Malcolm.

"I'm not your brother or father. You do not need to check in with me," Malcolm said as he walked the rest of the way to his door.

"You sure you don't want to come?" Leo continued to speak to Malcolm's back.

"I said no!" Malcolm snapped. His body tensed as his stomach twisted more; his thoughts went to leaving the girl.

"Fuck, Malcolm, just asking. You don't have to get all bitchy." Leo grinned. He loved getting under Malcolm's skin.

Malcolm was always calm and collected. Leo hated it. He loved the rare occasions Malcolm would give into the rage and chaos that boiled below his cool exterior. Malcolm had worked alongside Malcolm for years. He admired his work. He had brought kingdoms to their knees, manipulated father against son. Brother against brother. Collected thousands upon thousands of souls. Now he had vanished from the demon world. Locked himself away in his dark manor and spent time at a hole in the wall bar. He had done his share of work, was what Leo was told when he brought it up to the under-lords. It stressed and angered Leo.

"A high end CEO's son is going to be at one of the hotels in Vegas. Thought maybe you would want to take another empire down." Leo said as he tried to bait him.

"Why don't you do it?" Malcolm scoffed as he walked away from Leo.

"You're a waste." Leo growled at Malcolm's back.

Malcolm moved soundlessly; he vanished from the doorway, and his shadow appeared in front of Leo in seconds. Leo didn't even have time to blink before Malcolm had him by the throat and pushed him towards the window. Malcolm moved his hand, and the window opened. He squeezed tighter around Leo's throat and stepped out onto the balcony. He dangled Leo off the edge.

"A waste?" Malcolm spoke quietly as he watched Leo struggle.

"You're wasting away here." Leo coughed as he wrapped his hand around Malcolm's arm.

"You should worry about yourself," Malcolm muttered and dropped Leo.

Leo fell. Malcolm didn't even wait; he walked back inside and shut the balcony window. Leo crashed onto the brick driveway below. He let out a yell and instantly grabbed his ankle. Leo shut his eyes as the pain rushed over him. He narrowed his eyes as he looked at Malcolm's bedroom. The rage blocked out the pain. He was going to get him to come back. Leo shut his eyes and let his body phase.

Leo

"𝓜other fucker." Leo growled as he hit the stone floor.

"Fucking bastard." Leo gritted his teeth as he grabbed his ankle and snapped it back into place.

"Malcolm?" The voice was deep and had a chill to it.

"He's not fucking coming." Leo spat as he put his leg out straight and moved his foot in a circle.

"What does that mean?" The voice demanded.

"I don't know what to fucking tell you. He said no. He threw me off a balcony." Leo grunted as he got to his feet.

"'No' is unacceptable. The soul intake is being depleted. More and more are going to the light. The scale has tipped too far," he said as he stepped forward.

"Pavel, I don't know what you want me to do?" Leo asked in a desperate voice.

"You make him come back," Pavel said as he stood in front of Leo, his eyes glowed red as his body shook with rage.

"He doesn't want to. He is wasting away in that dark manor of his. He said he paid his dues." Leo laughed.

"Find something he wants. Something he connects with. Use it. Or you will be sorry…. Lazaros," Pavel whispered the name.

"How did you find out my name?" Leo's voice shook as he asked.

"I've been around a long time. All you demons do the same thing. Pick names that start with the same letter as your real name... Leo." Pavel scoffed.

"Stupidity. You will either get Malcolm to come back, or you will be my puppet. Now go… Lazaros," Pavel said with a sinister grin.

As Pavel finished speaking, Leo's body stiffened, and with the command, his body phased. Pavel's laughter rang behind him.

Jo

Jo shook her short chocolate brown hair back and forth in front of her mirror. The layers framed her face perfectly and bounced with the movement. She looked like a whole different person. She couldn't help but smile. Jo was unrecognizable. She touched the black v-neck, long sleeve top and dark jeans. Everything was the opposite of what she normally wore, no more flowery dresses. She gritted her teeth as she thought of the pale blue dress with white flowers speckled all over

38

it. The one he used to make her wear. She shut her eyes and clenched her jaw.

"Come on, girl, we got to get started. I only have so much time to teach you," Violet said from the doorway.

"Coming," Jo said as she stepped out of the bathroom.

"Oh, I like it. You're like a dark goddess. Come on." Violet smiled and walked out.

Jo bit her lip and didn't say anything as she followed Violet. Violet went behind the bar and motioned for Jo to follow.

"So, at the beginning of the night, make sure everything is stocked. Beer mugs, glasses, the kegs for the beer on tap go under here. We have a small fruit drawer over here for cherries and pineapples, blah, blah," Violet explained as she gave Jo the tour.

"Things don't really get busy, we have a few regulars. Tomorrow some local band will be playing and we might get a few more people. Cash register and card machine. No checks, no tabs, and no paying later," Violet said as she ended the tour.

"Got it." Jo smiled as she looked about the place.

The door opened, and a tall man with shoulders as wide as his waist walked in. His wheat colored hair was combed over to the side, and he scrunched his nose as he looked at Jo. He walked over to Violet and handed her an envelope.

"Change for tonight. Who's the girl?" He asked as he continued to stare at Jo.

"Iris, Mick, Mick, Iris. She's bartending for a little. I told you I need to go out of town, and because you

were not finding someone to replace me in the short term, I did." Violet snatched the envelope from him.

"What's her pay?" Mick's gaze narrowed suspiciously.

"Same as me," Violet replied as she turned and squared off with him.

"Dollarless," Mick said through clenched teeth.

"Fifty cents." Violet crossed her arms and matched his stare.

"Fine. I do not want to be bothered," Mick muttered as he took his eyes off Jo.

"Fine and she's staying upstairs." Violet said as she placed the money in the register.

"Fuck, Vi," Mick grumbled as he waved his hands in the air. He reached the door of the bar and walked out before anything else could be said.

"I was fine with anything, pay wise." Jo spoke up, confused about the whole interaction.

"No, and you need to learn that word and start understanding your value. He would be screwed without you taking my place. So, therefore, you are valuable. You name your price and your wants. When I get back, we are going to work on those things." Violet chuckled as she shut the register.

"Ok." Jo laughed back. A small part of her envied Violet and the way she handled everything.

Chapter Four

The night went by in a blur with few customers, just regulars, as Violet had said. She had it down, it was a simple job, and minus the chit chat that she was forced into by patrons, she liked it. The last person had cleared out when the bell chimed and the door opened. Jo looked up from the bar and locked eyes with a tall, dark stranger. He walked over to the bar and stopped in front of her. Jo lost her focus as she stared into his golden eyes that reminded her of sunlight. His hair was deep and dark, and as the bar lights reflected off of it, it shimmered blue. He stood silently in front of her, and it felt like all the air in the room had been pulled out. Jo's heart pounded so loud in her chest that it was the only thing she could hear.

"Bourbon." His voice was warm and chilled her all at once.

"Bourbon?" Jo whispered back; she couldn't look away from him.

"No ice," he said. His own body stood tense and rigid.

"No ice." She repeated back because his words were the only thing that bounced around in her brain. It had completely shut down.

"Iris," Violet said behind her in a harsh tone as she tried to get her attention.

The word never made it to her mind. She was locked to this stranger. She was in a trance, and no matter what, she couldn't make herself move.

"Iris." Violet reached out and touched Jo's arm.

"Uh?" Jo asked as she took her eyes off the man and looked at Violet.

"Bourbon, no ice." Violet smiled at her as she motioned to the counter behind her, with all the liquor stacked.

"Oh! Bourbon, no ice," Jo said as her blue eyes went wide and she spun on her feet to get the bottle.

Her hand clasped around the first Bourbon bottle she saw. She was panicked and embarrassed.

"Not that one." His voice made heat rush through her.

Jo's eyes narrowed as she scanned the bottles. She found another one and went to grab it. She lingered on it as she waited to hear his voice.

"No ice," he said softer this time. Jo could feel his eyes as they burned into her back.

Jo curled her fingers around the neck and turned. She set the bottle on the bar and then grabbed a short glass. She pulled the cooler open, found the metal scoop and dug out the ice. The ice cubes clanged as they dropped into the glass. She placed it on the counter and grabbed the bourbon. She watched warm brown liquor pour from the bottle into the glass. Suddenly his hand was over the top of it, and the liquid ran onto his hand and onto the counter.

"No ice," he repeated as Jo looked from the bottle to his face.

Jo dropped the bottle, and it smashed on the countertop. The neck of the bottle hit the glass, and it toppled over and shattered. Ice and glass scattered about. She stared at the mess, and her body immediately began to tremble.

She was back in the apartment, the soup bowl shattered on the floor, pieces of the white porcelain everywhere. She dropped to her knees and scrambled to pick them up.

"You fucking worthless bitch," Evan yelled as he captured her hair and smashed her face into the ground. Pieces of the broken bowl pressed into her cheek and drew blood.

"I am so sorry. I am so sorry. I didn't mean it. I'll fix it. Let me fix it," Jo said the words out loud as the memory flooded her mind.

She picked up the broken pieces of glass frantically; the glass tore into her skin. The clear color of the pieces began to turn red from her cuts, but she didn't feel it.

"Stop," he said as his hand captured hers.

"Let go," he commanded, his voice firm but soft as he watched her stop.

"I... I didn't mean to," Jo whispered, and her voice cracked.

"You're ok," he whispered as Jo looked up and locked eyes with him.

"You're safe; let go of the glass." Malcolm reassured her.

The pieces she held in her hand dropped back onto the countertop. The word "safe" bounced around in

her brain. Was she? Why did him telling her she was, instantly make her believe it?

"Iris, shit. Are you ok?" Violet's voice broke through the fog Jo was in.

"I'm so sorry, Violet. I didn't mean to break the glass or spill the liquor. I'll pay you back," Jo said as she tried to pull her hand from Malcolm's.

He held onto her as she pulled back. Malkcolm didn't want to let go. He wasn't going to. He stood and moved behind the bar.

"It's my drink and my glass. I will pay for it. Come," he ordered as he led her back around the bar.

"Hey, where-" Violet began to ask but watched Malcolm move to the bathroom, answering her question.

Jo didn't say anything. Her stomach dropped inside of her as she let Malcolm lead her away. As they stepped into the small bathroom, Malcolm let go of her hand. She fixed her eyes on the white title on the floor. Jo began to disassociate and let her body go numb so she wouldn't feel what happened next. She heard the water turn on as her eye traced a tiny crack in the floor title.

One…Two…Three. She said numbers inside her head as she let her brain focus on them.
Four…Five…Six. The rhythm of counting made her feel calm in high stress situations. It was a strange coping mechanism she developed so she could space out and not be in the moment. Seven…

She froze as she felt his hand on hers, and his touch was soft and gentle. His warm hand wrapped around her and he led her to the sink. He didn't say anything as he stood behind her and guided her

bleeding hand under the water. The small pieces of glass that had implanted themselves in her skin stung under the water. Some broke free and floated down the drain, following the red stained water.

Once all the blood was cleaned, Malcolm turned her towards him and brought her palm towards his face. Jo watched him with her fear and anxiety gone. A strange sense of calm and peace washed through her. She almost didn't recognize the feeling; it had been so long since she felt safe.

"I'm sorry I ruined-" Jo began to apologize.

"Accidents happen. It was stupid to hurt yourself," Malcolm said as his eyes fixated on a small piece of glass that stood straight up out of her palm.

"I'm so-" Jo went to say sorry again.

"Stop apologizing," Malcolm demanded as he tried to pinch the piece of glass and pull it from the cut.

"I..." Jo opened her mouth but then shut it as Malcolm's gaze flickered from her hand to her face, his eyes narrowed at her telling her she better not say she was sorry for being sorry.

"It's annoying," Malcolm muttered.

"I don't know what to say," Jo said, because the only words she was used to saying were apologies. "Then don't say anything," Malcolm said as he grew frustrated with the glass not coming out of the cut. Jo nodded and watched his brows press together; the small wrinkle in his forehead became more and more pronounced as the glass did not give into him.

"It's ok I can get it out la-" Jo said but then stopped as Malcolm's mouth went to her hand.

The warmth of his warm mouth against her skin made her shut her eyes, and a feverish feeling flushed through her. She felt his teeth capture the small shard of glass, and she felt it release from her skin. Her breathing became heavy as she leaned back against the sink. The mere contact with him overwhelmed her. Malcolm stepped closer to her and leaned towards the sink. He spat the piece of glass into it.

A drop of her blood hit his tongue, and he felt a rush go through him. His body went into euphoria as he felt everything. He couldn't help but press into Jo. He craved her. His hand went to her chin, and his thumb ran his finger over her plump lower lip. Sparks surged through him like electricity from the slight touch. With her eyes still closed, she leaned into his touch, and he knew she felt the same. His body vibrated from being this close to her. He had to have her.

"Thank you." Her lips moved against his thumb as she whispered.

"Iris," he said, her name. He had heard Violet call her earlier.

Iris. The name brought her back to reality. She was not Iris. He called her Iris. She opened her eyes, and a hint of sadness flashed in them. She wanted to hear her real name from his lips. But it could never happen. He could never know. She watched his gold colored eyes burn into her, and part of her didn't want to move from this bathroom.

"What's your name?" Jo whispered.

He was lost in her pure blue eyes. They were the color of the sky just after it had rained and the sun started to come back out. Cold but bright blue. He

traced her jaw, his hand going into her now short brown hair. His fingers weaved through it as he pulled her forward. His mouth pressed into her and another intense wave poured into him. Her lips soft against his response and began to follow his kiss. He pulled on her lip demandingly until her mouth opened and his tongue slipped inside. His hand gripped her waist and pulled her against him. He needed her, wanted her. She had to be his. A small whimper escaped her mouth, and he felt her pain. He pulled back in fear that he had hurt her. The feeling pitted in his stomach.

She opened her eyes; her body felt like jello. Jo had never been kissed like that. She was in a haze, and her body was on the verge of trembling.

"Did I hurt you?" Malcolm asked, his own voice heavy from the experience.

"The sink, my hand… I grabbed it by accident," Jo said with a small shake of her head.

Malcolm felt relief as he realized he had not hurt her. He went to step away, but her hand caught his shirt, keeping him in place.

"What's your name?" Jo asked again. She desperately needed to know.

"Mal'akh." His real name fell out of his mouth. He had not spoken it since the beginning of his existence.

A name is too powerful. It was a weapon. Something to be used against him, and he had just spoken it to some random human girl in a hole in the wall bar's bathroom.

"Mal-" She went to repeat it, but his hand fell over her mouth.

"No," he ordered quickly.

Jo froze. Her eyes went wide as she watched an array of emotions spread across his face. She nodded that she understood. He pulled his hand away from her mouth.

"Don't ever say my name.," he threatened as his eyes darkened and he straightened up to show his size.

"Are you in trouble, too?" Jo whispered innocently.

A smile rolled across his lips, and a small laugh escaped his mouth. He did not even intimidate her.

"More than you know." He touched her cheek again, and he could see himself getting lost in her.

"It's ok. I promise I won't tell anyone. Your secret is safe." Jo reassured him.

He studied her face, and he couldn't help but believe her. He looked at her hair and touched it with his fingertips.

"You changed your hair," he stated quietly.

"We all have secrets." Jo smiled and then patted him.

She flinched as she had used her hand that was cut. She pulled back and looked down at the small wounds on her hands.

"We need to bandage that," Malcolm said as he moved away from her.

"Iris, are you ok in there?" Violet banged on the door to the bathroom.

Jo smiled at her overprotectiveness. Jo stepped around Malcolm and opened the door with a smile still on her face.

"Hey, I'm good. I am so sorry I freaked out over there. It won't happen again," Jo said to her.

"Girl, shut up. You're fine. My first time, I smashed an entire bottle of some expensive rum Micky had brought specifically for him. You are fine. Are you ok?" Violet looked from Jo to Jo's hand and then lastly to Malcolm. Her eyes narrowed as she got to him.

"Yes, I'm going to go upstairs and wrap my hand." Jo nodded to Violet.

"Ok, well the bar's closed anyways, so you're good. I can clean up." Violet's eyes were still on Malcolm.

"Thanks Violet," Jo said as her hand started to throb like crazy.

"Um. Thank you for helping me clean my hand…" Jo began to say and paused.

"Malcolm," Malcolm said, speaking the name he had gone by all these years.

"Malcolm." Jo smiled, saying it as if it was just a secret between them two.

"Thank you again, Malcolm." Jo nodded to him and then squeezed around Violet to head upstairs.

Malcolm stepped out of the bathroom after Jo, and his eyes followed her until he could no longer see her.

"What's it to you?" Violet asked suspiciously, watching him.

Malcolm didn't acknowledge her. He reached in his back pocket, pulled out a stack of cash and handed it to Violet and started to go to the door.

"Hey, it's fine you didn't even get a drink," Violet said, both confused and annoyed.

"Replace the bottle. Tip the girl," Malcolm said dismissively, and just like that he was gone.

Chapter Five
Malcolm

The night air hit him full force. He had never felt overwhelmed before, and now his chest was tight, his stomach felt flipped and his mind raced. Malcolm needed distance. He needed to be away from her and this bar. He stepped out onto the street but stopped as the light flickered on in the room above the bar. His eyes watched the balcony. He was glued to his spot; he wanted to see her, and didn't want to leave her. What was wrong with him? His fingertips touched his lips. Why did he need her? Home! He needed to go home! He closed his eyes, not even bothering to check his surroundings as he let himself fade.

The minute he reappeared in his bedroom, he began pacing. His jaw clenched tightly as he tried to understand what had happened. She knew his name. She shouldn't know his name, but she did.

"Fuck," he whispered, knowing a demon's name was dangerous.

He would now have to listen and do whatever she commanded. She had no clue the power she could have over him. One person in all these years had found out his name. The man was obsessed with him, and once he uttered the word Mal'akh, he slit his throat and ended his life. After he was dead, he cut out his tongue just in case in the afterlife he thought he could speak his name. He couldn't kill her. She was innocent. She was pure. He saw how damaged she was. Even if he didn't know the cause of it. He could feel it, could feed off of it

if he wanted to, but deep down there was a light inside of her that flickered and wanted to burn bright. He wanted to make her come alive again. To see her light up.

"Fucking damn it." He growled as he clenched his hands into fists.

"She's just a fucking girl. She needs to die," Malcolm said out loud.

He had heard stories where demons had been controlled. Horrid stories of them treated like they were puppets. Told to do everything and anything. The longer the person held their name, the stronger the tie and bond became. He ended the man who discovered his name instantly; no bond could form yet. He had to kill her tonight. He would wait until she was asleep. It would be quick and painless. He moved his lips together as he thought. The feeling of her lips against his entered his mind. As he stood there, a mixture of emotions rushed into him — anger, panic, the need to kill, and there was one more. It struck him as odd as he sat back and thought about her. He was protective of her, and he wanted her. He snorted at himself and told himself it was her blood. The minute the droplet hit his tongue sent him into a frenzy. That's all it was. He ignored the pit in his stomach telling him that blood had never done this to him before. That it was something more, but he pushed it further down. He needed to get to her and kill her. He closed his eyes and thought of where he wanted to be and phased.

His feet hit the cement around the corner from the bar. He knew she would be up in her room just above it. He needed to make sure the room was clear.

That she was alone. He closed his eyes and let himself shift. His arms quickly turned into black feathered wings, and slowly he morphed into the crow. He took off to her room.

Jo

Jo stood in front of the bathroom mirror. The sound of the water that ran out of the faucet echoed in the silence that captured the room. Her eyes watched the bloodstained water go down the drain, lost in thoughts.

"I am so sorry." The words tried to draw her back into the dreaded memory.

"I can fix it." She closed her hand under the water and squeezed. The pain from the cuts on her hand pulled her from the memory. Her eyes flickered to the mirror.

"That is not you anymore." She told her reflection firmly.

"Never…ever…again," she whispered as she turned the water off.

She grabbed the beige towel and wrapped it around her hand as she walked back out into the main room. Jo let out a small sigh as she tried to get herself together. She needed to tell Violet she was sorry. That it wouldn't happen again. A soft tap on the front door made her breath stop in her throat. She wanted to talk to Violet, but not right now. Another followed the soft tap, but it was slightly louder.

"Violet, I'm sorry about that. I am ok and it won't-" Jo called as she began opening the door.

"Danny?" Jo asked as she saw his messy red hair as she opened the door.

"Sorry, I'm not Violet, but I wanted to stop by and update you on your car and, well, check on you." Danny smiled brighter.

"Oh yeah, umm.. come in." Jo's smile mimicked Danny's. He had a way of making her feel happy just by being there. It was like his energy just made you smile.

"Are you sure?" Danny asked as Jo shifted out of the doorway.

"Of course." Jo nodded and then walked back into the living room/ bedroom area.

"So, the car, it's…What happened to your hand?" Danny asked as he stopped mid sentence and walked over to her, holding his hand out for hers.

"Oh. I broke a glass at the bar and hurt myself trying to clean it up. I hope Violet isn't regretting me." Jo laughed as she shook her head.

"Violet's broken tons of glasses… some on purpose. Don't worry about that. Here, let me have a look," Danny said reassuringly as he took her hand and unwrapped the cloth.

"Ouch," he said as he looked at all the slices that the glass had put into her skin.

"It's ok. It's not that bad and doesn't hurt much. A regular at the bar helped me clean it up. I just need a bandage, if that," Jo said as she pursed her lips together.

"Hang on." Danny got up and walked to the bathroom. She heard him open something and come back.

"It was still there," he said as he held up a first aid kit to her.

"Still there?" Jo asked, now suspicious of him.

"Yeah. I fell on hard times awhile back, and Violet straightened me out. Put me up here so she could keep an eye on me. I've got into a few fights downstairs and so ta da first aid kit." Danny half laughed.

"Oh," Jo said softly as she watched him open the kit and pull out bandages and some ointment.

Hard times, the words echoed in her head. Danny seemed almost perfect and always happy. She couldn't picture him being sad or fighting.

"What's the look for?" Danny smirked a little as he peeked at her from the first aid kit.

"Picturing you fighting." Jo smiled.

"I didn't win them all." Danny laughed as he watched her face.

"All?" Jo chuckled as he reached for her hand.

"Let me see," Danny said as he took hold of her hand.

"Yeah, I didn't always know my limit, and it doesn't matter how big the fella was." Danny shook his head slightly with a small smile on his lips.

He applied the ointment to the cuts on her hand. She watched him move his fingers carefully against her skin. She could tell he was afraid to hurt her.

"You won't hurt me. You don't have to act like I'm breakable." Jo laughed as she watched him look so serious in the moment.

"It just looks like it hurts," Danny said with a small smile on his face.

"I have had worse," Jo whispered but then realized what she said.

"Worse?" Danny stopped and looked at her face.

"I'm clumsy." Jo gave a small smile as she tried to dismiss her comment.

"Clumsy?" Danny asked as he stopped treating her hand.

"Mm hmmm, bad on my feet. Are you really going to bandage it?" Jo asked as she nodded to the bandage material.

"Yes, I am," Danny said with a small frown on his face as he did not get an actual answer.

"So where are you from?" Danny asked as he rolled the cotton material across her palm.

"Um, you know what Danny, I don't think a bandage is a good idea. I'm gonna shower, and then I'll have to take it off. So I'll just do it after. Thank you for everything," Jo said as she slowly pulled back her hand.

"Um... ok. I..." Danny said as he stepped back and placed the bandage material down.

"All right. I'll go…I just..." Danny said as he tried not to be awkward.

"Ok." Jo nodded as she watched him uncomfortably walk to the door.

"I'll see you tomorrow?" Jo asked quietly.

"Yeah... yeah. Oh, um, your car, we got it to the shop, the battery is bad and we'll get that changed tomorrow." Danny fumbled with the doorknob.

"Thanks. If Violet still lets me bar tend, I'll be able to pay for it real soon." Jo smiled at him.

"Iris. If there… your past… I guess what I'm trying to say is if you need anything or if something happened in your past, I won't judge you. You can talk to me about it if you need to," Danny said quietly as he stumbled over his words.

"Thanks Danny." Jo smiled at him. He nodded and stepped out the door.

Jo let out a slow breath as she looked down at her hand, which was smeared with ointment. She shook her head at herself.

"Stupid.," she muttered as she looked around the room.

A soft clink came from behind her. She turned slightly and followed the noise to the window as it repeated. Jo narrowed her eyes as she walked to the sliding glass door. She squinted as she moved the curtain back. The same black bird sat on the rail and tapped the glass with its beak.

"You again." Jo smiled as she slid the door open.

"I don't have birdseed." She chuckled as she stepped out onto the balcony.

The bird fluttered over to her forearm and landed neatly. His talons dug into the skin of her forearm as he hopped down to her wrist and looked at her hand. He squawked in disapproval as he looked at it.

"Oh, sorry that my hand is injured. Strange bird." Jo laughed and shook her head.

The bird seemed to glare at her and then, without another motion, took off. Jo found the whole thing a little odd but stood out on the balcony a little longer. The night sky called to her as she looked upwards. Bright stars twinkled next to a large full moon.

Thoughts of what Danny said entered her mind as she looked upwards. Hopefully, it was only the battery on her car, and then she could be on her way. Thoughts of Evan entered her mind, and her stomach twisted.

The sound of metal screeching pulled her from her thoughts. She walked to the railing of the balcony and looked down. Her heart dropped to her stomach. Someone had pulled down the fire escape and now climbed the metal stairs to her. She panicked, not knowing who it was or what to do. She went to the entrance of where the fire escape would connect to the balcony. He was so fixated on climbing, he didn't see her. She came up with a plan to kick him down or off the stairs. She stepped onto the top stair and began to bounce on the step. The ladder began to swing and move side to side with each bounce.

"Get off!" Jo yelled as she bounced harder.

"Enough!" he growled as he continued to climb with the bouncing not affecting him.

"I have a weapon! You come up here, and you're getting hurt." Jo threatened.

"Sure, sure," he grumbled as he continued to climb.

"I mean it," Jo said as she slammed her foot down onto the ladder.

There was another loud growl from the man as he reached the top. Jo went to kick him in the head to knock him back, but he grabbed her ankle. He yanked back and pulled her foot out from under her. Jo tumbled backwards towards the cement balcony floor. She braced herself for impact, but instead of the cold hard

ground, she hit something else. She blinked and looked up into gold colored eyes.

"Malcolm?" she whispered as she looked up at him.

"Are you set on hurting yourself more? Isn't one incident a night enough?" Malcom snapped at her in annoyance.

"Umm... What?" Jo asked confusedly as she looked up at him.

Malcolm didn't say anymore but stood up with Jo still in his arms. He looked down at her hand, which was still not bandaged. He let out an annoyed sigh and then led her inside.

"Your hand," he demanded as he walked towards the cotton on the countertop.

"My hand?" Jo repeated as she walked behind him, still not processing.

"Are you a parrot? What is wrong with you? I need your hand." Malcolm angrily held his hand out to her.

"What's wrong with me? What's wrong with you? What are you doing climbing up the fire escape? I could have hurt you," Jo said as she held her hand out to him.

"Hurt me." He laughed as he repeated her statement.

"Yes. I planned to knock your lights out or at least off the fire escape," Jo said with a small smile on her lips.

"Sunflower, you couldn't hurt me if you tried." He smirked as he took the cotton material off the counter and began to wrap her hand.

"I didn't," Jo said as a confident smile spread across her lips.

"You won't need to," he muttered as he tore the cotton and then grabbed the bandage and wrapped her hand.

"Why didn't you use the door?" Jo asked as she looked at his face carefully.

"The bar's closed." Malcom answered shortly.

"Oh," Jo whispered.

Malcom tore the bandage and gently pressed it together. He looked up from her hand, and his eyes caught hers. He held onto her hand, and his fingertips brushed her wrist.

"Danny," he mumbled as he watched her face.

"Danny?" Jo asked. Her eyebrows furrowed as she felt her cheeks flush as his fingertips continued to brush against her wrist.

"Yes. Danny. Are you two together?" Malcolm asked, his voice harsh as he spoke.

"No, he's a friend," Jo answered as she shook her head.

"Good." His voice dropped as his fingertips traveled up her forearm.

Jo's stomach dropped as every part of her arm he touched intensified. She couldn't think, couldn't breathe. She licked her lips as she tried to come up with something to say.

"Why?" Jo whispered as she fought against the chills his fingers gave her as they made small circles.

"Because I would have a problem." Malcolm's voice deepened as he leaned closer to her.

"Problem?" Jo spoke softly, the word barely coming out.

"You're my problem," Malcom said, his voice and eyes full of desire.

Jo froze in place, and her mind went completely blank as she tried to find a way to respond. She didn't have time to even think of one. Within seconds, Malcolm's hand was on the back of her neck and his mouth crashed into hers. His warm lips pressed into hers, and a soft whimper escaped her. As her lips parted, Malcolm's tongue found hers. As his tongue explored her warm mouth, he pulled her against him. Jo's legs went weak, and she melted into him. Her fingers wrapped around his shirt to keep herself upright. Malcolm's hands dropped down and cupped her ass. Her pelvis pushed forward into his, and his kiss grew more demanding. He picked her up and placed her hard on the counter top. Her legs wrapped around him as his tongue danced with hers. Her fingertips traveled from his shirt and wove into his hair as she matched his desire.

A loud noise broke the kiss as the first aid kit tumbled to the floor. Malcolm pulled back and studied her dazed and confused eyes. He cleared his throat as he tried to focus on what he had come here to do. He clenched his jaw, and his mouth turned into a frown.

"What's wrong?" Jo whispered.

"You," Malcolm said in a quick breath. His hand left her hips and moved down over her legs, which were still wrapped around him.

"Me?" Jo pulled back, confused.

Malcolm grunted his response as he began to unweave her legs from around him.

"You climbed up my fire escape. I didn't come barging into your home," Jo said firmly as she scooted back on the counter and dropped her legs from him.

"I did not kiss myself." Anger sparked in her voice as she narrowed her eyes at him and crossed her arms.

Malcolm looked at her perched up on the counter, her arms folded across her chest. A small smile cracked across his face. Most people were scared of him. No one looked him in the eye. She was staring him down and scolding him with her eyes.

"No, but that's why you're the problem." Malcolm sighed and turned.

"Do you always answer or talk like this?" Jo snapped as she hopped down off the counter.

"Like what?" Malcolm asked as she paused in front of the sliding glass doors.

"Vaguely short… annoyed." Jo smirked at the word annoyed as it came out of her mouth.

"I don't talk to people much." Malcolm shrugged and then went to continue to leave.

"Wait," Jo blurted out as a sense of panic rushed over her at the thought of him leaving.

Malcolm said nothing but turned towards her. He scowled as he looked at her.

"Why are you here?" Jo asked and took a small step towards him.

"I don't know," Malcolm grumbled and then turned to the door, his pace quicker this time as he walked to it.

"Stay." Jo called to his back, shocked by her own words.

He didn't listen; he kept going to the door. Jo's chest tightened as she panicked. She didn't understand why, but she wanted him here.

"Mal'akh." His true name escaped her lips, and she watched him instantly freeze.

His back went straight, his stance went rigid as if some had dumped cold water over him. He clenched his hands into fists at his side as he turned sharply. He hardened his face as he moved toward her. Malcolm was in front of her in seconds, much quicker than it took him to get to the door. He towered over her as anger rolled off him.

"Don't ever say my name again," Malcolm snapped, his voice filled with ice as he spoke.

Jo looked at the ground, her body prepared for pain or something worse. She had experienced this type of anger before and knew what followed it.

"Don't," Malcolm said as his voice shook with rage as he spoke.

He watched her flinch, and something inside him hurt. Malcolm gritted his teeth at the odd feeling. He needed to leave. Jo curled her head further down as if it would somehow protect her. She waited, but nothing happened. A wind blew in from the glass sliding door and caused a loud bang. Jo didn't react and stood frozen, still waiting. Why was he taking so long? What was he doing? After several minutes, she looked up and was surprised to see that he had left.

She stood in the empty room alone as the curtain flapped in the breeze. She was confused,

relieved, and part of her felt hurt at the fact he was
gone.

Chapter Six

Jo

    Days passed by quickly, almost in a blur. She had mastered how to bar tend. She had made enough in tips and wages to pay for the car battery but save some money, too. Violet had left and would already be back tomorrow evening. Tonight would be her last shift alone. Danny had gotten closer with her, and she enjoyed his company. He spent the last few nights at the bar and helped her navigate things. He also kept some of the weirdos away from her. She truly appreciated his friendship. In the past few days, she had random thoughts of what it would be like to stay here.

    "Hey…so we're out of ice," Danny said as he stopped in front of the bar.

    "I told Micky earlier, but he never got back to me." Jo frowned.

    "That's ok. I know where Violet keeps the petty cash. I'm going to run and grab some," Danny replied and tapped the bar with his hands.

    "My hero," Jo said with relief.

    "For you, always." Danny shot her a wink as he walked away.

    Jo smiled. He had really been her hero lately. From the moment he picked her up on the side of the road. Danny was safe, kind, and handsome. Maybe… She stood behind the bar, zoned out her thoughts on what life might be like with Danny. Simple, safe. Then suddenly, her mind shifted to one moment. This moment kept coming back to her in flashes. The way his mouth

felt against hers, the way his hands felt against her skin. Her thoughts kept going back to Malcolm.

"Hey! Refill here!" A shout from the other side of the bar caught her ear.

She smiled and nodded to the man as she made her way towards him. She stopped and went to reach for his glass. His hand caught her wrist.

"Isn't your job supposed to be to fill my glass?" He sneered.

"I am trying to." Jo answered shortly and went to tug her arm away.

"You're not trying very hard." He smirked as he held tight to her wrist.

"Let go of me," Jo ordered as she leaned away from him.

She glanced around the bar; it was just him and her. Danny was gone. Micky was never here. Her mind started to panic as she tugged hard once more.

"I don't think I will." The man grinned and pulled her wrist to him.

Jo slammed into the bar hard. The impact made her let out a small whimper. The man leaned over the bar, his face inches from hers.

"We're alone here." He licked his lips as he looked at her.

"Danny, he's-" Jo started, but the man reached forward and grabbed her shirt.

"I heard him. He's gone to get ice." The man laughed.

He gripped the sides of it and began to try to pull her up over the bar. Jo began to fight back but struggled as the wooden bar dug into her ribs. She could hear her

shirt rip the more he pulled. With one hard tug, he pulled her across the bar. He pulled her onto his lap and locked his arms around her. He leaned his head down into her neck and inhaled. Jo tried to wiggle her way out of his lap.

"Oh yeah, baby, wiggle for me." He laughed as his lips brushed her neck.

"Let me go!" Jo yelled and dug her nails into his forearms.

Her fingernails drew blood as she clawed at him. She began to kick to try to create some space between them. As she fought, he became angry and tossed her to the ground. She landed on the ground and heard him knock the chair over as he got up. She looked back and watched him take a step towards her. Bright red blood leaked down his arms from the cuts she gave him. His eyes filled with anger.

"You're going to be so sorry," he said. His voice was like ice as he took another step towards her.

She rolled over and got on her knees and attempted to crawl away. Her eyes fixated on the door to leave. Her stomach twisted with fear as her heart pounded in her chest. She tried to stand when she felt his foot hit her in the back. She was launched forward. Her face scraped against the wooden floor. Her lower teeth went through her bottom lip. She could taste blood as it filled her mouth. She pulled herself up to her forearms as she tried to inch closer to the door. It was just in front of her. She stretched her arm outward to try to reach the threshold like it would save her. She felt the same foot that had kicked her forward press down on her back.

"Stupid girl." He laughed.

He moved his foot to the back of her neck and pressed hard on it. Her face pushed further into the floor as she tried to think of a way out of this. She tried to reach behind her to get to his foot but could not reach. "Don't worry, I'm not going to kill you. Just need you to not fight." He snickered as he applied more pressure. She felt something pop, and instantly her vision became cloudy. She was going to die, was the last thing she thought. His laughter circled around her as the world started fade. The pain overwhelmed her, then it was gone.

There was a loud crash behind her followed by a groan of pain. Then, there was a terrified scream that ripped through the surrounding air. She tried to turn over to see what was happening. She couldn't move. Her mind chanted, to get to the door repeatedly, as her body did not react. The noise stopped, and footsteps came towards her. She tried to pull herself to the exit, her vision blurry and body aching.

"Stop." His voice was abrupt as he bent down towards her.

"Stop moving." He ordered her again as he pulled her into his arms.

"Mal..colm," Jo said as she tried to make out his face.

"Why are you always getting hurt?" He snapped as he looked down at her bruised and bloody face.

"I'm sorry," she whispered.

"Can you stand?" he asked shortly but then scooped her feet out from under her.

She let out a small yelp as he pulled her into his chest. She tried to keep distance from him, but he grunted and made her lean against his chest. His arms held her steady as he walked to the door.

"Where are we going?" Jo asked as the pain radiated down her neck and into her back.

"I'm taking you," Malcolm said as he walked out the door.

Jo didn't argue. Her head started to spin as he carried her out of the bar. She shut her eyes and tried to focus on anything other than the pain. She leaned into Malcolm and felt the pain slip away. The motion from him walking made her realize how tired she was.

"Don't fall asleep," he commanded as he tried to walk faster but steadily so he didn't move her too much.

"I'm tired," Jo whispered back.

"Don't." Malcolm barked at her as he tensed his jaw.

"I'm tired of everything." Jo smiled hopelessly as she closed her eyes.

"Hey, stop. Everything. What's everything?" Malcolm grumbled as he tried to get her to stay awake.

"Life..." she muttered as her head slumped against his chest.

"Hey…No.. Hey!" Malcolm shouted at her as he went to shake her but stopped not knowing how badly she was injured.

"Fuck." Malcolm stopped short and looked down at her.

He could feel her life begin to fade. He let out a long sigh. His mind was telling him to drop her body on the ground and leave her there to die. His problem

would be solved, and she would be gone. The threat would be eliminated.

"Damn it." He groaned and then shifted her closer to him.

He closed his eyes and let his body begin to phase. He wrapped around her and let the phase take over. Within seconds he was back in his home. He let out a breath of relief as she was still in his arms. Malcolm could hear her heartbeat fading. He moved her over to his bed and laid her down carefully. His hand slid over the back of her neck, and he instantly knew it had been broken. His mind told him to leave her, but his chest tightened and his stomach twisted at the thought of losing her.

He gritted his teeth and moved his hands over her neck. He could feel the bones out of place. Malcolm slowly applied pressure and began to shift the bones back in place. He knew it hurt, but she didn't even groan. He watched her lips turn blue and the color in her skin fade. She was dying. Malcolm clenched his fists as he tried to think of something, anything, to save her. He pulled a knife out of his waistband and rolled the handle around in his hand. He looked over her, and as her breathing became shallow, he couldn't take it anymore. He ran the blade across his hand and cut his palm. Black blood began to leak out. With his free hand, he tilted her head back, and her mouth fell open slightly. He placed his cut hand over her mouth and closed his hand into a fist. Black blood dripped down into her mouth. As the blood slipped into her mouth, he could feel his power leaving him. He dropped to his knees on the side of the bed and watched her carefully. She was not

healing quickly enough for him. He squeezed his fist
tighter, and more blood dripped into her mouth.
He winced again as more of his power slipped from him.
He watched as her lip began to heal. Next, loud snaps
and cracks echoed around them as her bones realigned
and healed. The color returned to her cheeks, and her
lips turned pink once more. He let out a breath of relief
and he crashed onto his side.

Chapter Seven
Danny

"Iris?" Danny called out as he walked into the bar.

"Iris?" he called again, but as he saw the blood smeared across the floor, his stomach dropped.

He saw a bar chair shattered into pieces, and he began searching frantically for Iris. He moved quickly across the small bar. Danny followed the blood trail. As he rounded the bar, he saw a man curled into himself. He shook as he held his severely broken arm.

"Please don't hurt me," he cried as he looked at Danny.

"What.. what happened?" Danny asked as he hurried over to him.

"No, don't touch me! He said I must suffer. His eyes, his eyes. I can't unsee his eyes," the man said as he tried to move away.

His leg was twisted completely around, and blood leaked out from underneath him. Danny grabbed hold of the cordless phone on top of the bar top. He called for help as he looked down at the man.

"Where's the girl?" Danny asked as he waited for an answer.

"Girl? He… I'm sorry. I… she was so pretty," the man stuttered out.

Danny pulled the phone away from his ear as he looked at him.

"What?" Danny asked as he tried to process what the man mumbled.

"Where is she? Did you hurt her?" Danny demanded as he put the phone down on the counter and leaned down.

"I.. I don't know. It took her." The man flinched more from the pain.

"Hello, 9-1-1." The muted voice floated down from the bar top.

"Who took her?" Danny asked and then grabbed the man's twisted leg and pressed.

"The monster. He took her. He left with her," he yelled painfully.

"Hi yes, I'm at the old tavern. There's a man here who's been attacked, his leg and arm are broken badly. The girl bartending is missing. I need someone here quickly," Danny reported to the operator as his stomach twisted.

Monster…He looked around the bar and then moved to the door. Maybe he could catch up with them. His stomach twisted. He needed to know where Iris went. If she was ok. As he stepped outside, the red and blue flashing lights caught him. They had to have been already on their way.

"He's inside, behind the bar," Danny said as two police officers approached him.

"Any weapons? Anyone else inside?" One officer asked as he eyed the door carefully.

"No one else is here. There's a shotgun behind the bar but not within reach of him. There was a girl working, and she's gone." Danny was more concerned about where Iris had gone and not the broken man inside.

The officer went inside and, in a few seconds, he waved the EMTs in. Danny stepped aside for the EMTs to run past him.

"Do you work here?" the officer who stayed behind asked as he motioned for Danny to come towards him.

"No, I help out sometimes. Iris... She is about five six. She has short brown hair and blue eyes. She's not from here. She was working. I went to get ice. We need to find her," Danny said with urgency in his voice.

"Where is she from?" the officer asked.

"I don't know," Danny answered with a shake of his head.

"Do you know her last name?" the officer asked with a raised eyebrow.

"No." Danny realized he didn't know much about Iris.

"So… Iris…no last name, don't know where she came from. Just showed up one day and you gave her a job with no information?" The officer sounded annoyed.

"She needed help. Her car broke down. She looked like she was…" Danny stopped talking; he didn't know what Iris was running from.

"She needed help? Where's her car?" The officer asked, now suspicious.

"It's around back." Danny nodded to the back parking lot.

The sound of EMTs wheeling the man out on a stretcher tore Danny from the cop's attention. They rushed him to the ambulance and slammed the doors. "I think he's on something. I'm going to follow them to the hospital to see if I can get some more answers. He

keeps talking about a monster," the other police officer said as came out of the bar.

"All right. Danny here's going to take me to the missing girl's car. I'll run her plates to see if I can get more info," the police officer who was talking to Danny told his partner.

"Close up the bar and come show me her car," he said as he looked at Danny.

Danny nodded and pulled a key from his pocket. Violet had left him a spare just in case Iris had any issues. He locked up and then nodded to the officer to follow him.

Jo

She curled into herself. She was laying on something soft and cozy. She knew as she ran her hand outwards that she was in a bed. Jo stretched her hand out, feeling for the edge. She couldn't find it. She inhaled as she stretched. The bed smelt like a warm liquor, like rum or whiskey. There was a deep, smokey smell, too. Jo opened her eyes. She knew that scent. She could still taste him on her lips. Jo sat up straight and looked about the room. The deep gray walls matched the dark vibe the room gave off. She pulled the black bedding around her. She was in a gloomy cave. Where was she?

"Malcolm?" The word escaped her mouth before she even registered that she would call out to him.

Her body knew she was in his room. That this place was his. She heard a small grunt and leaned over the side of the bed. Malcolm had collapsed on the floor.

"Malcolm!" Jo yelled as she hopped off the bed and went to his side.

He groaned as she reached out and touched the side of his face. He pressed his cheek into her hand, and her touch felt good.

"Hey, open your eyes. Look at me," Jo said firmly as she rubbed the side of his cheek with her thumb.

Her eyes wandered over him as she searched for any wound or clue as to what happened. Her worry increased with each second he was not responding to her.

"Malcolm." Jo shook him lightly with her free hand.

Malcolm's hand snatched her by the wrist, and he sat up forcefully. As he did, he took her arm with him and ended up making her fall across him. His other hand caught her head. She was sprawled across him, confused, as she looked up at him. His eyes were jet black.

"Iris." His face softened when he realized it was her.

"Malcolm… your eyes.," Jo said as she reached up and touched his cheek with her other hand.

"Did you get hurt?" Jo asked, her eyebrows frowned.

"Hurt… No," Malcolm said as he remembered what happened.

She was dying, and he gave her his blood. He shut his eyes as the realization of what he did hit him. They were now bound.

"Does your head hurt?" Jo asked as she watched him close his eyes. She moved her hand from his cheek to his forehead.

"No," he grumbled as he opened his eyes.

"What happened?" Jo asked and then pulled her hand back as she watched his eye color change back to yellow.

"You hit your head. You were attacked. I took you here and made sure you were ok," Malcolm said shortly.

"But I feel fine. You're on the ground with black…your eyes…" Jo said as she pulled back further to look at him.

"Fine," Malcolm said dismissively.

"But…" Jo went to protest, but Malcolm pulled her against him.

"You talk way too much," he grumbled as she landed against his chest.

"You don't talk enough," Jo whispered,I. It was meant to come out stronger sounding, but being this close to him made her voice hitch in her throat.

Before she knew it, he was on his feet cradling her against him. She didn't even understand how it was possible for him to move that fast or even get up from the position they were in. He moved over to the bed, and her heart pounded in her chest. Her eyes grew wide, and everything began to hit her. She was in a room alone with him, in a place she didn't know, and he was putting her on a bed.

"Please," she whispered, as she became afraid of what was about to happen.

Malcolm looked down at her as he placed her gently on the bed. She scooted back quickly. His eyes narrowed at her.

"I'm not gonna hurt you." Malcolm's voice became soft.

"We didn't need to be on the ground anymore. It's…hard." Malcolm smirked.

Jo nodded, still unsure of where she was and why she was there. Malcolm sighed. He saw the questions flash across her face, and he hadn't figured out any of it himself.

"I… the bar, the guy. What-" Jo began to stutter out.

"I took care of it. Brought you here. This is my home, yes, this is my room, and no, none of that will happen unless you …ask me to." The smirk still lingered on his lips.

"Why?" Jo asked quietly as her eyes flickered around the room. She was looking for a way out.

"I need you here," Malcolm whispered. The truth came out effortlessly.

"Need?" Jo asked as she began to feel the room close in on her.

She felt like she couldn't breathe as her chest tightened and her eyes followed the solid walls. Malcolm watched her with confusion. Her eyes darted about as they searched the room.

"Yes…You're staying here," he said as he watched her panic increase.

"I can't. I have to go. I have…" Jo said as she got dizzy.

Malcolm watched her curl into herself as she tried to slow her breathing down.

"What's happening?" Malcolm demanded as he became frustrated that once again she was hurting herself.

"Closed… space." Jo managed to get out in between hyperventilated breaths.

Malcolm looked around the room. A thought hit him, and he realized she had always left the sliding glass door to the apartment open. He walked across the room, his eyes focused on the window. He grabbed the dark black curtains and tugged. They crashed to the floor and revealed a set of three windows. He stepped through the black curtain and pulled open the window. The night breeze came rushing in. The cool air hit her, and she felt herself relax. Malcolm stood by the window and watched her. Something had happened to her. Something wrong and horrible. He felt his blood boil. Malcolm clenched his jaw and walked across the room silently. He reached the bedroom door and hesitated. Malcolm wanted to ask, wanted to demand to know who or what had done this to her, but he couldn't find the words. He walked out of the room and slammed the door. Jo leaned back against the headboard as the panic started to leave her. She glanced at the door… Was she locked in?

Chapter Eight
Malcolm

He collapsed back against the door as he shut it. What the fuck was he doing? He couldn't let her go now. He couldn't kill her now either. Malcolm ran his hands down over his face. He had placed himself in an impossible situation. If others found out about her, that they were bound. He clenched his jaw. His hands went into fists as he struggled to control all the rapid emotions flooding through him. He needed to do something. Anything. He needed air and space. He walked away from the door.

Malcolm, open your eyes. Are you ok? Hurt? Her voice flooded through his mind. She was in a stranger's home and had just been attacked, but she was worried about him. She had been through something. It angered him that something or someone had hurt her. He would kill them, and if they were already dead, he had ways to make souls pay for the torment that had been caused in this life.

He shook his head as he walked down the stairs and towards the kitchen. He didn't know what he was doing or where he was going, but he found himself in his empty kitchen. Malcolm opened the fridge. It was empty, too… He had nothing to offer her. He closed his eyes as if the empty fridge represented him and the nothingness

he had. Malcolm grabbed a glass out of the cabinet and turned the sink on to fill the glass. He needed to come up with a plan. He had to keep her… not just because she knew his name or now they were bound. Malcolm just wanted her. She had a light within her beneath it all, and it called to him. This was like nothing he had ever felt in all the time he had spent wandering this earth. He felt whole next to her. Malcolm felt his stomach twist. He was going to fuck this up somehow. The water from the sink spilt over the edge of the glass, and he let out a slow, steady breath as he shut the water off. He looked up at the ceiling, wondering what she was doing, what she was thinking.

He didn't even think twice; he walked to the door and opened it. As soon as the air hit him, he felt himself transform. His black feathers shimmered in the moonlight. He needed to be away from her but still needed to check on her. He found his way up to the windowsill and looked in.

Evan

"Hello?" Evan placed the phone to his ear as he answered the out-of-state number.

"Mr. Matthews?" A man's voice came through the phone.

"Yes? Who is this?" Evan asked, concerned.

"Evan Matthews?" The voice asked again.

"Yes. This is Evan Matthews. Who are you?" Evan asked as he became irritated.

"Mr. Matthews, this is Detective Jamison from the Paris PD. We need to ask you some questions. We got your information from your car," Jamison said quickly.

Evan's stomach bounced with excitement. She had screwed up. She didn't ditch the car. He grinned and had to take a moment to ensure the happiness didn't come through in his voice.

"Oh, thank God. That's my fiancée's car. I've been looking for her. She took off." Evan made his voice sound worried.

"Took off? Sir, there was an incident at a bar here in town. She had started working there, and now she appears to be missing," Jamison said quietly.

"Incident? Please tell me she's ok," Evan's voice was on point - frightened, concerned, but all he really wanted was information.

"A man at the bar got a little rough with her. Somehow, he ended up with a broken arm and leg. She is nowhere to be found. Do you have any information on how to get in touch with her?" Jamison asked.

"No, she's not well. She goes through manic episodes. She took off in the middle of the night. I didn't report the car stolen because I was hoping she would just come back. She left her medicine and everything. Paris… What state?" Evan asked as he grabbed a pen.

"Idaho. Can you tell me if she has family out here? Somewhere she may go? We don't know if she's hurt." Jamison pressed.

"No, I am all the family she has. We're located in Oregon. I will start heading that way. Do you need anything else from me?" Evan asked quietly.

"Any identifiers would be great tattoos, scars. Does she tend to gravitate towards anything when she feels scared?" Jamison interrogated.

"She's five, six, has bright blue eyes, long honey blond hair. She likes to be secluded. Always liked music. She self harms so she has several scars throughout her body. No tattoos. She has pierced ears, ummm…" Evan rattled on like a concerned partner should sound; he threw in the self harm comment to seal the deal and cover any scars he may have left on her.

"She's blond?" Jamison questioned, confusion in his voice.

"Yes.. Her hair goes down to just above her butt, and it's a deep honey color." Evan repeated his voice, mimicking the detective's confusion.

"The girl who was working had short dark brown hair…" Jamison stated, his voice puzzled.

"She may have cut and dyed it. She does odd things when she is manic. Please find her officer. She is not well," Evan pleaded. He shook his head, and anger washed through him. She cut her hair and dyed it. He gritted his teeth; how dare she!

"We are going to do everything we can. When you get to town, stop by the office," Jamison said quietly.

"I will, officer," Evan said firmly.

"Mr. Matthews…there's no one she would be running from, is there? Changes in one's appearance can sometimes indicate…trouble." Jamison sounded suspicious.

"Just herself, sir," Evan replied quietly.

"All right, we'll see you when you get in." Jamison ended the call.

Evan clicked his cell phone off and placed it down on the counter. He grinned. He knew where she was, and she was stuck now. No car, no way out. She would pay for cutting her hair. She would pay for taking off. He walked to his bedroom in three long strides. He would be in Idaho shortly, and by tomorrow night he would have her back.

* * *

Jo

Panic rushed through her, and she couldn't breathe. He just left. She looked around the room wide-eyed. Jo couldn't think straight. She was spiraling, and any minute she felt like she was going to fall out. Her breath became rapid, and her chest burned. She could feel the world start to fade. Just as everything was about to go black, she heard a small chirp. It started out soft and then slowly broke through the chaos in her mind. She glanced at the window. The open window. She took a deep breath and saw the same blackbird from the apartment perched on the windowsill.

"You," she said breathlessly as she walked over to the window.

She kneeled down next to the window; seeing outside made her instantly feel better. She wasn't completely enclosed and shut in.

"Thanks," she whispered to the bird as he moved closer to her.

83

"I really hate being locked in places. I... I can't be trapped anymore." She confessed her fear to the bird.

The bird took off into the room and circled around. Jo watched in confusion as to why it would do such a thing. It landed on the handle of the door and chirped at Jo again. Jo narrowed her eyes at the bird. It squawked louder and then took back off out the window. The door. The bird wanted her to try the door. She stood slowly and gathered the strength to walk to the door. If she touched it and it was locked, the realization of being locked in would crush her. She didn't know right now, and maybe she could just pretend. She took a deep breath and walked to the door; her legs shook with each step. Her stomach twisted as she wanted to vomit the closer she got. She tried to ignore the closed door. Jo told herself not to check. She held her hand out to the silver doorknob. Her fingertips twitched as she curled them around the handle and pulled. The door creaked open. He didn't lock her in. She stood frozen as she looked out into the dark hallway. Jo stepped out carefully into it and looked around. She saw the stairway to the first floor and walked towards it. The next step she took creaked loudly in the silent house. She stood still and shut her eyes as she tried to listen to see if he heard her and where he could be. Nothing. There was no noise. She let out a slow breath and opened her eyes.

"Aaahh." She screamed and stumbled backwards.

Malcolm didn't hesitate as Jo started to fall backwards. He took three steps and caught her. She

was back in his arms again. Her face filled with confusion as she stared up at him.

"You weren't there," Jo said quietly as she searched his face for answers.

"You need to be careful," he muttered as he put her upright on her feet.

"What are we doing here?" Jo asked quickly as she tried to put distance between them, but the only way to do that was to step back in the room.

"Are you hungry?" he asked as he ignored her question.

"No." Jo shook her head as she waited for him to answer her.

"I brought you some water." Malcolm suddenly held a glass out to her.

Jo looked at the glass, her eyes filled with fear and suspicion. She shook her head no. Malcolm sighed loudly and shook his head as he put the glass to his mouth and took a drink.

"Here." He held it back out to her.

Jo took the water cautiously from him and then held it close to her. She looked from the water to him, unsure what to do next.

"I don't know. I need to figure something out. If you could just go rest while I do that. It would be great." Malcolm blurted out as if he read her thoughts.

"No... I can't. Look, I need to go. I have to get back to the bar. Violet isn't back yet. I can't stay here." Her voice shook as the thought of being trapped somewhere again entered her mind.

"You need to stay. I can't have you running about with what control- " Malcolm snapped, almost saying too

much. He moved towards her and she instantly stepped back into the room.

"You're staying.," he growled at her as he watched her eyes grow wide.

"No, please. Mal'akh. Please, just listen to me," Jo begged.

Malcolm froze. She did it again. She said his name. He clenched his jaw as he waited. He had to listen to her. She looked at him, not sure what to do next.

"I'm listening," Malcolm said through his gritted teeth.

"I don't know what you want or what you think you need, but it's not me. I can't do this again. Please," Jo begged.

He unclenched his jaw and felt relieved she had not told him to do anything. He stepped towards her, and she inched back. She was now far enough into the room that he could close the door.

"I can't. I need you close until I figure this out. Once I do, you can go. Until then, relax, go to sleep. Anything, just stay." Malcolm ordered as he reached for the door.

Jo shook her head no quickly as tears slipped from her eyes. Her body shook as she watched him start to close the door.

"I'm not going to hurt you," Malcolm said; the words felt odd and gross as they came out of his mouth.

"Don't close the door, please," Jo whimpered.

Malcolm paused, not sure why the plea made him stop in his tracks. He looked at her and nodded.

“I won't. You stay in this room and don't leave. I won't close the door,” Malcolm whispered. She reminded him of a caged animal.

Jo nodded as she went and sat on the bed. Malcolm felt sick as he watched her behavior. He didn't understand what would cause her to act like this. Malcolm pushed the door the rest of the way open and watched her breathing return to normal. He stared at her for one more moment before he turned and walked away.

Chapter Nine

She stared at the open door, not moving from the bed. What was he planning? What was it that he needed from her? She needed to escape. Jo felt drawn to him, and there was an underlying feeling of safety with him, but she was not going to allow herself to be in this situation again. She watched the door as she stood up slowly. Jo was afraid to move. She took her first step and felt her stomach twist. She took a deep breath and moved towards the window. Jo needed to get a sense of where she was. She stood in front of them and peered out. There was nothing to see but tall trees. She pulled her bottom lip into her mouth as she stepped away from the window. Maybe she could just get out? Run to the nearest street, pray someone would stop for her? Like Danny did. Danny. He would notice she was gone.

Her footsteps were light as she walked to the door and, without hesitation, dashed to the stairs. She placed her foot soundlessly on the first step. This time she was zoned in on being quiet. She moved down them, and no noise came from each step she took. She had months of practice from sneaking away from Evan. As she reached the bottom landing, she saw a brown wooden door with frosted glass windows. It led to the outside. She moved to it and reached out to the black handle in seconds. She squeezed the latch and slowly opened the door. No sound came from the door. She was in the clear.

She opened it enough for her to step out. Her feet hit the concrete steps, and she rushed down them.

The pebbled driveway hurt as she rushed across it in her bare feet. Her eyes fixated on the faded iron gate. She would climb it and be on the road in no time. Jo ignored the sharp pain in the soles of her feet as she rushed to the gate. She paused just in front of it and then the gate slowly opened. She was confused and stared at it. Was it automatic? On a sensor? She looked over her shoulder and saw Malcolm in the driveway. He held the control to the gate. She looked from him and to the open gate. She scolded herself, not sure if this was a trap or not.

"You can go… but it's a far, hard walk," Malcolm yelled to her.

Jo shut her eyes, and her mind yelled that this was a trap. She didn't know what she should do. She felt fear and adrenaline rush through her. Her body was not sure how to respond.

"I'd rather you stay but I won't make you. It will be easier if you're with me." He whispered just inches from her ear.

Jo opened her eyes and looked into his gold ones. He leaned towards her as he spoke. She didn't understand how he got in front of her so fast. He blocked the way to the gate now and her mind screamed danger.

"How…" Jo whispered as she watched his face.

"I'm fast," Malcolm responded and then stepped aside to give her the view of the gate.

"That's not just fast," Jo said, her eyes going back to the gate.

She was met with silence as she looked at the gate. He waited to see what she would do. His heart pounded in his chest as he waited.

"Why do you… you said you need me?" Jo asked. She was scared of being trapped again, but something in her wanted to know.

He stepped in front of her and held out his hand. She looked to his open palm and back to him. Her body wanted to reach out and touch him, but her mind warned her. She licked her lips as she nervously put her hand on top of his. Tingles rushed through her, and her fingertips wrapped around his hand instantly. He watched her face and the rush of emotions that flooded through her.

"You feel it," Malcolm whispered as he stepped towards her.

She nodded as her other hand reached out and touched his chest. She felt this force pull her towards him. Jo needed to be near him. It was stronger than anything she had ever felt. She felt as though her soul belonged to his, and she could literally feel herself wanting to connect with him.

"I feel it, too." Malcolm's other hand covered her hand on his chest, keeping it there.

"What is it?" Jo whispered as she watched his chest rise and fall beneath her hand.

"I don't know. That's why I need you here… Stay," he begged. His voice shifted from harsh to soft and vulnerable.

"I'm tired," she whispered. She could not bring herself to look up for fear of what would happen if she locked eyes with him.

"Stay. Rest. If you don't want to be here come morning. I will drive you back to the bar, not another request for you to stay," Malcolm said as his hand squeezed hers slightly.

Jo nodded. She couldn't deny she felt it. Couldn't fight the need to be near him. She was exhausted and just wanted to sleep and be safe.

"Are you hungry?" Malcolm asked quietly as his hand traveled to her hip.

"I…" Jo started to say, but her stomach let out a loud growl.

"Come on." Malcolm chuckled, his usually firm, serious mouth let a smile crack through.

His chuckle made Jo's stomach flutter around like butterflies were trapped inside. She couldn't stop the smile that spread across her own lips at the sound of it. She nodded and stepped back from Malcolm. He let her go. Malcolm badly wanted to snatch her hand back, but he was careful not to force anything on her after seeing her previous responses. Malcolm watched her start walking and noticed she winced slightly. He frowned and in two long strides; he was at her side. He scooped her up into his arms and cradled her as he began to walk.

"I can walk," Jo said firmly, but her protest fell on deaf ears.

Malcolm chose to not acknowledge it and kept walking to the house. He set her down on the concrete steps and motioned for her to go inside.
"You were going to take off barefoot? You should have planned that better." He shook his head as he spoke.

"It was a fight-or-flight thing." Jo laughed with a shrug as she stepped into the house.

"Kitchen," Malcolm said as he followed behind her and nodded to the left.

"Kitchen." Jo repeated and waited to follow Malcolm.

Leo

What had he just witnessed? Leo leaned against a tall oak tree, his back pressed into it as he watched. He came back to try to find a way to convince Malcolm, but what he saw was far more intriguing. Malcolm had never shown an interest in anyone but himself. He flinched in disgust as he watched him scoop the girl up and carry her across the driveway. A human? He scoffed in his mind as he wrinkled his nose. Leo shifted his stance as he debated moving closer to the house to see. He phased and reappeared near a window. He leaned against the stone mansion wall as he tried to listen. Leo could not hear them. He closed his eyes and tried to focus on the noise inside the house. He heard a small noise coming from the back of the house. Leo phased again and reappeared by the kitchen window. He smirked, realizing he had found them. He closed his eyes and listened.

Leo's face twisted as he listened. There was a giggle and more laughter that came through the wall. What was happening? Malcolm was fear itself. He was dark, hated people, life, and could not stand humans…

Now he was making one giggle. He tried to peer through the kitchen window.

Malcolm

He carried her into the kitchen tightly against his chest. He got near the marble island, dropped her legs and held her by the waist. He placed her down on the kitchen island. A look of shock flashed across her face as her butt hit the stone counter top. He didn't even say anything before he grabbed her foot and lifted it up so he could see the bottom of it. His thumb rubbed against the inner sole as he looked for a wound. Jo let out a loud giggle as she tried to pull her foot away. Malcolm gripped her foot tightly and raised an eyebrow at her as a smile spread across his lips.

"Don't!" Jo ordered as she tugged her leg away.

"Dont?" Malcolm's smirk turned into a grin as he brushed his fingertips down her foot.

"Stop… No… I'm ticklish," Jo begged as she laughed and wiggled.

"So, you're not hurt?" Malcolm smirked.

"No… ssstop." She laughed and then yanked her foot away, nearly kicking him as she did.

"Still hungry?" Malcolm asked, his eyes were brighter and Jo noticed a warmth in them as he watched her.

"Yeah… I'm not picky." Jo smiled back at him.

Malcolm nodded and then turned to the cupboards. He didn't spend time on food. He didn't need a lot. Malcolm simply existed. He frowned as he saw

93

mostly empty shelves. There was peanut butter and bread.

"It's fine." Jo laughed from the counter as she watched him stress about the lack of food.

"Are you barely home or just don't eat?" Jo smirked as she watched him twist the top of the peanut butter cap off.

"Both," Malcolm said quietly as he pulled out a butter knife and spread the peanut butter on the bread.

"So… I need some answers," Jo said quietly as Malcolm handed her the peanut butter sandwich.

As she took the sandwich, her stomach let out another loud grumble.

"Do you not eat?" Malcolm asked. His eyes scanned her body. She was on the thinner side, but he didn't think anything of it until this moment.

"I do now," Jo said quietly as she happily took a bite out of the sandwich.

"Now?" Malcolm eyed her suspiciously.

"Yup… You live here alone?" Jo asked as she changed the subject.

"Yup… So you're just not hungry in life 'til now?" Malcolm smirked, changing the subject back.

"You just like being lonely?" Jo narrowed her eyes at him as she played his game.

"Love being alone. I don't like people." Malcolm stepped towards her.

"People suck." She agreed as she finished the last bite of the sandwich.

His hand ran up her leg gently as she froze and looked at him. He had stepped between her legs and now caressed them. She felt her breath catch in her

throat. She could feel the heat rise in her cheeks as her body flushed.

"Mal-" His hand covered her mouth. A small glimpse of fear flashed in his eyes as she almost said his name.

He was afraid she would say his true name, and she needed to stop. He watched her eyes grow wide as she waited for an explanation.

"Don't say my name," he whispered to her as he took his hand off her mouth.

She watched his face as his eyes seemed to darken as he spoke about his name. She wondered what power a name could hold? What could be so bad about his name?

"Iris, do you understand?" Malcolm asked her. The hand that had covered her mouth now laid on her hip.

"My name's not Iris." She blurted out as she watched his expression change, his eyebrow raised as his look asked her to explain.

"It's a long story, but my name is... Jo," she breathed. An immense weight lifted off of her as she said her name; her stomach twisted in fear.

"Jo?" Malcolm asked as his thumb rubbed her thigh as he tried to comfort her.

"Yeah... as in Josephine. I...I'm... I don't want anyone to know who I am," Jo admitted.

"Josephine." He repeated her name, and this time her finger went to his mouth and pressed against his lips, a small smile on her lips as she copied his action.

"Shhh... don't say my name." She grinned, half serious, half teasing him.

Malcolm looked at this fragile creature that sat in front of him in amazement. She surprised him. There was courage in her. No one would dare do something like this to him. He caught her by the waist and pulled her against him. Her pelvis pressed against his as a small gasp escaped her lips. Jo, legs on either side of his waist. Her legs wrapped around him possessively as he moved his mouth away from her finger and towards her ear. Her body tingled as she felt the heat from his body so close to hers.

"What are you running from, Sunflower?" he whispered into her ear.

His warm breath against her ear sent chills through her as she unknowingly leaned towards him; she needed to be closer to him.

"I... I'm-" his hand interrupted her sentence as he covered her mouth.

A noise caught his ear. There was something outside the kitchen window. No one knew where he was. This was something different, someone with some power. He could feel the energy shift in the world now that he focused on it. His eyes darkened as he formed the noise shh with his mouth. He then closed his eyes and phased. Jo gasped as his body turned to smoke in front of her and he was gone. She covered her mouth with her own hand to hold back the scream she felt in her chest. She pushed herself across the countertop away from where he was just standing. How did he disappear? What was happening? Her mind couldn't understand what she had just seen. Jo's stomach

twisted and her legs felt tingly as she realized that this was something unnatural. Her mind screamed danger as she reached the end of the counter. She toppled over the other side of the island and hit the floor. Jo tried to catch herself, but it didn't stop her fall. She crashed to the floor. Pain rushed through her as her wrist broke her fall, and pain radiated up her arm.

Jo ignored the pain as she cupped her good hand around her wrist that throbbed. She needed to get away. She needed to go. Jo got to her feet and rushed to the exit of the kitchen. Once out of the kitchen, she made her way to the front door. She grasped the handle and pulled the door open.

"What are you doing?" His voice called from behind her.

She spun towards the kitchen to see Malcolm standing in the entrance. She didn't realize how tall he was and how much bigger he was than her until this moment. His body was tense, and his eyes narrowed at her.

"Are you ok?" he asked as he took a step out.

"What… How?" Jo asked as she cradled her hand.

"Jo, let me see your wrist," Malcolm said quietly as he walked to her.

"Where did you go? How did you do that? You just disappeared. How is that possible?" Jo asked as she took a step backwards towards the door.

"I don't know what you're talking about." Malcolm continued to walk towards her.

"No… No, you were there and then you weren't," Jo said firmly as she kept her distance from him.

"I was there the whole time. What did you do to your wrist?" Malcolm said as he reached her and placed his hand above hers, resting on the door to keep it closed.

"I'm not crazy. You vanished." Jo looked up at him.

"I think you're tired," Malcolm whispered as he went to touch her side.

"Don't touch me. No... No... If you were there the whole time, you would know what happened to my wrist." As she finished her sentence, she elbowed him in the gut and took off towards the stairs.

Malcolm grunted as he doubled over from the impact. Hunched over, he watched her run up the stairs. He shook his head at her. She was running up. There was no way out of the upper floor. He closed his eyes and phased. He reappeared where the stairs met the top floor just as Jo got to them.

"Boo." He smirked as he watched her face flush with fear.

She let out a small yell as she jumped back and tumbled down the stairs. Malcolm's smirk turned to panic as he watched her lean back. He reached out and grabbed her forearm to steady her. A look of relief rushed across her face as she gained her balance. She then looked up at him, her face a mixture of fear and confusion.

"What are you?" Jo asked, her voice part curious and part afraid.

"Do you really want to know?" His lips curled into a devilish smile.

"Yes…" she whispered. She stared at him, expecting him to disappear again.

In an instant, he turned into black smoke in front of her eyes. His hand that once held on to her drifted away into nothing. She let out a small gasp as she looked down at her arm and where he once stood. He was gone. There was nothing. This was impossible.

"I'm a demon," he whispered from behind her.

Jo glanced over her shoulder. He stood behind her, ready to catch her if she fell. Her eyes widened with fear as her brain was slow to process the words that came out of his mouth.

"No," Jo said quietly, and before Malcolm could respond, she raced up the stairs.

"No questions?" He laughed as he watched her get to the top of the stairs and take off down the hall.

His laughter followed her as she continued to flee him. He got to the top of the stairs as he saw her duck into his bedroom and slam the door. Malcolm heard the door lock in place. He let out another chuckle. Malcolm could easily phase into the room. He would let her feel safe, give her a minute to process. He had other things he needed to figure out. Someone was outside his home. Someone who held power. A demon. He knew it was another one of his kind. He needed to find out who and why.

Chapter Ten
Leo

    Leo's lip curved into a sinister smile. He had finally found something, or he should say someone, to use against Malcolm. This girl. He was not sure what she held over him, but he knew that she was special to Malcolm. It was strange that she was at his home. He had to find out more about this girl. Leo overhead him call her by two different names. First Iris and then Jo. The girl was hiding something. That would be the key. Find something he could use over the girl and then used her to get Malcolm to do what he wants. He could have laughed out loud as he trembled with excitement. The sudden silence inside the house grabbed Leo's attention. He paused outside the window. His excitement disappeared as his gut told him something was about to happen. He felt the surge of energy, and his stomach twisted. Someone was phasing, and he knew it was Malcolm. Leo panicked and phased quickly, going to the last place he was. He hit the cold, hard stone floor; his nose brushed against it. He phased so quickly that he didn't control his landing.

    "Leo… back so soon? I didn't expect you to be such a quick and fast worker." Pavel's voice hissed as he stood over him.

    "Ugh… I…" Leo pushed himself off the floor.

    "You what?" Pavel growled as his eyes narrowed at Leo.

"I have found a way to get Malcolm back in business." Leo grinned as he ran his finger down his nose as if to rub out the pain.

"So, you haven't done it?" Pavel was unimpressed with the little news Leo had brought him.

"No, but it will work. I just needed-" Leo began to explain, but Pavel wrapped his hand around his throat.

"I don't care what it is or how you do it. I want it done. Do not keep coming here empty handed!" Pavel yelled. A rush of hot air hit Leo in the face as spit speckled his cheek.

All he could do was nod slowly before Pavel dropped him. He crashed to the floor and stared up at him. Pavel's hood dropped back and revealed his face. Leo looked confused, he had not seen Pavel's face in a long time. He always covered himself. Now Leo realized that his skin had turned ash gray and his head was completely bald. Pavel looked like he had begun to rot away. He looked as if at any moment a piece of his body could fall off. Leo did not know this was even possible, but as he stared at Pavel's face he could see the effects of the decades of not fulfilling his end of his bargain. The one he made for power in exchange for his soul.

"What's wrong with you?" Leo asked as he stood up.

"We all have reasons as to why we became what we are… mine needs souls. Get me souls or I will ruin you." Pavel growled.

"Go, Lazaros." Pavel grinned and waved his long, fragile hands at him.

Leo grumbled as he felt his body phase without his control.

Jo

The door slammed behind her, and her hand went straight for the lock. She clicked it into place as her hand shook. She glanced around the room. Jo needed to block the door. Her eyes landed on a wooden chair in the corner of the room. She rushed to it and gripped the wood in her hand as she hurried back to the door. Jo wedged it under the handle and prayed he wouldn't be able to get in. She looked around the room again, and the feeling of hopelessness settled in. Her eyes spotted the window, and a small spark of hope nestled within her. She walked to it, her chest tight as she hoped for a way out. As she got to the window, her eyes spotted the ground so far away.

There was no way she could jump without hurting herself. The spark was smothered. She reluctantly walked back into the room. She had traded one prison for another. One monster for another. She went to the door and placed her hand against it, as if it would tell her something. Jo wanted to open it, but she didn't want to let him in. Whatever he was. She turned her back to the door and sank to the floor. She let out a deep sigh and pushed back against the door beside the chair. Jo tried to think up a plan to escape, but nothing was coming together. She felt a weight on the other side of the door. As if someone was directly on the other side with their back against it. She tensed as her breath held in her chest.

"Jo?" Malcolm's voice came through the door.

Her eyes widened, and she felt her heart pound against her ribs. He was there, just on the other side of the door. What if he wanted in? Could he get in? Worse, what did he want from her? The questions plagued her as she tried to calm herself.

"I know you're there." Malcolm teased. She could picture a small smile on his lips.

"You should answer, or I might have to come in to check if you're still there." Malcolm continued as his lips turned up into a grin.

"What do you want?" Jo whispered as she pulled her knees up to her chest.

Malcolm was surprised by the question. He didn't know what he wanted. Until recently, all he wanted was to exist alone, quietly, hoping for a day that would end him. He was done with it all. He was tired, and the world had nothing left for him. Then he saw her.

"You." The word fell effortlessly out of his mouth. He didn't even realize he was about to speak it until he couldn't take it back.

"Me. Like my soul?" Jo asked faintly, the words barely fell out of her mouth in fear.

Laughter rumbled the door as Malcolm chuckled, the warmness to it made Jo feel at ease.

"Why are you laughing? Isn't that what demons do? They steal souls…work for the devil…are evil?" Jo asked, her voice frustrated because of his laughter. Malcolm laughed more as he leaned his head back against the door. His laughter rattled the door again, and it fueled Jo's frustration.

"Hey!" Jo said and elbowed the door.

"What?" Another chuckle came across.

"Don't laugh. That's what you do, right?" Jo demanded.

Malcolm imagined her face scrunched up and offended. A cute sparkle in her eyes. He tried to hold back another laugh. Her lips pressed together in frustration. Her eyes narrowed in disapproval.

"Answer me," Jo grumbled as she bumped the door again.

"I'm retired." Malcolm answered. His voice still had a touch of laughter in it.

"Retired? Demons retire?" Jo asked. Her voice was a mixture of confusion and shock.

"This one did." Malcolm shrugged as he shifted from the door.

"How does that work?" Jo urged. She felt him move away and wondered what he was doing.

"Simple. I did my part and what I needed to... to relieve the debt that I owed," Malcolm explained, his voice now came from the bed.

Jo jumped at the sound and pushed back into the door, her eyes wide as she found him sitting on the bed, comfortable as can be, like he had been there the whole time.

"How did you do that?" Jo questioned as she slowly stood up.

"Demon." Malcolm smirked as he laid back on the bed.

"So you can just appear anywhere you want? Just think of a place and you're there?" Jo asked as she boldly took steps towards him.

"Pretty much." Malcolm yawned as he closed his eyes.

"Pretty much." Jo repeated his words as she reached out and touched his knee.

It was a knee, solid and felt no different from hers. She didn't know what she was expecting. Malcolm sat up and looked at her in surprise. The warmth from her hand on his knee sent chills through his body. He had never in his entire existence responded to someone like that.

"Sorry… I just-" Jo began to pull her hand back.

Malcolm caught her wrist and sparks shot through his hand as he touched her.

"Don't," he whispered. The words were a pure reaction, and he didn't want her hand to leave his.

Jo's face flushed as she felt heat radiate through her. She looked down at his hand on hers and couldn't help but feel the need to be closer to him. She moved slightly closer, her body acting on its own. His hand pulled her close.

"Don't?" Jo repeated his words as her thigh now brushed against his knee.

"Don't be sorry… don't move," he said as his hand let go of her wrist and moved to her waist as he pulled her into him.

Jo's hands went to his shoulders as he pulled her against him. She felt her heart speed up in her chest and her stomach flip in anticipation. Her eyes locked with his. The warm gold color of his eyes made her lean forward to look. As she did, she felt the hand that held her waist lift her and pull her forward. Her legs wrapped around his back, and she straddled him. Her body

screamed for his touch. She could hear her pulse vibrating in her ears. His hands ran up and down her sides, caressing her as his eyes remained locked on hers. He watched her intensely as if he was judging her response.

His head leaned forward into the crook of her neck. He watched her skin as it turned to little speckles of goosebumps in response to his warm breath. He brushed his lips against her skin and felt her shudder.

"I'm going to tell you a secret," he whispered. His lips continued to brush against her skin, and each time she felt her body beg for more.

Jo could feel herself inching towards his lips; she wanted them to touch her more. Her skin craved their touch. She could barely focus on what he was saying.

"All you have to do is say my name and what you want and... I'll do it." The brushing of his lips against her skin turned into soft kisses as the sentence ended.

"Hmm?" Jo muttered as she adjusted her neck to let him have better access.

"If you want me to stop, just say 'Mal'akh stop,'" Malcolm said. His tongue ran up her neck and brushed her earlobe.

"Use my name and I'll have to," Malcolm whispered into her ear.

"You said not to." Jo shut her eyes and enjoyed the warm tingles he was causing in her.

"I know what I said." Malcolm growled as his grip on her hips tightened.

"I'm giving you a way out," Malcolm said as he pulled her earlobe into his mouth and sucked on it.

She felt this ache inside her growing with each touch. There was a need at her core. The chills and tingles overwhelmed her. She wanted him, wanted more.

"Mal'akh…" she said breathlessly.

Malcolm froze, his stomach twisted and waited for her to order him to stop. It would be hard, but he would. He would walk away.

"Mal'akh, don't stop," she whispered as she gave in.

The words sent a fire through him, and his body reacted to her. He pulled her tightly towards him and picked her up. In one quick motion, he turned her around and laid her on the bed. She felt the soft bedding buckle under her weight and then, in an instant, she was staring up into his golden eyes. He leaned over her and studied her as he fought against the command she had given him. He wanted to be sure. She watched his eyes fade from gold to red and back. Jo narrowed her eyes as she watched his eyes. She could see him fighting with himself. Concern and worry filled his eyes.

"Demon," she whispered as she watched his eyes darken again.

He swallowed hard as he stayed above her. He clenched his jaw as he waited for her to continue. She watched him, waiting, and then he slowly nodded.

"Evil?" she asked and reached up and touched the side of his face.

He shut his eyes as she touched his cheek. His stomach fluttered at the feeling of her skin against his. He forced himself to answer.

"Goes with the title, Sunflower," he muttered as he felt his chest tighten, afraid of what she might say next.

"I've seen evil." His eyes fluttered open at the sound of her voice.

"You're not evil." Jo's voice was steady as she said the words.

Malcolm looked down at her in surprise and confusion. He started to say something back to her. She saw him about to argue, and her hand moved from his cheek to his hair. Jo's fingers threaded through his black hair, and she pulled his face down to hers. Her lips pressed against his as she began to kiss him. Her body arched towards his as his lips parted and he deepened the kiss. His aggressive and demanding tongue explored her mouth. He kissed her back fiercely, like he couldn't get enough of her. His mouth moved over hers and pulled her bottom lip into his mouth. His tongue brushed against her lip as he sucked on it. She felt her body quiver, and an ache began at her center. She wanted him, all of him.

His mouth moved against the delicate flesh of her neck and made her knees weak. Everywhere his mouth touched sent a warm rush through her. A soft growl vibrated against her skin as he reached the beginning of her shirt. He gripped it in his hand and pulled it. The shirt split down the middle. The cold air spread across her skin and sent a rush through her as she felt his warm mouth traveled down her body. She arched up into him, eager to feel his lips across her skin.

He ran his finger up her black bra strap and slowly slipped it off her shoulder. He watched her face

as he did. She pulled her bottom lip into her mouth and bit down on it in anticipation. He teasingly went slower, pulling off the other strap and he could see a flash of frustration on her face. He smirked and pulled the center of the bra down and her breasts came free.
She lifted towards him, wanting to feel his mouth on her breasts. The instant satisfaction that shivered through her as his mouth captured her nipple made her let out a moan. He squeezed her breast as he sucked. She let out a sharp inhale as his teeth grazed over her nipple as he let go. He ran his tongue down the middle of her stomach. Her body shook with the feelings that rushed through her. Her toes curled into the bed as he kissed down her stomach. He gripped the sides of her pants as he reached them and pulled. Her underwear went with them. He chucked the clothes behind him, and they landed on the floor with a thump. The coldness made her legs want to close. Malcolm's hand caught her thigh and pushed them open.

"Uh, uh, uh." Malcolm smirked as she locked eyes with him. He leaned his head down towards her center and caught a glimpse of her as she bit her lip and tilted her head back.

He ran his tongue down the center of her lips and watched her legs quiver. He pushed his tongue past her lips and rubbed small circles against her bud. Her hips rocked as they followed his motion. He felt her grow wet and found her entrance with his fingers. He pushed inside her and moved them slowly. His tongue still played with her bud. He heard her let out a soft gasp that turned into a low moan. He began to move faster

and felt her grow more excited by the moment. She felt her body throb more and more.

"Oh my God," she whispered as the sensation overwhelmed her.

She longed for him. Her body shook with need, and only one thing could stop it.

"Mal'akh... fuck me... please." She groaned as her hips arched.

She felt him move away from her. She heard some noise and then felt something large at her entrance. Malcolm pressed into her, and she instantly felt relieved. It was what her body waited for. He began to move, and her legs locked around him to hold him in place. His pace quickened, and her body clenched around him each time he moved. Her hips followed his movements. He moved faster and thrusted deeply into her. She held on to him as she felt his member begin to throb inside of her. Her own body tightened around him in a spasm of ecstasy. A warm feeling washed over her as all her muscles contracted. She let out a moan and clung to him as a wave of intensity rushed over her. He felt her orgasm, and it instantly made him release. He caught himself with his forearms on either side of her. Her face was flushed, and lower lip swollen from her biting on it. He moved to the side of her and watched as her face went from satisfied to embarrassed. She covered her face with her hands. He smirked and reached over. He pulled her hands from her face. She smiled as she looked up at him.

"Don't cover your face," he ordered as he placed her hands down to the side.

"The afterglow looks good on you," he said with a coy smile on his face.

She looked at him, still embarrassed. He pulled her into his arms. She turned as he wrapped his arms around her.

"Sleep," he murmured as she let out a small yawn.

She nuzzled into him, and the feeling of safety and warmth took her over. She instantly gave in, and sleep came quickly. Just before she nodded off, she felt his lips press against her forehead.

Chapter Eleven
Evan

His black truck came to a rolling stop outside of the police office. He had driven straight here. He only stopped for gas and didn't even waste the time to use the bathroom. His bladder wanted to burst but the pain only fueled his anger. He would never let her out again. They would move. Someplace with a basement. Some place he could lock her away for ever. This would be the last and only time she ever attempted this. He turned the key and the loud roar of the engine stopped. He glanced at himself in the rearview mirror and checked his reflection. He reminded himself to be concerned, be worried as he stepped out of the car. This is the worst thing that has happened to you, he directed himself. He let out a breath and tried to get into character. He walked to the front door of the police station as the sun just began to shine. The loud beep rang in his ear as he stepped through the doorway.

"Can I help you?" A voice called out from behind a thick glass partition.

"Hi, I'm Evan Matthews. Detective Jamison found my car. My fiancée is missing." His voice started off annoyed but then he remembered he was playing the role of a concerned and worried partner.

"Oh! Mr. Matthews. Yes, you got here very quickly. He wasn't expecting you so soon. He just got into his office. Let me give him a buzz," the short red headed woman said quickly as she reached for her office phone.

He heard her have a quick conversation announcing his arrival and then the click of the phone.

"Mr. Matthews, have a seat in one of those chairs and Detective Jamison will be right out." She smiled at him and nodded behind him.

"Thank you," Evan said as he walked over to the off white chairs.

He couldn't sit. His body vibrated. He had too much energy. His mind repeated to him over and over again, "Find her. Find her. Find her!" He could feel his hand twitch as he was on the verge of snapping.

"Mr. Matthews." Detective Jamison's voice pulled him from his thoughts.

"Hi… Detective Jamison?" Evan asked as his eye twitched and he held out his hand to shake Jamison's.

"Yes… Mr. Matthews are you alright?" Jamison asked. He picked up on his tense body language and the eye twitch.

"Not really, I'm tired. I've been looking for Jo for over a week now, fearing the worst. So I'm a little stressed. Please tell me you found her and I can take her back home to get some help." Evan's voice flooded with emotion.

"Let's go back into my office and talk," Jamison said with a nod and started to move towards the door.

Evan clenched his jaw. The longer they took the longer she was away from him. He let out a long puff of air from his nose as he followed Jamison. Jamison's office was down a long hallway. The ugly brown carpet made Evan cringe. Why would they not have white tile or better flooring? This must be a shit hole of a town.

They're never going to find her. Evan's mind was spiraling. He was so close to her yet still did not have his hands on her.

"Have a seat, we need to talk about a few discrepancies. Do you have a picture of… Jo." Jamison asked as he sat across his desk from Evan.

"Discrepancies? Here," Evan said. His heart pounded in his chest. What if Jamison found her and he believes what she's telling him?

Evan pulled out his clean black leather wallet and flipped to the front space. He slid a picture of Jo out. She was wearing his favorite blue sun dress. The baby blue color always made her eyes stand out. That's why he painted the room blue. The room she wasn't supposed to escape, the room she was meant to stay in! His hand trembled as he passed the picture to Jamison.

"Do you need some coffee? Are you going to go to a hotel after this to get some sleep?" Jamison asked as he watched the tremor in his hand.

"No, coffee will make it worse. Yes, I have a room booked at your inn," Evan said as he watched Jamison look down at the photo.

"So, the woman who had your car, was calling herself Iris. The other person at the bar said she had short brown hair and blue eyes." Jamison said. He had only spoken briefly to Danny who had blurted out her description. Jamison watched Evan's face carefully.

"Think of something!" his mind screamed as he adjusted himself in the chair.

"Jo may have cut her hair and dyed it. She thought someone was after her. She has paranoia.

Maybe even multiple personalities. We haven't confirmed it. She started refusing to go to doctors and I couldn't bear to have her hospitalized. I thought I could handle it at home." Evan's voice sunk to a defeated tone which played right along with his helpless and hurt fiance act.

"We have word out at the local hospitals in case she shows up there. Can I keep her photo? Just for now. I want to confirm that this is Jo with the people at the bar. Unfortunately, this is all I have for now. Don't worry too much. We are a small town and everyone knows everybody here. We will find her," Jamison said, falling for Evan's act.

"Thank you so much. I just want her back home safe," Evan said with a nod as he stood up.

"I understand. You go get some rest for now. I'll be in touch," Jamison said quietly.

"My car, can I have a look at it? I might be able to figure out where she would go. It might be helpful to you," Evan asked as he got to the door.

"Right now it's part of the investigation. Let my guys go through it and then we will bring you in," Jamison responded as he stood up.

"Ok… one last thing, Do you have any local parks in the town? I'm going to get some rest and then try to clear my head. I like nature." Evan explained.

"Yeah, there's a local park right off of Main and First." Jamison smiled at him.

"Thank you." Evan nodded and he was on his way.

Jo cut her hair! Her long, golden hair. He remembered from the phone conversation that he had

said the woman had short brown hair. She dyed it brown. That bitch. Anger flooded through him as he walked to the car. How dare she. He would shave her bald and she could live out the embarrassment until her golden locks grew back. The fact she thought she could even do that made his stomach burn with fire. He reached the truck and jerked the door open. The handle threatened to break in his hand.

"First and Main," he repeated as he sat down and pulled up his GPS.

Jo liked nature and liked the parks. She would gravitate to them. If she was going to go anywhere to breathe or relax or feel better, it would be there. He would take her and disappear. They may need to move. This local cop might be a pain in the ass and he has his address. They would move somewhere Jo didn't know. Someone in the middle of nowhere. So if she ever ran again she wouldn't be able to get anywhere.

Danny

Danny didn't know what to do. He cleaned the bar after the police had given him the go ahead. He walked the outside of it. Trying to find any bit of evidence where Iris would have gone. His stomach twisted with worry. Violet would be back today and he was a bundle of nerves. Something was wrong, why would Iris just take off. He needed to know she was ok. That nothing horrible had happened to her. After searching the nearby roads and streets, he found

116

himself back at the bar. He wanted to be here in case she came back. In case she needed him. The police had taken her car and said they would be back by this morning to look through her room.

"Knock, Knock."

"Come in?" Danny replied back to the odd saying as he watched Detective Jamison step through the door.

"Jamison… Anything?" Danny asked eagerly.

"No… Unfortunately. Do you have an extra key to the upstairs? That's where you said she was staying," Jamison said calmly.

"Yeah, I can get you in… But, nothing?" Danny asked, having trouble believing that there was nothing. People just didn't vanish.

"I have a photo I need you to look at." Jamison reached into the front pocket of his shirt and pulled out the small wallet size photo.

Danny took it in his hands and looked down at a picture of Iris in a blue sun dress. She was standing beneath a tree and you could tell the day had been windy from how her dress swayed to the side. Danny looked up from the photo with his eyebrow raised, not sure what Jamison was needing.

"Is that the girl?" Jamison asked as his own eyebrow mimicked Danny's.

"Yeah, this is Iris. Her first night here she cut and dyed her hair brown." Danny handed the photo back over to him.

"Her guy's in town. The car registration came back and we made contact. He must have driven all night and drove like hell to get here. He says her name

is Jo and she suffers from some mental health stuff."
Jamison frowned.

"Look, she definitely was trouble. I wouldn't say she was not with it. There's something more she didn't say. She was pretty banged up when she got here. Someone roughed her up. She was running from someone. I didn't ask questions but I wouldn't trust this guy of hers," Danny said his eyebrows furrowed as he spoke.

"Banged up?" Jamison asked.

"Look, I know what domestic violence looks like when I see it. My gut tells me she was running from this guy. I wouldn't trust him or help him. Why give a fake name and change your appearance? Run her real name, she's not a criminal." Danny defended Iris.

"We're not jumping to conclusions and if we find the girl and she doesn't want to go back, we will help her. Let's take this one step at a time. We need to find her," Jamison said quietly.

"Room?" Jamison asked as Danny's silence filled the room.

Danny didn't say anything but reached under the counter and pulled out a spare key. He slid it across the bar top to him.

"Up those stairs, it's the only room." Danny's tone was flat.

"Danny, I promise if this guy is what you say he is we will help her. But we need to rule out first that she didn't have anything to do with our friend that was on the bar floor and that she doesn't need mental health help," Jamison said quietly as he took the key.

Danny didn't respond. He nodded slowly; he knew that Jamison had to do his job but his stomach turned at the idea of this guy searching for Iris. There was something not right.

Chapter Twelve
Malcolm

Soft cries wrapped around him in his sleep.
Someone was hurt. He strained to listen. Was it real? Or
was it just the cries from his past coming back to greet
him? The faces of the innocents he convinced to sell
their souls in the very beginning of his demonhood.
They plagued his dreams. What he once pridefully
considered an honor now filled him with nightmares and
guilt. He would watch the light fade from their eyes.
They would beg and plead for more time. Then their last
screams as the hellhounds dragged them off. The
screams were now etched into the inner workings of his
brain.

There was another soft cry. It was full of fear and
pain. He then felt a vibration. It tore him from sleep. His
arms trembled as he looked down at her. Her face was
scrunched up in a painful look. Her body shook as she
whimpered in her sleep. Something or someone was
hurting her. He went to pull her closer to see if comfort
would make the bad dream stop, but she began to
cower more.

"Stop. Please. Don't. I'm sorry," she cried out.

Rage settled into Malcolm's stomach as he
shook her lightly. She let out a loud cry, and he shook
her harder. She tried to curl into herself to protect her
body. Malcolm frowned deeply as he tried to wake her
once more; he rubbed her arm fiercely. She winced as if
it hurt.

"Jo, wake up!" he said firmly.

His voice snapped her out of her dream. Her eyes jolted open, and she pulled her arms up over her head to block imaginary blows that came for her. Her body shook from the adrenaline and fear from her vivid dream.

"You're safe," he said as he reached out and rubbed her arm.

She uncovered her head and looked up at him. He watched her eyes change from fearful to confused as she looked up at him.

"Mal'akh?" Jo spoke softly as she looked up at him, she needed to know he was real.

"It's me. You're okay. You're safe." Malcolm pulled her back into his arms.

She was trying to stop her body from shaking. Jo looked around the room quickly to make sure it was not blue. She looked up at him and placed a hand on his cheek. Jo let out a small breath of air, relieved that she was not dreaming this.

"Who?" Malcolm asked, he tried to hide the anger in it.

"Who, what?" Jo responded, but she knew what he was asking.

"Who hurt you?" Malcolm asked again, his voice calm.

"They don't anymore. It's okay." Jo smiled; her thumb moved across his cheek.

"Who hurts you in your sleep?" Malcolm asked, his jaw clenched.

"Malcolm, I don't want to talk about him." Jo quietly begged him not to press the conversation.

"Him." Malcolm's eyes darkened, and Jo realized her mistake.

"Yes, it was a him. I left. I'm never going back. It's in the past. He'll never hurt me again," Jo said as she tried to get him to let it go.

"He hurts you in your sleep," Malcolm growled.

"Trauma. We all have it." Jo let out a small laugh as she played it off.

She saw his brows frown and his lips turned thin. He was about to argue and demand to know. She didn't want him to know. Jo didn't want him to see how broken she was. She felt embarrassed and ashamed. There was a strange sense of guilt, and it ate at her. She didn't want him to see the ugly pieces of herself.

"They are nightmares. They will pass. I just need to have some better things to dream about." She smiled at him.

Malcolm's face didn't change. He clenched his jaw at the thought of this 'him' hurting her. He wanted revenge. Malcolm wanted him to be in pain. He wanted to inflict suffering and terror on him.

"You could help me…. make better things to dream about." She smirked. Her thumb went to his lip and pulled his lower lip out from the thin line his anger had created.

He raised an eyebrow at her comment. She thought he could give her better things. He felt his heart soften and the anger subside. He leaned forward and pressed his lips to her forehead.

"Did you want to try to go back to sleep?" he asked, his lips still against her forehead. They sent tingles through her as they brushed her skin.

"No. I usually get up when… I don't like going back to sleep once I wake up… Gives me a headache," she lied.

He pulled back sharply and looked down at her. His eyes narrowed and darkened as he stared at her. She went to ask him what was wrong.

"Don't lie to me. I hate lying. If it's something you don't want to say, then don't say it. Just simply say no, I don't want to go back to sleep," Malcolm said firmly.

"I don't want to go back to sleep," Jo said. Even though his voice was sharp, she did not feel like he would hurt her.

"Ok." Malcolm nodded as he waited to continue, as if she was going to tell him what she wanted to do.

"Sir… if you don't remember you've kinda kidnapped me and told me you're a demon… so, the ball is in your court as to what to do." Jo burst out laughing seeing his face.

"What do you like?" Malcolm asked as she rolled over into him.

His arms wrapped back around her as he pulled her against him. She fit perfectly to him. Her every curve hugged him and he thought for a second that he could get used to this. Her warmth radiated into him, and he wanted so much more now.

"Like?" Jo sighed in contentment as she curled into him more.

"Yes. What do you like?" Malcolm asked as he pressed his face into her neck, inhaling sharply.

"I…I like, umm." Jo tried to think straight, but Malcolm's warm breath on her neck sent crazy waves of

heat and chills through her. Her body was on an emotional roller coaster.

"You don't know what you like? Has anyone never asked you before?" Malcolm's lips now brushed against her skin, and when he was finished speaking he pressed his lips into her neck.

"No… Not really," she whispered as she moved her head, giving him better access to her neck.

Malcolm placed soft kisses up her neck to her ear. He lightly pulled on her earlobe with his teeth. Another chill shuddered through her body. He pulled her earlobe into his mouth and sucked on it. She leaned into his mouth; her mind went blank as she focused on the sensation of it. He pulled away and his teeth slightly nipped at her earlobe as he did.

"Tell me what you like," Malcolm ordered. His hand traveled up her bare skin and captured her breast. He held it firmly and squeezed.

"I like… you," Jo whispered. Her eyes were closed as she leaned back into him, enjoying the feeling of his hands on her.

"Me?" Malcolm repeated in surprise.

"Mhmm." Jo sighed breathlessly.

Her soft hum of confirmation stopped him in his tracks. He had never been liked. He was always feared and hated. That's what demons were. It didn't bother him; he enjoyed it for the most part. The rush of someone cowering and begging in front of him used to make his skin vibrate. He looked down at her for a moment with worry. What if she feared him? She turned in his arms and looked at him.

"What's wrong?" She put a hand to his cheek.

"You're not afraid of me?" His voice was confused and almost vulnerable as he spoke.

"Yes." She nodded, but there was no fear in her voice; her eyes held no fear.

"Because I am a demon," he said as if it was all normal.

"No. Although that does sound terrifying." Jo smiled slightly.

She watched his eyebrows frown, and deep lines of worry appear across his forehead. His eyes squinted slightly, and there were crow's feet at the corners. Her smile widened as she watched him process what she had said.

"I'm afraid because I don't know what this is. I have been in one bad situation after another," Jo said softly, her eyes taunted him.

"Demons don't frighten you. Evil doesn't scare you." Malcolm studied her face.

"Evil. I have seen and experienced evil. Evil is a matter of perspective. From my view, I don't see evil when I look at you." Jo ran her hand down his face and traced his jawline.

"I'm worried, though… Are you going to be bad for me?" A dangerous smile played on her lips as her thumb brushed his.

"Only in the best ways." Malcolm grinned.

"Best ways?" Jo's eyes sparkled with mischief as she looked up at him.

"Hmmm… One condition," he said as he leaned forward. His lips came close to hers, just barely touching them.

"Condition?" Jo asked, her mouth begged for
him to move forward.

"Yup," he whispered as his lips brushed against
hers.

"You stay," he continued. His mouth captured
hers, and he kissed her quickly.

The intense rush she got from the quick kiss left
her wanting more and then disappointed when he pulled
away.

"Stay?" she asked, confused at why he would
want her.

"Stay. As in I am Keeping You," Malcolm said
firmly and then pressed his lips hard into hers.
His kiss was forceful and demanding, as if the statement
he said was echoed in the kiss. Her tongue eagerly
greeted him, and a battle for dominance erupted in her
mouth. She moved her hand up into his jet black hair
and tugged tightly as she kissed him back just as
wanting. He broke the kiss suddenly, and she
breathlessly sucked in air. She looked at him, confused
as to why he stopped.

"Come on. I want to show you something," he
said as he detangled himself from her.
She looked at him and pulled the blanket around herself
as she stood. He glanced at the blanket then her.
Malcolm moved to his closet and grabbed a dark t-shirt
and a pair of his boxers. He walked back to her and
handed them to her. She grabbed the clothing and then
slowly let the blanket slip. He stepped back as he
watched her. His eyes traced every curve of her body.
He didn't actually want to show her anything; he would
rather stay wrapped up in this room with her. But one

thing she said kept repeating in his mind. She didn't know what she liked. No one had ever asked her. She slipped the boxers up and then looked at him. Her short brown hair bounced lightly from the wiggle she did to pull the boxers up. He held his hand out. He was still naked, and she felt her cheeks grow warm.

"No one else is here." He grinned as she caught her looking.

"Hang on." He laughed and then walked to his closet and slipped on a pair of boxers and shorts. He looked back over his shoulder as he walked out and held his hand out to her.

She smiled and took it. He led her out of the bedroom and down the hall. She was amazed at how big the house was. He paused at one door and pushed it open. He moved aside for her to step in. She hesitated but went inside. The room was dark in color with warm hues of amber. There was a grand piano in the center, and the walls were lined with every instrument. Guitar, bass, cello, violin. He had trumpets, flutes, and even a saxophone. She looked curiously back at him.

"Music? Instruments?" he asked her quietly as he looked about the room.

"Do you play all these?" she asked, amazed.

"I can." He nodded as his hand ran over the piano keys.

"Do you?" Malcolm asked from the piano. His fingers played a small riff.

"No." She smiled as she watched him.

"Ok, then… Let's go." He smiled and moved towards the door. She looked at him, puzzled, but followed.

He stopped at the next room and pushed the door open. The room was lighter in color, soft off-white. There was a large window overlooking the woods, letting natural light in. There was an easel by the window and all sorts of paints and tools.

"Paint? Art?" he asked as he watched her wander over to the wall where some of his old paintings hung.

"You paint?" She reached out and touched a painting.

"Do you?" he asked as he raised an eyebrow and she shook her head once more.

"Hmm… Come on, then," Malcolm said as if he was trying to crack a puzzle.

He walked down the hall and made a sharp turn. Malcolm stopped in front of two large doors. He pushed them open. Light flooded out of the room as she stepped in. She entered a floor to ceiling, wall to wall covered library. She looked around in amazement.

"You read?" Malcolm laughed as she looked around.

She nodded, still overwhelmed. Jo did love reading. She walked among the books. Reading was her one escape inside the blue room. Malcolm watched her and then frowned.

"What?" Jo asked as she looked back and saw his frown.

"This isn't it. It's close, but no." Malcolm motioned her to follow.

"What? What could you possibly have left in here? You have an art studio, a music room, and a library," Jo said as she began to follow him.

128

"I've been around for a while and like to change hobbies often." Malcolm smirked.

Jo followed him down the flight of stairs and out the glass french doors. She was confused as he led her outside. As soon as she stepped outside she felt at peace. Her eyes wandered around at a magical garden. She wandered over to the reddest rose she had ever seen. She walked under an archway of climbing wisteria. The purple flowers flowed down the arches and blew in the slight breeze. Passing through the arches, she found herself in a field of sunflowers. They reached up towards the sky trying to catch all the rays of the sun. She walked over to them, her fingers reached out and brushed their golden petals.

"There it is." Malcolm grinned as he came to her side.

"What?" Jo laughed as she looked out over the garden. There are flowers, plants, and trees everywhere.

"The spark. Everyone has it, Sunflower." He smiled with a wink as he looked from her to the sunflower.

"I love nature, flowers and gardens. I had this dream of having a small cottage nestled in the woods where I could grow anything I wanted." Jo smiled, looking around in amazement.

"It's yours," Malcolm whispered.

"What?" Jo asked him with a confused laugh in her voice.

"I said I was keeping you. So, the garden is yours. Plant whatever you like, whatever makes you

happy. Spend all the time out here you need," Malcolm explained.

"It's gorgeous," Jo whispered as she looked back at the field of sunflowers, and then she paused.

"Wait..." His words finally settled in.

"For?" Malcolm asked as he stepped to her.

"When you say you're keeping me, is this... Are you forcing me to stay here?" Jo questioned as she tried to find the right words.

Malcolm let out a quick sigh and caught her by the hand. He spun her towards him. They were face to face. The chills his fingers etched into her skin ran up her arm and curled into her neck as if that's where she wanted him to touch next. She felt her heart speed up in her chest as she leaned into him.

"Let me explain clearly. I am a demon. There are rules in the demon world." His voice hushed as it rumbled through his chest. Jo found herself excited as she tried to focus on his words.

"One, don't let anyone know your name...your real name," Malcolm muttered as he stepped closer to her.

"Mal..." She went to say, but he grabbed hold of her chin and his thumb pressed into her lips.

"Two, don't share your blood with anyone," he said firmly.

"Share blood? What?" Jo asked, confused.

"You were hurt pretty badly by the man at the bar. I took you back here and broke the rule." Malcolm's voice became deeper.

"Blood... share blood? Explain," Jo demanded.

"Demon blood can heal," Malcolm said quietly.

Jo's face scrunched up in confusion as she tried to process what he just said.

"Ironic. I know, evil creatures that we are, our blood can heal." Malcolm cracked a smile as he waited for her to catch up.

"You gave me your blood… how?" Jo muttered her question.

"Does it matter? What you need to know now is that I am bonded to you. We do not tell our name and we do not share blood. If we do that, one person is connected to us. So… you stay," Malcolm demanded.

"Bond… what does that mean? Why is your name important? I can't just stay here. I have-" Jo snapped as she stepped back. Her head and her world started to spin.

"You have what? What exactly do you have? You're clearly running from some type of past. You were working at a bar, you have a car that doesn't work… Why wouldn't you stay? Look at what I have," Malcolm said, the demon of temptation slipping out of him. This was a conversation he had thousands of times. Show them what little they have and what they could have, and in seconds their soul was his. He waited with a smug look on his face as he knew the outcome of this game.

"No. I may be running from some... thing. I may not have a lot. My car is actually working, and even though that may not be for long or enough. And you have all this. I have more," Jo said with anger in her voice.

"Demon or not. I have freedom now, and I am not giving that back up for a garden, library, music room or art studio…. Or you." Fire was burning in her eyes.

"What?" Malcolm asked in disbelief.

"You are not taking my freedom from me. I say where I go… where I stay," Jo said to her, hands now in fists at her side.

He tried to process how his power didn't work. How she could not give in to what he was offering. He watched her turn sharply and began walking into the sunflower fields.

"Wait! Where are you going?" Malcolm called after her and began to follow her.

"Don't you dare follow me, Mal'akh!" she shouted back at him as she marched on.

His feet froze to their spots. She said his fucking name! He clenched his jaw so tightly he could feel the muscles spasm in his cheek. He stood there long after she was out of sight.

Chapter Thirteen
Evan

He walked into the park. The white flowered trees swung in the crisp breeze. Their petals fell down onto the stone path and danced under his feet as he walked. His eyes scanned the park. It was pretty much empty. An elderly man walked his speckled brown and white dog, but other than that, no one was there. He knew Jamison had said she cut her hair but his eyes looked for her golden locks. When it dawned on him that they were no longer golden nor long, he felt anger bubble up inside of him. He narrowed his eyes and looked once more for short brown hair. It still didn't change the fact that the place was empty. He grumbled and sat down on the bench.

The grass looked almost damp from how green it was. His eyes fogged over as a memory came to mind. The soft checked blanket was sprawled out across the vibrant grass. The wooden picnic basket he had set in the middle. She sat opposite him in a white dress. Jo looked around, her skin pale from being kept from the sun for so long. She smiled, excited to be out. He opened the basket and pulled out sandwiches and chips. He placed them on a plate and handed it to her. She smiled brightly at him as she took the plate and waited for him to make his.

"Thank you," she said, her voice genuine.

"You're welcome. It's nice to get out, isn't it?" Evan said back to her.

Jo nodded and shut her eyes as she tilted her head back. The warm rays of the sun danced across her

face. She savored the moment, trying to ignore the fear that seeped in her stomach. Fear that this might be the last time she felt their warmth.

"Does the sun feel good?" Evan laughed as he poured red wine into two long fluted glasses.

"Amazing," Jo said as she let it warm her skin.

"This could happen more." Evan smiled as he reached out and touched her hand.

Jo moved her head back and opened her eyes. She looked at him, torn between wanting to bolt and wanting to convince herself that he loved her. That he meant what he said. That the "this time will be different," was true.

"That would be nice." Jo smiled weakly, not wanting to ruin the moment. He held the glass out to her, and she took it.

Her eyes scanned the liquid, looked for traces of powder or anything suspicious. It wouldn't have been the first time he drugged her. He laughed and took a sip of his wine. She let out a small breath and took one.

"If you behaved more often, we could do this more. I would love to take you to the new breakfast place soon," Evan continued.

'Behaved more?' The anger that fluttered in her stomach at the words shocked her. She forced a smile and nodded. Evan picked up his sandwich and took a big bite. She hated the way he ate. He would chomp and slurp every time. Even with a sandwich. She had brought it up once politely in the beginning, and that was the first time he threw something. His plate went flying across the room. He blamed it on past experiences, and she ignored the red flag.

"I heard they have crepes." Evan grinned, his cheeks full of his sandwich.

"That would be lovely," Jo said as she looked down at her sandwich.

The sound of laughter caught her attention, and she looked across the park. A group of guys was playing frisbee golf. They were all about her age. She watched them for a second as they laughed and carried on. She wondered what it was like to be that free. Evan cleared his throat. For a second, she had forgotten his jealous nature.

"So... how are things going at work?" Jo asked as she tried to recover.

"Good, actually-" Evan started to say when he was cut off.

"Hey, watch out!" A yell erupted from the direction of the men playing frisbee as the frisbee came sailing towards Jo.

The frisbee bounced to the ground and skidded towards Jo. She looked from the frisbee to the guy running towards them. She picked it up and held it out to him.

"Hey, sorry about that." The man grinned, his brown hair slicked back from sweat.

"No worries." Jo smiled back as the man took the frisbee.

"If you guys want to come play, you're more than welcome to join." He said, lingering just a moment, his eyes locked on Jo.

"We were just having-" Jo started to say, but a loud slam drew her attention to Evan.

"We were just leaving," Evan snapped bitterly as he shoved things back into the picnic basket.

"Maybe next time. We meet here every-" he continued, confused by Evan's reaction.

"Thank you, but-" Jo started to try to turn him down. Her mind screamed for the words to come out faster, reject him quicker!

"Leaving." Evan snatched Jo's hand.

The car door slamming echoed around inside her brain. One minute it was gorgeous and almost normal; the next she knew what would happen. The blue room. She couldn't breathe. She watched Evan throw everything in the back of the truck. Her mind said she couldn't go back. To get out of the car and run. Call for help. Ask the frisbee golf guys. Anything! But she stayed frozen in the chair. She didn't even hear Evan get in, her mind in utter chaos as the engine roared and they sped out of the park.

He shook his head as he chased the memory from his mind. He thought she would be here. His stomach knotted as he scanned the park once more. His mind replayed the conversation he had with Jamison. The bar. That would be his next stop. Make friends with someone, get more information. He would find her.

Malcolm

It felt like forever. He hadn't moved. His first thought was to find a way to chase after her. To make sure she stayed. Malcolm could phase to where he thought she was going. He knew his property, and the

136

sunflower field ended up by the brook that ran through it. He could phase there and then walk to meet her. It wouldn't be following her, more cutting her off. He started to, but the words she spoke hit him in the chest. She had freedom. Freedom. As if she had been a caged and trapped animal. This was something deeper. Something that had hurt her. He couldn't hurt her. Images of her twitching and sobbing in her sleep flashed in front of his eyes. Malcolm would not be that. He was many things and had done horrible things, but he would not do that. He gritted his teeth and decided that if she would go, he would let her.

He wandered over to the stone bench and sat down, his eyes watched the field. His chest twisted with aniexty, and hoped that she would come back. He didn't know what he would say if she did. Worse, he didn't know what the right action would be if she didn't. He heard a small snap and watched as she walked out of the sunflowers. He stood and took a step towards her. She pulled her lower lip into her mouth and nervously chewed on it. Her hands were clasped together and watched her anxiously pull on her pinky finger.

"You came back?" he asked quietly.

She nodded as she watched him. Her eyes judged him like she was trying to make a decision.

"Why?" Malcolm asked as he took another step towards her.

"You didn't follow me," Jo said, her voice surprised.

"You told me not to," Malcolm stated. His voice held a bit of defensiveness .

"I know. That's why I came back. You let me go…" Jo said, pausing and not explaining what she meant.

"I don't want you to." Malcolm's voice dropped low as he spoke and took another step towards her to close the distance between them.

He reached out and took her hand. Malcolm watched her forearm as the faint blond hair stood up at his touch. He knew the shiver that ran through her as their hands touched because he felt it, too. He watched her unintentionally inch forward to him, her own body pulled to his.

"I know you feel this, too. I don't want you to go because I don't know how I could stand not having you here. There's something in me that needs you," Malcolm whispered.

"I feel it, too." Jo's hand went to the side of his face, and another chill rushed through him.

"Stay," he whispered, the word a silent plea.

She just nodded because she could not find the words to speak. Her voice caught in her throat from the intense rush of feelings coursing through her. He moved his hand from her forearm to her waist and pulled her against him. His eyes darkened and flashed possessively as he looked down at her. He watched a small flicker of fear pass through her eyes, and he felt his chest clench.

"I won't hurt you. Never. You can leave whenever you want. I won't stop you. You're not trapped here," Malcolm whispered. His thumb brushed her cheek as he spoke.

"This… this feeling, is it because of what you said that we're bonded?" Jo asked, her voice barely above a whisper.

"I've felt it from the moment I saw you. Before I shared blood with you. Now it's intense and I can't escape it." He leaned down and pressed his forehead into hers.

"You're trapped?" Jo whispered as her nose brushed his.

"Without mercy," Malcolm said. As she leaned in his lips brushed hers ever so softly.

She pulled back a little, but his hand captured her waist and held her in place. He saw guilt in her eyes and cracked a smile.

"Sunflower… I'm a demon. Nothing is trapping me where I don't want to stay," Malcolm said as he ran his hand down the length of her arm.

"Sunflower… why do you keep calling me that?" Jo smiled as she tried to suppress the tremor he was causing in her.

"I think you are the light in the dark that I have been looking for," Malcolm said as he wrapped his arms around her and his mouth moved to hers.

This kiss differed from the ones before. It was demanding but soft, as if he wanted to show her some secret part of himself. It was vulnerable. She kissed him back eagerly, enjoying every moment of it.

"I'll stay," Jo whispered as the kiss broke.

"Good," Malcolm answered quickly.

"One condition." Jo smirked.

"Hmm… do you know what happens when you negotiate with a demon?" Malcolm grinned.

"This is not negotiating. It's a condition." Jo grinned.

"State your condition." Malcolm laughed. It was deep and grumbled through his chest.

"I want to see which room is your spark," Jo said, and her heart began pounding in her chest.

"Condition reluctantly accepted." Malcolm laughed as he stepped back and held out his hand for her.

Jo laughed at his comment and entwined her fingers with his as they began to walk back to the house.

Chapter Fourteen
Danny

He paced the bar long after Jamison left. Violet was still not back. No word on Iris. His stomach was twisted, and all he could feel was the acid as it burned his insides as the anxiety of it all crept over him. He glanced at the clock, and it had not been very long. The sound of the front door opening caught his ear. The small spark of hope immediately fizzed out as he saw a man step in.

"Sorry, we're closed," Danny said quietly from behind the bar.

"Sorry. I was just needing directions," the man said as he came towards the bar.

"Where are you needing to go?" Danny asked as he reached the bar.

"The Inn? I think. I'm passing through and need a place to stay this evening." He smiled, his brown hair was neatly combed to the side, his green eyes wandered about the place.

"Oh yeah. That's Priscila and Lenny's place. If you keep going past the bar towards the square, it's the street right before it. Turn right, and then it will be the large brick building on the left." Danny explained, his hands moved around while he talked.

"Gotcha." He smiled, not really sure where he was headed.

"Are you sure?" Danny asked as he raised his eyebrow at him.

"Yeah, I think so." He laughed with a shrug of his shoulder.

"Danny." Danny held his hand out to him.

"Evan," Evan said as he shook his hand back.

"Nice to meet you," Danny said as they dropped each other's hands.

"What are you in town for?" Danny asked as he nodded to him.

"I'm-" Evan went to make up a lie when the door opened again.

"Danny! Oh, I'm sorry. I didn't know you had someone here," a man said as he walked into the bar quickly.

"It's ok, Roger. How can I help you?" Danny asked with a smile.

"It's more I think I can help you. My shop across the way. We have security cameras… I heard a girl was missing? The new one who's been bartending?" Roger started to explain, his voice sympathetic as he spoke.

"Yeah, Iris. I'm not sure what happened," Danny said, the worry and anxiety started to slip through his voice.

Evan narrowed his eyes on Danny. Why did he care so much? Who was this boy to Jo? He tried to mask his anger. He needed to hear what this Roger knew, needed to get leads.

"I think I saw someone carry her out. Come see." Roger motioned for Danny to follow as he made his way to the door.

Danny started to follow him but then paused and looked back at Evan. His mouth hung open a bit as he searched for something to say.

"No, no, it's ok. Go. You gave me directions. I will find it. Thank you," Evan said to Danny with a firm nod.

"Danny, come," Roger said as he walked through the door.

"Come back if you get lost," Danny said to Evan as he followed Roger.

Danny was out the door before Evan could even respond. Evan waited a few seconds and then moved to a window. He watched Danny and Roger cross the street. Evan needed to see the video and needed more information. He waited for them to go into the building, and then he opened the door and crossed the street.

Evan moved to the side window and tried to peer in. He watched them gather around the small TV screen, and he could tell by Danny's body language that there was something wrong. Evan watched him tense his shoulders. He clapped Roger on his back and began heading to the door. Evan pressed against the wall. He would follow him. He would find something out.

"Danny, where are you going?" Roger called after Danny as he began to cross the road.

"To find out more. Thank you Roger. If you could, call the police and show them," Danny yelled back.

"Oh... ok." Roger ducked back inside.

Evan waited until both men were out of sight and rushed to his car. Then he waited. Evan saw Danny pace outside on the phone. He was so committed to finding out what happened to his Josephine. He might have to do something about this but for now he would let the other man do the work for him. Evan watched Danny shove his phone into his pocket with a deep frown on his face before he fished his keys out of his other pocket and turned down the alley.

"What do you mean, you're not sure?" Danny grumbled into the phone.

"The only place I can think of is that old mansion, that creepy house on the outskirts of town," the voice said back.

"Your family has lived here longer than anyone else, and that's the best you got?" Danny murmured.

"Look, Danny, that's all I got. I can double check with Grams, but as far as I know, the only place that he could be at is that old creepy place. We know everyone else," Mac said back.

"All right, Mac, if you think of anything else, give me a call back. I'm headed that way." Danny sighed, hung up and walked down the alley to his car.

Danny pulled open his truck door and slid inside. He couldn't have pulled out of the alleyway fast enough. His only thoughts were on getting to the house and finding Iris.

The old mansion sat on the outskirts of town. It sat on a broken concrete road that the earth had started to reclaim. His truck creaked down the road as it became dark. The tall trees that stretched towards the sky blocked the sunlight. The air felt lighter as he turned down the old white rock driveway. They were kids when they found the old house. It was tucked away beneath the trees, and its back was against the lake. They had carried their fishing poles all the way out here one day and stumbled upon it.

The house was set back in time. Most of Paris was, but this house was older than that. Someone had been working on it though. The roof was no longer missing shingles, and the garden was kept up nicely. Danny drove past a field of sunflowers that reached up to the sky searching for its light. He rolled his truck to a stop in front of the stone steps. He got out and quietly shut his door. His body was on high alert. He didn't know what he would find, but the determination and need to find Iris pushed him. He walked up to the wooden door and knocked on it hard with the side of his hand. His knock echoed back to him. He waited a few more seconds and went to knock again when the door was opened.

"You," Malcolm said as he looked at Danny. "Looks like I got the right house." Danny narrowed his eyes on him.

"What do you want?" Malcolm sneered.

"Where is she?" Danny asked. The anger in him vibrated his voice as he spoke.

"Who?" Malcolm asked sharply as he shifted his stance in the doorway.

"What have you done with her?!" Danny yelled as he stepped towards Malcolm, his hands in fists.

"I have done nothing with her," Malcolm bellowed back as he bowed up.

"Woah! Hey. What is going on? ...Danny?" Jo asked as she came to the door and wedged herself between Malcom and Danny.

"Iris. You're ok. Thank God!" Danny said and then wrapped his arms around her.

"Yeah. I'm fine. Sorry to scare you, I know with the whole thing at the bar. I'm still trying to wrap my head around it. I was just going to tell Malcolm I need to reach out to you and Violet." Jo hugged Danny back.

"What? Yeah. You…. We should go." Danny let go of Jo and looked at Malcolm.

"She's not going anywhere," Malcom threatened.

"Who do you think you are?" Danny growled as he bowed back up.

"Ok… She is right here, and she gets to say where she goes," Jo said loudly as she stood on her tippy toes between them to give herself more height.

"Iris, you shouldn't stay here," Danny whispered as he went to reach for her hand.

"Danny, I appreciate you so much. Really, I do." She patted Danny's hand.

"Why is there a but in that sentence?" Danny looked at her, dumbfounded.

"Danny, I'm going to stay here with Malcolm for a little bit." Jo winced slightly, knowing it would hurt Danny.

"What? What about your stuff? The apartment? The bar? Oh, and the cops! They think you're missing!" Danny said with a hint of anger mixed with the disbelief in his voice.

"I.. I-" Jo tried to answer, but the word 'cops' twisted her stomach.

If the cops knew, then Evan might find her. Her mind began to spin, and the urge to run overwhelmed her.

"I will talk to the sheriff personally. Everything will be cleared up. She will be safe here," Malcolm said as he placed his hand on Jo's shoulder.

Jo felt his hand and the warmth it provided, and she leaned back into him. She immediately felt safe. She let out a slow breath.

"Are you kidding me?" Danny asked as he looked at Jo for answers.

"Danny, I will be back at the bar in a few days. I just need some time." Jo surprised herself with her statement.

"A few days, what's that mean?" Danny wanted a timeline; he wanted a point where he could come here and demand her back.

"Umm, two days?" Jo said with a shrug.

"Fine. Look, I'm just trying to look out for you. No one knows anything about him. Here," Danny said as he pulled his cell phone out of his back pocket.

"Take my phone. You need anything, you call the bar," Danny forced his phone into her hand.

"Danny, but-" Jo said as she looked down at the phone.

"I'll get another one. Keep it. If I don't see her in two days, I'm coming back." Danny threatened Malcolm. Malcolm didn't respond; he just grinned. Danny let out a huff, and before Jo could even attempt to give back the phone, Danny had stormed away.

"He's annoying," Malcolm said shortly as he watched Danny leave.

"He's nice," Jo whispered and looked down at the phone.

The word 'cops' came into her mind again, and the panic crept up.

"Stop worrying… I said I'll take care of it," Malcolm said; his arm brushed hers gently.

"How?" Jo asked as she turned around to question him. Her eyes held fear that she tried to hide, but he saw it.

"I know the sheriff. He owes me." Malcolm's hands went to her sides as he moved her towards him.

"I will keep you safe, Sunflower," Malcolm promised.

She let out a small sigh and stepped into him and wrapped her arms around him. He was a bit surprised by her action, but he held her tightly. He meant it. Malcolm wouldn't let anything happen to her.

"If you are so worried about the police, I can go now and make sure this whole thing is dropped and be back in no time." Malcolm stroked her back.

"Are you sure?" Jo whispered as she took a small step back so she could see his face.

"I'll be back in the blink of an eye. Don't worry. Make yourself some tea or coffee, go sit in the garden. Breathe, relax, and I'll be back before you even miss me." Malcolm smirked.

"That actually sounds really great." Jo nodded and leaned into him.

"Be back soon." Malcolm said as he stepped back.

He leaned forward and kissed her forehead before he phased out. Jo stared at the spot where Malcolm had just been in amazement. She knew he was a demon, but it still hadn't penetrated all the way through her subconscious. Jo reached out and brushed the air as if it would feel different somehow. She shook her head softly and rubbed the back of her neck. Then she retreated inside.

Chapter Fifteen
Evan

He followed Danny's car until he saw him turn into the driveway. He drove past it and parked on the road to stay out of sight. Evan backed track quickly until he spotted the driveway and crept down it. He wasn't sure what he had planned. Evan had a gun in his back pocket. He made sure to stay on the edge of the driveway in case he needed to duck into the trees. A cloud of dust floated up in the air and he knew that Danny's car had just passed through here. Evan moved quickly, and before he could control himself, he had taken off into a jog and then a run. He rushed down the driveway. He nearly fell at the end of it. Evan squinted his eyes as he tried to catch his breath. His eyes narrowed in on the scene in front of him. He felt his heart speed up in his chest as he watched Jo come out behind a tall broad shoulder man. Evan felt his body twitch as anger and rage rushed through him. He had to force himself to step off the driveway and hide. Everything in him wanted him to go over and drag Jo away.

Evan watched Danny become very tense and angry. He was not liking anything Jo was saying. He knew Danny was trying to convince Jo to leave with him. Evan was torn between deadly jealousy and wanting Jo to go with Danny. If she left with Danny and went back to that stupid bar, he could easily take her home. He watched Danny grab the cell phone out of his back pocket and force it into Jo's hand.

No. No. No. No! The words screamed inside his mind as he watched Danny stomp off to his car. "What the fuck!" he screamed inside his head. He ducked behind the bush to hide as Danny's car went by, kicking up rocks as if it was angry.

He looked up to see the man that had been embracing his Josephine was gone. Jo looked out onto the driveway as if she were looking for someone who had left. Evan narrowed his eyes. Did he leave while he was hiding? He observed Jo as she walked back into the house. He looked around, and the excitement grew in his stomach. The man left. Jo was alone. He was going to get her and they were going home.

Jo

The whistling from the tea kettle drew her from her thoughts. She grabbed a simple white coffee mug from the cabinet. Malcolm didn't have much. She smiled as she thought about it. If she was going to stay here longer, they desperately needed to go shopping. Jo poured the water and dunked the only tea bag he had into the hot water. She watched it turn a light brown hue. Jo looked around for sugar or honey, but there was none. She shook her head lightly with a small smile on her face as she took the cup and headed towards the garden door.

The warm breeze rushed around her as she stepped outside. The sun warmed her skin and danced across the white pebbled path. She made her way

towards the sunflowers. Jo smiled as their long stems reached up high into the sky. She sat on the white bench just beside them and shut her eyes as she let her body soak in the sun. She hadn't had a moment like this in so long. Her mind wandered to Malcolm, and she was eager for him to come back. She found herself wondering what life might be like with him. Tea in the garden every morning. She grinned as she opened her eyes.

The happiness faded as she opened her eyes. Her hand let go of the teacup she held and it fell in slow motion to the ground. Porcelain shattered around her feet. The tea spilled onto the white rocks. She couldn't breathe and her body began to shake.

"Hello Josephine," Evan said as he pulled the gun out of his back pocket.

"Ev..Ev..Evan." Jo stuttered out his name. Her mind was still not convinced he was there but her body told her it was true. Fear rushed over her, her legs and stomach felt shaky.

"Let's go," Evan said as he motioned for her to stand up.

She shook her head as a small tear slipped out of her eye and rolled down her cheek. She shook her head again as Evan stepped towards her. He took the gun and pointed it at her.

"How?" she whispered.

"I told you, there was nowhere you could go. I told you that you are mine, and that's it. Now let's go home," Evan said as he closed the space between them.

"No," Jo said as she avoided looking at him.

"Now, Josephine!" Evan demanded and pressed the gun to her forehead.

"Do it," Jo whispered, her voice shaky as more tears ran down her cheeks.

"What?" Evan asked, confused.

"Do it. I am not going back. I am not going anywhere with you. I would rather be dead than with you!" Jo yelled as she locked eyes with him.

"Dead… Dead… you'd rather be dead!?" Evan yelled. Spit came flying out of his mouth and hit her in the face.

She took a deep breath and wiped her cheek. She narrowed her eyes at him as she slowly stood.

"I am not yours. I will never be yours… again." Jo said as she pushed the gun away from her and started to walk.

There was a loud grunt, and then something hit her in the back of the head. She stumbled forward as she tried to keep her eyes locked on the door to the kitchen. Her gaze got heavy, and she felt her world start slipping. Her hand went to the back of her head and she felt something wet. She fell to her knees as the world went black.

Evan watched her body slump to the ground as he clenched his jaw. He wiped the handle of the gun on his pants. The blood seeped into his jeans. Evan shoved the gun into his back pocket and walked over to Jo. He looked down at her. Blood seeped through her short brown hair. He had hit her hard with the butt of the gun. He wasn't sure how hard but she was out. She was still breathing, so that's all that mattered to him. He bent

down and slung her over his shoulder and began walking towards the driveway.

Malcolm

He phased into the sheriff's office. He heard a loud gasp as he materialized and grinned as he saw the sheriff shrink away behind his desk. Malcolm rolled his eyes as he stepped forward.

"You…you said you…you didn't work anymore. You…I thought-" the sheriff rambled on.

"Max…enough." Malcolm growled.

"What do you need?" Max asked as he tried to regain his composure.

"To collect." Malcolm grinned, he was being vague because he still enjoyed watching people squirm at the sight of him.

"I... Collect... what?" Max sank further into his chair, rolling it away and into the wall behind him.

"Relax. I don't want your life or soul. I am here to say we will be even if you do one thing." Malcolm rolled his eyes.

"What is it?" Max asked as he tried to control the shiver in his voice.

"The girl, the one missing from the bar. The one where that guy…well." Malcolm chuckled before continuing.

"The guy was me and the girl is no longer your concern. Drop the case, let it go," Malcolm finished firmly.

153

"I would, but-" Max started to say but in a blink in an eye Malcolm was in front of him, his hand clasped around his throat

"There is no 'but,'" Malcolm snarled.

"There…is… she... has someone looking for her." Max struggled to say the sentence.

"Who?" Malcolm asked as he loosened his grip.

"She has a fiancé, she's mentally unstable according to him and needs help." Max said as he sucked in air.

"Fiancé." Malcolm repeated and he got a weird sensation in the back of his head.

It was a dull, painful ache. It made him let go of Max as he stepped back, he put his hand on the back of his head expecting something to be there.

"You will drop this. If you don't I will be back and I will collect the right way." Malcolm locked eyes with Max and let them turn dark.

"Ok. Ok." Max nodded fiercely.

The feeling was getting worse as Malcolm stood there. He didn't understand where it was coming from. He needed to get home. He then realized that the feeling wasn't coming from him. It was from Jo. With their bond he could feel her pain. He shut his eyes and phased as quickly as he could.

He slammed into the kitchen island. His hand clasped it to steady himself as his knees slammed into the wood. He looked around in the empty kitchen. He spotted the kettle and remembered the conversation about the garden. He stumbled towards the garden door. His shoulder scraped against the door jamb as he fumbled to push the door open. His whole body was

weak and he tried to keep the pain at bay. He squinted and his head throbbed as he looked out over the garden. His stomach twisted as he did not find her.

He walked quickly out onto the white pebbles pathway. He tried to see anything that would tell him where she was.

"Jo," he called out as he looked around.

His eyes landed on a few spots of bright red against the white pebbles. He kneeled and knew before he even got close it was blood. A surge of adrenaline pushed through him as his mind realized that Jo was hurt somewhere. He followed the small blood trail out to the front of the house and back down the driveway. His stomach twisted, the rage in him boiled over. His eyes darkened as he phased to the end of the driveway. There was nothing and no one. Jo was gone.

Fiancé. Jo was hiding her identity from someone. The images of her twitching in her sleep, the cries, the pain flooded his mind. He had been here in his home, he took her. He promised to protect her and she was back with the man who was hurting her. He would find him. He would kill him. He shut his eyes and phased.

Chapter Sixteen
Malcolm

Malcom phased back into the sheriff's office. He appeared right in front of his desk. He slammed his fist hard into it. His knuckles smashed against the wood and the desk buckled inward. The power behind his fist shook the desk, and Max fell out of his chair.

"I already stopped the investigation! I swear!" Max yelled as he covered his head with his hands.

"The fiancé. I need his information now!" Malcolm bellowed at him.

"Umm, it's in the file, hold on." Max scrambled from the ground.

"Faster!" Malcolm growled. His mind screamed that he needed to find her now.

He imagined her being hurt and alone with some asshole. The longer he took to find her, the worse it could get. He could be hurting her now as they spoke.

"Evan Matthews, he's from out of state. Here's his phone number. I think he's staying at the Inn," Max said as he slid the file towards Malcolm.

"The Inn," Malcolm said as his eyes glossed over and began to darken.

"I don't know anything else about him. What are you going to do?" Max said as he saw Malcolm begin to turn dark.

"He has something that's mine," Malcolm said and then began to phase.

"Wait, we can do this the legal way. Let me help you," Max said to the dark shadow that turned to nothing. Malcolm was gone.

Jo

The pain in the back of her head vibrated down to her jaw and across the bone. She felt pain drill into her teeth. Everything throbbed. She groaned as she tried to move her hands. The clinking sound of metal moving caught her ear. She realized there was cold tightness on her wrist. Jo went to move her legs and was met with the same sound and feeling. She knew they were handcuffs. Images of what happened moments before the world went dark flashed through her mind. She felt sick, not because of the intense headache, but because she knew when she opened her eyes he would be there. Evan would be sitting there watching her. Waiting for her to open her eyes. Her stomach twisted in fear, was she back in the blue room? She fought the tears back. She wanted to scream, to cry ...to not exist. The tear slipped out of the corner of her eye and rolled down her cheek. She prayed he didn't see it. The longer he thought she was asleep, the longer she wouldn't have to deal with anything more.

"Josephine," Evan said in a sing-song tone.

She didn't respond. She tried to focus on anything else. There was a fan going in the room, and she counted the low rumble noise it made each time it circled. She tried to count the sounds. Tried to calm

herself. There was a ceiling fan. There was no ceiling fan in the blue room. A small flush of relief washed through her, and a little bit of hope. She was not in the blue room. He had not taken her back yet.

"Josephine, I know you're awake." Evan's chilling voice whispered in her ear.

She stayed silent and as still as she could be. She prayed that he would give up and just let her be. At least for a little while.

"Josephine!" Evan screamed, and his fist hit the side of the bed and caused the bed to rock.

Jo stifled a scream, but she winced and knew it was all over. She couldn't pretend to be asleep. His face hung over hers.

"Open your eyes," Evan whispered as he watched her face.

"Josephine, look at me," Evan muttered harshly.

Jo could feel his breath on her face. She moved her face away from his. He grabbed hold of her jaw and squeezed. The pain shot into her eyes, and she let out a muffled cry. Everything hurt, and the pressure he applied to her jaw rattled her.

"Please," she whispered.

"Oh, there she is. Your favorite word…please. Please, Evan, no Evan. Please don't." Evan snickered as he squeezed tighter.

"Evan," Jo whispered and opened her eyes.

"You cut your hair," Evan growled.

She didn't say anything. Jo saw the rage in his eyes. She knew what he was like and that talking or answering made it worse. He let go of her jaw and grabbed a handful of her hair and pulled. Jo let out a

scream as she felt the roots wanting to give away. The burning sensation rushed over her, and it was unbearable.

"It's fucking ugly!" Evan yelled in her face as he let go of her hair.

"We are shaving your head as soon as we get home. That way your blonde will come back, and in the meantime you'll realize how stupid you were," Evan said as he got up and moved away from her.

"Do you have any idea what you put me through?" Evan said from the end of the bed.

"I was searching all over for you," Evan muttered in disgust as he began to undo his pants.

"Do you understand?" Evan yelled as his pants dropped to the floor.

"Do you know how…alone I have been. You left me, knowing my needs," Evan hissed.

"Are you wearing his fucking clothes? Are those his…his boxers!" He screamed so loud the bed vibrated with his anger.

"Did he touch you? Do you know what will happen if he touched you! We will have to cleanse you. Jo, he better not have!" Evan bellowed.

She cringed. Jo didn't know what he was going to do next. She wished that he would just leave her be. She felt pressure on the bed and knew he was kneeling near her. He felt him move between her legs.

"Evan, can we talk?" Jo asked as she tried to find some way to make him stop.

"Now you want to talk? You should have said something to me before you took off. There's no talking now." Evan laughed.

"You're lucky we're not home." A loud growl that echoed through the room cut him off.

Evan stood up, confused by the noise. He looked around frantically trying to find the source. Was there a wild animal in the room? He quickly pulled his pants up and tried to focus harder on the room. Jo strained to see what was going on. She couldn't see anything. She had heard it too. Maybe she was losing it. Maybe there is a wild animal in the room. Maybe it would end this all. She thought quietly.

"Who…Who.. are you?" Evan stuttered as he backed away.

He came out of the shadows. His eyes glowed a deep red. They were the color of hot coals. His presence made the air in the room feel heavy and hard to breathe. Fear and power leaked out of him. Evan backed himself into a corner as he shook. Jo felt it too, and she tried to sink further into the bed. Maybe whatever it was wouldn't notice her.

"Evan Matthews?" Malcolm sneered as he moved across the room.

Jo heard his voice, and the fear immediately left her. Excitement and relief washed over her. He was here. He would save her. She tried to sit up but the best she could do was raise her head as she tried to see him.

"Yes. What and who are you?" Evan cowered further into the corner.

"Malcolm?" Jo called out. She needed to see him, needed to know he was really there.

She heard heavy footsteps come over to the bed. She felt his hand on her face before she saw him.

He looked terrifying, but he didn't frighten her. His face was filled with calm anger, his brows narrowed at the sight of her and his eyes glowing would have made anyone cower, but she leaned into his hand.

"We'll be back home in a second, Sunflower," he whispered to her.

"Sunflower? Who do you think you are?" Evan yelled.

The personal nickname struck a nerve, and the anger he felt made him push past his fear. He went charging towards them. Malcolm's hand left Jo's cheek, and he simply turned and caught Evan by the throat. He picked him up as he squeezed and shoved him into the wall. A loud crack erupted from behind Evan's back as the impact broke the wall. A gurgle noise filled the air along with the sounds of Evan's feet hitting the wall as he struggled to try to breathe.

"You will be going to a place far worse than this." Malcolm grinned.

"Malcolm, don't." Jo said from the bed. She knew what those sounds were even if she couldn't see it.

"Why? He deserves to die. He deserves to suffer. He deserves a fate worse than death," Malcolm growled as he squeezed even tighter.

"He will. Malcolm being alive will be worse for him than you killing him," Jo said calmly from the bed.

The thought hit him, and he knew she was right. He would come undone at the thought of not having her. Malcolm knew his type; the controlling, obsessive behavior would consume him. Not having what he wanted would drive him mad. Malcolm dropped Evan and as he did, the handcuff key came bouncing out of

161

his pocket. Malcolm kicked him aside. His body slumped sideways and slid into the wall. Malcolm didn't even look back at him as he picked up the key and moved to Jo. He didn't say a word as he undid the cuffs. The metal fell away from her wrists, and she flung her arms around his neck. Malcolm didn't even hesitate as he took her into his arms and cradled her to his chest. He stood and began to walk out.

"Wait." Evan coughed from the ground.

"You're alive because of her. Make no mistake about that. If you so much as think about her, I will be back to finish what I started," Malcolm threatened as he held Jo close.

Evan went to grab Malcolm's foot. As he reached for it, Malcolm's foot slammed into his chin, and he kicked him backwards. Blood spilled out of his mouth as his teeth bit through his lip and tongue.

"I'm gonna phase, hold tight to me," Malcolm whispered to Jo.

"What?" Jo whispered fear in her voice.

Malcolm saw the fear and panic flash over her eyes. He leaned his head down towards her and pressed his lips to hers. As he began to kiss her, he could feel the worry and fear melt away. He hugged her closely and phased with her.

Chapter Seventeen
Evan

Evan cupped his face as he rolled on the ground. His tongue and lip throbbed from where his teeth had bitten into them. Blood dripped onto his hands as he stood up. He looked around the room confused. Malcolm and Jo were just there, and now they were gone. They didn't leave through the door. They were just gone. What was he? The glowing eyes, the dark presence, the way he just disappeared. This couldn't be real. He stumbled to the bathroom and looked at his lip. A gaping hole flapped at him as he looked into the mirror. He slowly stuck out his tongue, and there was another hole. He shook his head as blood dripped down his chin. It would be fine; he needed to get to Jo. He needed help. He stumbled towards the front door and grabbed hold of his keys. He didn't even clean the blood off his face as he got in the car.

It didn't take long to get to the small police station. Evan didn't even care that he skidded into a handicap spot. He left the car running and rushed inside.

"Mr. Matthews!" The woman behind the glass shouted as she looked at him covered in blood.

"I need the sheriff." Evan demanded at the window.

"Mr. Matthews, what has happened?" The woman asked as she hit the page button.

"I want the sheriff now." Evan demanded as he slammed his fist down on the small counter.

"Please calm down." She said as she backed up from the window.

"I won't be calm. Do as I say! I need the sheriff now!" Evan shouted, blood droplets smeared across the glass window.

"Mr. Matthews, I think you need to calm down." Max's voice came from the far door.

"Are you the sheriff?" Evan turned towards the voice.

"Yes, sir, and if you would take a breath and tell me why you look like a bloody mess, we might be able to help." Max said as he observed Evan.

"Malcolm." Evan said his name and watched the sheriff's face grow uncomfortable.

"Ginny, it's ok. That won't be necessary. Mr. Matthews, please come into my office." Max said as he moved aside for Evan to come in.

Ginny drifted her hand away from the panic button under the desk. She was not sure what had just happened. The door slammed, and she nearly jumped out of her skin.

"This Malcolm guy, he took Jo." Evan fumed as soon as he slammed the door shut.

"We need to-" Evan started to demand.

"We don't need to do anything. You need to leave this alone." Max cut Evan off.

"No…No..No! Jo is mine!" Evan said as his fist shook.

"Jo was yours. Now she belongs to him. Evan, I can't make this anymore clearer. Forgot about Jo. Go home. You don't want to mess with him." Max advised him calmly.

"What is he? What kind of power does he hold? Why does his eyes glow?" Evan asked a ramble of questions as he tried to process.

"He's a… Damn it. He's a demon, Evan. Leave it. Go home." Max said as he shook an icy chill ran through him as he said demon.

"Demon?" Evan asked as he looked at him confused.

"Shhh. Yes. You best let this go," Max said as he nodded to the door.

"Whatever." Evan grumbled and turned towards the door.

"I am trying to warn you, boy. He's not one to cross. He's powerful in a way you don't understand or can be. Let it alone." Max said one final warning as Evan walked out the door and slammed it closed.

Evan stormed out of the police station into his car. Demon…he knew nothing about demons. There had to be something. Someone he could ask. He sat down in his car frustrated, He was not going to let this go. Evan gripped the steering wheel in his hand and squeezed. He wasn't letting her go. Malcolm was not taking her from him. All the work and time he put into her. She was his, and that was it.

He let out an angry growl as his body shook from the rage that coursed through it. He pulled out his phone and began searching for demons, anything and everything he could find on them. His eyes landed on something called a crossroad demon. A crossroad represents an in between realms. This was where you could summon a crossroad demon and he saw the word wish. Were crossroad demons like genes? Could he get

what he wanted by simply asking for it? Evan grinned if
he couldn't beat Malcolm himself. He could get
someone on his level to do the work for him. He started
his car and began to drive. His destination was the
nearest crossroad.

Leo.

     Leo had been watching the scene. He had easily
followed Evan from Malcolm's home, back to the inn,
and now watched him speed off from the police station.
He was overjoyed when Evan had taken the girl. It
would have been so simple to take the girl from Evan
and then bend Malcolm to his will. Now everything was
a mess. The dumb boy had messed up, and Malcolm
had got the girl back. Leo thought for sure the fear of
Malcolm would make him run away scared, but there
was too much rage in this one. Too much evil; he could
smell it on him. It was a bitter smell, almost sickly sweet.
He now watched him as he stomped out of the police
station and into his car. Leo looked at him wondering
what his next move was. He had to know now that
Malcolm was a demon. He surely wouldn't pursue him.
There was this deep seeded anger that ate away at him.
This boy had a hole in his belly, and there was no way
he would give up. He watched him speed off. Leo closed
his eyes and tracked him in his mind. He had his scent
now, and he could tune in on it, he could follow him with
little effort. He phased to the outer part of town as
Evan's black truck sped past. Leo grinned as he heard

166

the loud screech of his brakes as he skidded to a stop in the middle of the crossroads.

"You're not going to, are you?" Leo laughed out loud.

This was perfect. He watched Evan get out of the car and began to pace around the cross road. He was really trying to summon a crossroads demon. Leo shut his eyes and phased closer. He tried to remember whose turf this was. Who he was about to piss off. He then saw her. She was gorgeous. Crossroad demons usually were. She had long red hair that swayed down to her hips. She wore it slightly pulled back with two free pieces to frame her face. She wore a long flowing black dress, and her eyes glowed as she appeared to him. Leo was not about to let Evan get away from him. He smirked and shut his eyes to phase to the center of the crossroads.

"Maria. I'll take this one." Leo said as he appeared.

Maria turned on her heels ready to fight, but as she locked eyes with Leo, she ducked her head in submission. She didn't say one word or objection. Leo could see the rage and disappointment on her face even with her head bowed. She stepped back and quietly phased. Even demons have a hierarchy. Leo was an older and more powerful demon than a mere crossroads demon.

"What the hell? Who are you and exactly why did you chase her off?" Evan yelled as he turned to face Leo.

"Easy boy. You don't want her help; you want mine. Now what are you thinking? Money? Glory,

riches?" Leo said acting like he did not know what was going on.

"No…I want to be strong." Evan said as he tried to think of a way to explain.

"Strong…who are we trying to be stronger than?" Leo laughed.

"Do you know Malcolm?" Evan asked, as he looked around like saying his name would summon him.

"I know Malcolm. He's pretty powerful." Leo said acting like he was impressed.

"Exactly I want to be as powerful if not more. He took something of mine. Something I am going to get back." Evan said the hint of anger and rage rolling through again.

"As a human you will never be as powerful or more than him." Leo said as he led the conversation where he wanted it to go.

Leo watched the tiny seed he planted blossom in Evan's eyes. He didn't even have to say the words. Evan was easily manipulated. This was going to be easy.

"Human…Then I want to not be human…Make me a demon too." Evan said as everything clicked into place.

"You want to be a demon?" Leo asked with a coy smile.

"Yes. How do we do this!" Evan yelled at him as his anger built by the moment.

"I take your soul…demons don't need them..and in exchange, I'll make you a demon." Leo smirked.

"Soul…Fine. I'm not going to a good place after I leave this world anyways. Might as well hang around for a while." Evan smirked.

"Perfect. That's looking on the bright side. Now shake." Leo grinned as he held his hand out to Evan.

Evan in return held his hand out. Leo grasped Evan's hand and squeezed tightly.

"Now you have to say you give me your soul of your own free will in return to become a demon." Leo instructed him.

"That's it? Just a few words? I don't have to go find a goat to sacrifice or something." Evan asked, confused.

"Nope now say it!" Leo yelled at Evan.

"I Evan Matthews give my soul to you in return to become a demon." Evan said as he looked at Leo.

"Perfect." Leo muttered and threw his head back as a force rushed through Evan.

He could feel something in him begin to peel away. A soft light glowed within Evan burning outwards in his chest. The pain radiated from his center and grew with each moment. As if his chest would burst.

"What's happening?" Evan yelled in pain as he clung to Leo's hand.

"Marking your soul. It will go dormant till you die and then it's mine." Leo smirked as he let go of Evan's hand.

Evan dropped his hand and shook out the strange pins and needle feeling in it. He looked at Leo, not feeling any different. He stepped towards him in a threatening manner.

"Hey-" Evan started to say as he pointed at Leo. As the words left his mouth he felt a force rush through him. It was as if someone had pushed him and his legs went weak. He stumbled backwards.

"Hang on." Leo chuckled as he watched Evan's eyes grow wide.

Evan buckled over to his knees as a searing, hot burning pain flooded his skin. His bones felt like they were about to snap and break. An icy feeling began at his toes and spread upwards dulling the fire that plagued him. When the feeling reached his eyes, they turned black. The pain was replaced by power and strength. Evan looked down at his hands and closed them into fist. He felt like he was invincible, like he could do anything and nothing could stop him.

"This is incredible." Evan said as he moved his arms.

"You feel like this?" Evan asked him, still in amazement.

"Eh give or take." Leo shrugged, the feeling was old to him he had been a demon so long.

"I feel so, so I can't even explain it." Evan let out a loud growl at the end.

"Ok so run along now. Go do your evil plan." Leo said with a yawn tired of Evan's dramatics.

"Josephine." He said her name in a whisper form and turned to walk back to the car.

"Oh and you know demons can only be killed by one thing." Leo said the question once again leading him, he wanted to tell Evan.

"What's that?" Evan asked as continued to walk.

"A demon blade." Leo said as the sound of metal rubbing against something came from behind Evan.

Evan turned quickly, his eyes narrowed on Leo, he was not sure what Leo's intentions were. Leo twirled the long black blade in his hand before turning the handle towards Evan.

"What's that?" Evan asked cautiously.

"A demon blade ... .You might be a little dumb. Maybe I wasted this gift on you." Leo rolled his eyes as he started to pull the blade away.

"No..no. I'll take it." Evan spoke quickly and held his hand outwards towards Leo.

Leo grinned and placed the bone handle into his hand. Evan grasped it, the weight of it felt good in his hand. He nodded to Leo and then started to make his way back to the car, blade in hand.

"You can phase now..." Leo said as he rolled his eyes.

"Phase?" Evan stopped and turned back to look at Leo.

"Mhmm." Leo said and then shut his eyes, one minute he was there, the next he was standing beside Evan.

"How?" Evan asked, amazed.

"I'm not your fairy fucking god mother figure it out." Leo said annoyed and phased out.

Evan looked at where Leo once stood and tried to process what he did. He closed his eyes. He focused on what he thought it would feel like and he felt his body grow light. Then he had a strange sensation and then pain. It was like his body had broken down into molecules and he became nothing. He let the feeling go

and he reappeared in the same spot he stood in. How do they travel like this? He thought as he tried again, before he let his body go light he focused on a spot behind the car and then let the sensation run its course. He faded away and in a panic he let the feeling go quicker than he wanted and he landed on the hood of the car.

He groaned as he rolled to his side. There had to be a simple way to do this.

Chapter Eighteen

  A surge rushed through her body, and she squeezed her eyes shut. Her skin heated up, but her insides felt cold. She sharply inhaled and clung to Malcolm. Her skin rattled and vibrated as they reappeared at Malcolm's home. It was over before she could process. The entire experience left her shaken, and her body felt out of place. Malcolm felt her tremble in his arms, and he pulled her closer to him. She was confused, and her mind raced. How did this even happen? She tried to calm herself. Adrenaline mixed with fear rushed through her. Her body trembled as it felt weak and drained. Malcolm held her tightly and gave her a second to adjust. She let out a slow breath and let the comfort from Malcolm slip into her. She finally felt normal again, and that's when thoughts entered her mind about Evan.

  How did he find her? Was this really over? Would Evan let her go? Malcolm…how did he save her? He saved her? Doubt rushed into her mind. She had lived in hell for so long. Could her mind finally be slipping away? What if she was still in the blue room and made all of this up? That she escaped, that a demon came and rescued her? It did sound like one giant delusion.

  She pulled her head back slightly and looked up at him. Her big blue eyes stared into him, and he found himself stuck in the moment. She reached up and

touched his face softly. He leaned into her hand. He could see all these questions and fear in her eyes.

"Are you ok?" Malcolm asked as he looked down at her.

She nodded her eyes and studied him intensely. He narrowed his brow at her as he tried to understand all the feelings coming from her. He wanted to make sure she was ok.

"Are-" Malcolm went to say, but Jo shook her head and cut him off.

"Are you real? Is this real?" Jo blurted out, her voice cracked, and then she struggled to get out of his arms.

"What?" Malcolm asked as he put her feet on the ground, but his hands went to her hips.

"Are you real!" Jo shouted, and her voice quivered as she spoke.

Malcolm could see the panic in her as she began to breathe rapidly. He reached out to touch her, and she stepped back. He put his hands up as if to say he wouldn't hurt her.

"Hey." He whispered as he held out his hand to her.

She kept her hand withdrawn to her chest as she watched him with careful eyes. He took a small step towards her.

"You're safe." He said calmly as he waited for her to respond to his movement towards her.

"I would never hurt you," Malcolm said quietly as he took another soft step to her.

"I'm real." He whispered as he held his hand out to her.

"You're real?" Jo whispered as she looked at his outward stretched hand.

"I'm real," Malcolm said firmly as he continued to wait for her.

"I'm not in the blue room. Finally, so broken that I've made up a demon as my savior." Jo laughed as a small tear slipped out of her eye.

"No, Sunflower. You're here with me. This is real," Malcolm stated and took her hand in his.

Jo didn't pull back or fight. He gently pulled her towards him. He took her hand and placed it on his chest. She looked at him confused. She then felt a small thudding underneath her hand.

"You have a heart?" She cracked a smile as she felt it beat beneath her palm.

"Shh don't tell anyone." He smirked with a wink.

"Tell me something you can see." He asked her, seeing the panic still in her but not as less.

"What?" Jo asked, confused.

"Tell me something you can see." Malcolm repeated.

She scanned the room they were in his kitchen. Her eyes caught a gold chandelier in the dining room across the way.

"The chandelier in the dining room." Jo whispered.

"Good, tell me something you can smell." Malcolm said as he kept his hands on top of hers.

She closed her eyes and focused on her sense of smell. A deep, earthy smell floated in a cool breeze. She opened her eyes and looked at the window above

the kitchen sink. It cracked open, and she could smell the earth outside.

"The dirt." She laughed a little at her answer.

"What can you hear?" Malcolm asked as he nodded to her first answer.

She closed her eyes once more and listened. The small opening in the window let the noise of birds in. They tweeted happily in the background. She felt a surge of joy as she listened to them.

"Better?" Malcolm asked as he saw her face relaxed and calm.

"Thank you." Jo said as she opened her eyes, and although she was calm and felt better, he could see a question floating on her face.

"It's called grounding. When you're panicking, you focus on things around you. Something you can see, smell, hear, and feel." He said calmly to her, his hand stroked hers that laid on his chest, still feeling his heart beat.

"Well, aren't you just full of surprises?" Jo said with an impressive smile.

"Tons." He smirked as mischief flashed in his eyes.

"He's never coming after me again." Jo said, but the sentence felt like more of a question.

"Never, and if he does, I'll make sure he won't be able to. Nothing and no one is ever going to hurt you again. I vow this to you," Malcolm said as he reached up and put his opposite hand to her cheek.

She believed him. Since she had been with him, her heart had felt calm, her skin no longer crawled with anxiety, and she felt safe. She belonged with him. There

was something inside of her that was drawn and deeply connected to him.

"I believe you," Jo said softly as she leaned into him.

He wrapped his arm around her and kissed the top of her head. He felt her melt into him, and he knew that she felt what he had been feeling since the moment he laid eyes on her. She let out a sigh of contentment.

"How's your head?" Malcolm asked as he looked over the top of her head; it had healed.

"It feels fine. I know that he hit me with something, but it doesn't even hurt." Jo said, confused.

"Good," Malcolm said shortly.

"Demon perks?" Jo asked with a small laugh.

"Yes, I'm not sure how long it will last. I'm honestly impressed it has lingered this long," Malcolm said, puzzled.

"Speaking of surprises." Jo said as she pulled back slowly.

"Surprises?" Malcolm asked as she stepped back but held on to his hand.

"Yes…you owe me a spark." Jo grinned as she said the word spark.

Malcolm let out a small sigh and shook his head. He closed his fingers around hers; he nodded for her to follow him as he led her out of the kitchen and up the dark wooden staircase. He stopped in the hallway of closed doors and raised an eyebrow at her.

"I'm not letting you know this easily." Malcolm smirked and waited for her to see he wanted her to choose the door.

She looked from one room to another.
Musicians, artists, she thought as she looked at each
one. Her eyes stopped at the library, a small grin as she
thought of the word explore. She turned back to the art
room and music hall. She turned and looked at Malcolm.
It was one of those; she knew it, but which?

"You grinned at the library." Malcolm stated, but it
was more of a question.

"I was trying to determine if you were an artist,
musician or explorer." Jo said as she watched him.

"Explorer?" Malcolm asked, his brows came
together.

"Well, books explore new worlds and uncharted
areas of all things. You want to experience something
but can't go, there's a book. You want to get lost in
something more than yourself. There's a book. But I feel
like you'd rather go and do it versus read about it." Jo
said as she reached for his hands.

"Your hands." Jo said as she ran her fingers
along his, she knew they were skilled and she could see
callous but she still wasn't certain.

"My hands." Malcolm stated back.

"Artist or musician, it's so hard to pick." Jo smiled
and then looked up to him; she searched his eyes and
then placed a hand on his cheek.

Malcolm closed his eyes as she touched his
cheek.

"Music," Jo said as if that simple movement told
her what she needed to know.

Malcolm opened his eyes; a small look of
surprise and uncertainty flashed in them. Jo's hand
dropped away from his face, and she stepped

178

backwards into the music hall door. Her hand is still holding his. He had a look of amusement on his face as she bumped the door with her butt it did not budge. He stepped into her, pinning her between him and the door. She felt chills rush through her as her body vibrated in anticipation.

"Here… Let me help." He whispered as his hand found the door handle and the door cracked open.

"Very helpful." She smirked as she stepped backwards into the room.

He watched her eyes twinkled with amusement and lust as she pulled him into the center of the room. She then looked around the room of various instruments.

"I bet you play them all." Jo said as she looked around, her hand still held him tightly.

"I do…I'm pretty good with my hands." Malcolm smirked as he pulled her into him.

His hand let go of hers and found her waist as he pressed his pelvis into hers; there was barely room for air between them. She found herself caught up in his eyes, which held hers intensely.

"Piano." Jo said as she watched his face change from intense want to curious.

"How did you know it was this room and not the other?" Malcolm asked as he leaned his face towards hers.

"You… like to feel," Jo whispered, her eyes now fixated on his lips that were so close to hers.

"Feel?" he asked as his lips barely brushed hers.

"Artists see, musicians feel." Jo said, trying not to give into the urge of pressing her lips to his and taking the kiss for hers.

"Mhmm," Malcolm murmured as his lips pressed into hers.

She eagerly met the kiss with her own lips. Her hands found the way to the back of his neck and looped around him. His hands dropped from her hips to her firm buttocks. He lifted her up and her legs wrapped around his waist. Malcolm kissed her deeply, his tongue searched her mouth, tangled with her tongue as he carried her over to the piano bench. He dropped to his knees as he sat her down on it. His hands traveled back to her waist until his fingertips found the ridge of the boxers he let her borrow; two tiny buttons kept them to her. He kissed her while his hands played with the soft fabric, and with one quick tug the button popped off. His hand fumbled with the fabric, and then Jo felt a rush of cold as her pants fell to her ground.

Malcolm moved away from her lips. Malcolm's lips trailed down her neck; Jo leaned into her skin, came alive underneath his lips and begged for more. He kissed a trail down over her collarbone; his fingertips grabbed the bottom of her shirt and pulled it up over her head. His lips left her skin for a second as he tossed it to the ground. A chill passes through her from the cold air. She went to reach for him, but his hand captured her breast and squeezed lightly. She leaned into it, and soon his wet, hot mouth was on her breast. He pulled her nipple into his mouth and sucked as he massaged her breasts. Jo let out a soft moan as a sensation rushed over and she felt an ache grow in her core. He

ran his tongue over her nipple before he pulled on it with his teeth. Jo inhaled sharply as the sharp feeling sent a shiver down her. Her hand went to the back of his head and tangled in his hair, begging him not to stop. Malcolm let go, and her nipple bounced in front of him. He squeezed her breast and moved his mouth closer to her nipple once again. He watched her lean forward and inch her nipple closer to his mouth, wanting him to take it.

He pulled her nipple into his mouth, and a satisfied moan escaped her lips as a rush of warmth spread through her. It was short lived as he pulled away. She went to protest but felt his mouth move down over her skin. His hands ran over her thighs as he spread them apart. Malcolm's hand slid up to her ass and cupped her cheeks as he pulled her forward. His mouth moved down over her stomach. As he reached her core, he watched her legs tremble in anticipation. He moved over her and licked down her center. She tilted her head back and leaned into the piano. Chimes of the keys from the piano field the room as she pressed back into them and he buried his face into her.

He ran his tongue over her bud; the sensation sent chills through her. She lifted her hips trying to meet his mouth. His warm, wet tongue began to rub against her. A loud moan escaped her as he pulled her bud into his mouth and sucked on it. It sent her into ecstasy. His hand moved towards her entrance, and he slipped a finger inside her. He began to slowly move his finger. His mouth continued to taste her. He wanted to taste more of her. He moved his fingers from her and then pushed his tongue inside her. She let out a cry of

pleasure as he thrust his tongue in and out of her. She grabbed onto the piano keys; another loud chime played out with her moan. He felt himself begin to throb, he needed inside of her badly. Malcolm moved from her and stood. He stepped towards her and was about to pull her into him when her hand caught his hip. Her eyes looked at him with longing and lust as a small smile curled to her lips. He looked at her confused as she slipped to her knees in front of him.

Her fingers grasped the sides of his pants before he could react, and she pulled them down. Malcolm's ejected member was inches from her lips. She leaned forward and watched him tense in anticipation. She brushed her lips over the head of his member and heard him let out a small breath as she moved her lips slowly over the tip of his head and pulled him into her mouth. He let out a groan as she pulled him further into her mouth. Her tongue wrapped around his shaft as she began to move up and down. His hand went to the back of her head as she moved.

"Fuck." He muttered as she moved faster and took him deeper into her mouth.

She pulled back and let him slip from her mouth. She swirled her tongue around the head and back down before she placed him back in her mouth. Malcolm pushed himself deep inside her mouth; the warmth and pressure made him twitch inside her mouth. He slowed the movement, not wanting to let go of control. He gripped her hair in his hand and pulled to let her know to stop. Jo stopped and looked up at him, her mouth filled with him. He let out a small groan as he looked down at her. She was gorgeous, and he couldn't help but move

in and out of her mouth once more as he watched. He then paused and pulled himself out completely. His hand caught her chin with his hand. She looked up at him from her knees. She was a sight to see, lips swollen, her blue eyes stared up at him; he brushed her lips with his thumb and watched them tremble.

He leaned down and grabbed hold of her firmly but gently as he lifted her up. His hand went to her ass and lifted her up into him. Her legs wrapped around him as he placed her on top of the piano. His hand captured her face as he kissed her. Her legs pulled him into her. He pushed deep inside of her and filled her. She let out a moan against his lips. He moved in and out of her, her body pulsed around him as she moaned into him. Her body quivered with each movement. All of her muscles began to contract. She felt an intense buildup as her body flushed. Her toes curled as she felt a release coming. She closed her eyes, her nails dug into his shoulder blades as she clung to him. Her body arched toward him. Her muscles tightened as he felt her build up. He felt her explode around him. He couldn't take any more, and he let himself go.

She melted against him as they stayed still for a moment. Malcolm leaned forward and kissed her forehead softly. She was still wrapped around him. He slowly pulled her off the piano, still inside her as he carried her to the couch. Malcolm could feel her body twitch in the aftermath. He laid her down and pulled out slowly as he did. Jo curled into herself, a smile of satisfaction on her lips. She reached for him, and he laid down beside her and pulled her into his arms. She let out a small sigh as she gave into exhaustion.

Chapter Nineteen
Danny

Danny didn't know what to do, so he slammed the truck into park outside the bar. He felt anger and worry try to take over his body. His hand twitched a little. Two days was too long. A lot could happen in two days. He didn't want to leave her there. Why couldn't she see it was not safe? He sighed as he got out of the car as he tried to think of anything just to go check on her. He walked into the bar and heard her before seeing her. Violet slammed her open hand down on the bar top.

"Four days! I'm gone for four days! What the hell happened, Danny?" Violet yelled at him as he walked in.

"You act like I work here, but what-" Danny started to say but Violet threw up her hand.

"What happened?" She repeated her question as she took a deep breath to calm herself.

"Some drunk got handsy with Iris. I'm not sure what happened. The guy got taken care of, and Iris is with Malcolm at his place." Danny blurted out.

"Is Iris ok?" Violet asked, concerned, and replaced her anger.

"No…well yes but no because she's at Malcolm's place. She didn't want to come back. We don't know anything about him. I can't just leave her there." Danny rambled as he rubbed his forehead anxiously.

"Take a breath. Malcolm…he's never shown an interest in anyone before. All the time he's been here…That doesn't mean he's a bad person though, Danny. Also, if he saved her from the guy, then he can't

be that bad." Violet said as she thought things over in her head.

"We don't know if he did." Danny grumbled as he leaned on the bar.

"Did Iris look ok? Did she sound scared or frightened?" Violet asked, her eyes searched his face as she spoke.

"No, she made it clear she wanted to stay with him." Danny sighed as he placed his head in his hands.

"I just want to make sure she's ok." Danny said as he held his head.

"So go," Violet said quietly; she reached out and grabbed his hand as she saw the distress on his face.

"Vi, I can't just go. She's running from a terrible life. I don't need to go storming over there like some weird guy who thinks he has some claim to her…but I also can't sit here and not make sure she's ok." Danny grumbled as he became frustrated.

"She has things upstairs….things she probably needs." Violet smiled at him.

"Violet, you're so smart. So smart." Danny grinned as he stood up.

"Be careful; don't get yourself into trouble." Violet winked at him as he was already moving towards the stairs.

She shivered as the warmth that she was curled into became cold. She stirred slightly as she tried to find him. Jo then heard a soft melody that began to fill the

room. She opened her eyes and looked to where the sound was coming from. The room was dark; the only light leaked in from the window. It danced across the floor and across the piano. Like a spotlight, it highlighted Malcolm. The moonbeam bounced off his firm back and trickled down his muscular arms. Malcolm sat at the piano in just his boxers, his eyes closed as his fingers worked across the keys. Jo pulled the blanket around her and sat up quietly. Something yellow caught her eye, and she looked over. A bright yellow sunflower laid next to the couch cushion. He had left it there for her. Jo picked it up and slowly brought it to her nose. She inhaled the smell of the earth, which made her smile. She glanced back at Malcolm, who had not noticed she was awake yet. Jo wanted to watch him in secret. See the pieces of himself that he kept hidden.

The music was soft and light, but there was a depth to it. It was dark and haunting. She watched his shoulders move as he played. She could see them tense and relax.

"It's still night time Sunflower." Malcolm said not opening his eyes.

Jo got up off the couch, blanket still wrapped around her, and walked over to him. Reaching him, she couldn't help herself. She reached out and ran her hand down his back. She felt him lean back as she touched him. His body wanted to feel her touch. He stopped playing as he leaned back into her.

"No, don't stop." Jo said as she ran her hand down his arm and placed his hand back on the keys.

"I'm a little distracted," Malcolm said as his other hand began to run up her thigh.

186

Jo smirked and leaned into him. The blanket fell open slightly. She caught his hand with her other hand and moved it from her leg. She placed it on the piano keys.

"I was right. Music is your spark," Jo said quietly and then leaned down towards his ear.

Her naked breast pressed against his back as he felt her lean into him. He let out a small groan as one of her hands still held his to the piano.Malcolm felt himself grow stiff as he felt her skin against his. He wanted her again, to be inside her. He felt himself throb as he pictured her legs back around him and pushing himself deep into her.

"Play for me." She whispered as her warm breath hit his ear.

He was quick; he slipped his arm around her waist and pulled her around to his lap and placed her on it. The blanket fell down around her, and she sat completely naked in his lap. Her mouth hung open in surprise. His arm securely around her, he brought his free hand to her face and ran his thumb down her lip. It bounced as his thumb released it. He moved closer to her, the keys chiming as she brushed them.

"You have no idea what you do to me." He whispered, his voice full of want and possessiveness.

She pulled her bottom lip into her mouth and bit it. Her eyes contemplated something as she told herself to be brave. He watched the decision flash into her eyes, and he looked at her curiously. She pulled back from him, and he let her go, wanting to see what she was up to. She stood up slowly, and the blanket fell completely to the ground. His eyes wandered down her

perfect curves. His hands itched to touch them. Jo raised her leg and placed it on the bench just in front of his swollen member. He tilted his head at the action, and his eyes watched her. Jo then placed her hands on his shoulders and scooted herself onto the top of the piano. She steady herself with arms on the side of her. She did not block any part of her body from his view. She opened her thighs and let her feet dangle just above the keys. Jo felt a surge of excitement, her stomach twisted, her heart raced and the dull throbbing ache began in her core. He said she had no clue what he did to her, but she wanted every inch of him every time her eyes locked with his.

She watched his eyes wander over her. She could see the desire in his eyes grow as well as the bulge that the cotton boxers barely contained. His eyes locked on her core, and he wanted to taste her all over again. He went to lean forward to bury his face in her, but her foot caught his shoulder.

"No. No." She smirked as she watched him narrow his eyes at her and his own mouth turned into a smirk.

"Play for me." Jo said firmly; she tried to control herself because all he would have to do was barely touch her anywhere right now and she would melt.

"I can see you want me," Malcolm said, his voice deep; she knew he was talking about the growing wetness between her legs.

"Play for me…please." Jo said, trying to hold on to her control, but she was losing to her body.

"Good girl, using your manners," Malcolm said as his fingers ran up the side of her calf.

She shut her eyes and trembled at his touch. She couldn't hold on much longer. A small chime caught her air as Malcolm began playing. Her foot still pressed against his shoulder and his eyes fixated on her center, he could barely play. His mind wasn't on his fingers stroking the piano; his mind was on what he wanted to touch and feel. He leaned forward and ran his tongue down the side of her calf. Her head instantly dropped back, and he watched her hold back a moan.

He stood suddenly, his hand caught her ankle and in one swift motion he pulled her forward onto the piano. His hand dropped her ankle and caught her chin. His other hand traveled up her thigh.

"Don't ever hide noises from me; they are mine." He growled as his hand found her center.

She inhaled sharply as she felt his fingertips run down her slit. He purposely teased as he just brushed her bundle. She let out a small moan.

"Mmmm, that's it." He said and then rewarded her by rubbing her bundle with his thumb, moving in soft circles.

Her whole body quivered. She felt like she was losing all control. Each time he spoke, each touch she felt herself unravel more. He pushed a finger inside of her, and he felt her clench down around; wetness spilled out of her as he began to move. She let out a loud moan and inched closer to him, her hips wanting to move with him. He sat back on the bench and pulled her to the edge of the piano as he wanted to taste.

"Mal'akh, wait." Jo whispered breathlessly. She said his name, and he froze, his face inches from his prize. He let out a groan and looked up at her, his

eyes locked with hers. He caught a flash of mischief as she slowly moved down from the piano. She was trying to control her breathing, trying to calm herself down so she could send him over the edge. He helped steady her off the piano and onto his lap, his hands wrapped around her, ready to take her.

"Wait," she said as she pulled back and moved his legs apart as kneeled in front of him.

Malcolm looked down at her below him, and his arousal grew. She took his boxers into her hands and pulled. His underwear hit the ground, and his hard cock stood inches from her lips. She kissed the tip of his penis. Jo felt him move closer to her mouth. She licked the tip of his head and watched him shudder. She pulled him into her mouth, taking his length .

"Fuck." He groaned as his hand from the back of her hair, his fingers wrapping it as she began to move up and down.

She swirled her tongue around his shaft and up over the tip of his head; his breath quickened. She began to move faster as she tasted a small bead of salt. He was close, and she could feel him beginning to pulse. She went to take him, all of him, when his hand in her hair stopped her. He pulled her back by her hair. Jo looked at him confused, but he grabbed her and pulled her up to his lip. She felt his member brush against her core, and she craved to feel him inside of her. She shifted her hips and moved him back. He lifted her by her hips and eased her down on top of him.

"Mal'akh." She let out a moan as he pushed inside her, filling her.

190

She was so close to her climax already. She held on to him as he began to move. Every part of her flushed and felt like he was the missing piece to her. He began to move quicker, and she felt it coming. Jo tilted her head back as she felt her body tense. She clamped down around him as she felt her wave buildup and release. She clung to him as her body shook. That was all he needed; her own orgasm caused his, and he was shook from it.

She stayed holding on to him, him still inside of her. Jo could feel his cock still pulsing in the aftermath. She let out a small happy sigh and leaned her head on his shoulder.

"I'm never going to let you go," Malcolm whispered.

"I know…you said you were keeping me." Jo said as she nuzzled into his neck.

Chapter Twenty

"Lazaros." Pavel bellowed his name, summoning Leo to him.

Leo hit the stone floor as he phased in. He let out a low groan as he rolled onto the floor. The phase happened so quickly he was not prepared. Everything hurt as he stood up and let out a cough. His lungs burned from the impact.

"What is taking so long for you to do what I have asked!" Pavel yelled again, his hand shook violently as he did.

"I have a plan. It's been set into motion." Leo said as he straightened up.

"Explain." Pavel said, his voice unimpressed.

"I turned someone into a demon who badly wants the girl Malcolm is so obsessed with. He's going there to kill Malcolm. Obviously, he won't be able to. Malcolm is stronger and older. The girl most likely will be hurt or, hopefully, worse, and then Malcolm goes dark. You welcome him back with open arms," Leo stated his thought out plan.

"Hmm, I'm surprised you have a plan that may actually work." Pavel said with a smug look on his face.

"Why are we doing this? What does having Malcolm do for you anyway?" Leo asked, annoyed and confused.

"Because we're gonna be on the same team, come this way." Pavel said as he motioned for Leo to follow him down the hall.

Leo hesitated as he watched Pavel start down a long, dark hallway.

"Lazaros, follow." Pavel said as he turned the corner.

"I could fucking kill you for knowing my name." Leo muttered to himself as he started down the hall.

"You could try." Pavel's voice snickered down the hall away, an unsaid threat in his words.

The hallway was dark and made of stone; it felt like they were walking further and further into the earth. The hall narrowed downward. After several twists and turns, the hall opened up into a room. Leo stepped inside the open room and looked for Pavel. He stood in the center as he waited for him. Behind Pavel was an odd glass cell. There was a light floating inside it. Leo couldn't make out what it was. He stepped to the glass when suddenly a face appeared. Leo jumped back, and then it all clicked.

"Souls," Leo whispered.

"I doubted you too much. Correct. Souls." Pavel grinned.

"What? Why?" Leo asked as his eyes fixated on a somber face that floated by.

"Lost souls. I am collecting them. They will generate power. Enough power where I will be in control and darkness will overthrow the earth." Pavel announced.

"You sound like what Nyx tried to do." Leo whispered.

"I am not like Nyx! She was clouded. She didn't want the Earth; she just wanted revenge. She was angry and spiteful, and it made her misjudge. I am calm,

collected and know what I want. What I deserve. Nyx fell short, but only a little. She was using the souls wrong. Just to escape. If only she realized that harvesting souls gave power. We wouldn't be having this conversation." Pavel explained.

"Lazaros, you are to be quiet about this," Pavel ordered.

Leo nodded, not sure what more Pavel wanted from him, but he was not going to ask. Pavel snapped his fingers.

"Leo, go, make sure what you have planned for Malcolm goes down," Pavel said as he waved him off.

"Fine, fine. This is a lot. All right." Leo muttered and shut his eyes and thought about the cross road before he phased.

Silas

Anger flooded through him as he looked down at the empty body. This murder was done on purpose. It was not part of the design. He felt the call, a soul taken before its time. A soul that was going to be lost without him, but now he arrived and there was no soul. Something was happening. He knew someone was behind this. He looked up at the sky as the night sky began to twinkle.

"Kere," he said to the black velvet that stretched across the sky.

"Brother." Her voice came from behind him as if she knew he would call here.

194

She stood dressed as dark as the night sky, her hands folded neatly into each other as she waited for him to say what she knew he was about to say. She then watched his eyes narrow as he looked past her.

"I don't recall saying your name." Silas said dryly.

"Oh, you know you miss my handsome face." Balor smirked as he stepped out from behind Kere.

"Handsome. You've always thought so highly of yourself, but now you might be pushing it." Silas mimicked his smirk.

Balor walked over and bowed up to Silas. Silas's chest tensed as well as he followed Balor's movements. Baylor reached out and clasped Sila's forearm and squeezed. Silas grabbed hold of Balor's and did the same. A smile broke across Baylor's face as he slapped Silas on the shoulder.

"I've missed you." Balor laughed.

"I've missed your stupid ass too." Silas laughed as he shook his head.

"Hey now! I have a very nice ass! Your sister thinks it's perfect!" Balor laughed.

"Ok that's enough of that." Kere announced as she walked over to the body.

"The soul's been taken." Kere said with a frown.

"Before I got here. This isn't the first one. They are all deaths that would produce a soul doomed to be lost. I take the call to guide them to the afterlife, and I find empty shells." Silas grumbles as he explains.

"What did you fuck up this time?" Balor groaned as he rubbed the back of his neck.

"Shut up." Silas growled.

"Seriously, I am not going all hero again. We just did that not too long ago. I did not enjoy it. It was supposed to be a one and done thing." Balor said as he walked over and looked at the body.

"Maybe you just lost it? Maybe it's around here somewhere." Balor said as he nudged the body with his foot.

"Here soul! Come here, soul!" Balor called as he looked around.

"Shut the fuck up!" Silas said as he grabbed Balor by his collar.

"All I'm asking is if you looked hard enough." Balor smirked.

"I swear-" Silas said, wanting to lash out at him.

"Enough. Silas is right; something is happening. This is not a lost soul wandering. It's gone. Someone's taken it. I can't feel a presence." Kere said as she shut her eyes.

"Wonderful," Balor grumbled as he yanked himself away from Silas.

"Silas, you need to let Nora know. Maybe she can help. The In-between must feel something. Maybe she'll get a reading on this and be able to point us in the right direction before this gets out of control." Kere said and then looked to Balor as she held out her hand.

Kere took hold of Balor's hand, and all his protesting went out the window. Her touch softened him, and he sighed.

"Fine…I'll help. I might still have some connections to the local demons down here. I'll look into it…Silas…You're lucky I love her." Balor said as he kissed Kere's hand.

"You're lucky she's my sister; you wouldn't be in this realm or any for that matter." Silas said and phased before Balor could shoot another comeback at him.

"He thinks so highly of himself." Balor grumbled.

"I know someone else who does too." Kere smirked at him.

Balor grabbed hold of her and pulled her into his arms. He kissed her fiercely as he held her. He pulled back before she was finished.

"Save the rest of that for me for later. Give me the motion to get back to you quickly." Balor smiled as she pulled her forward and his lip touched her forehead.

"I love you, my goddess." Balor winked at her as he stepped back.

"Balor, are you sure?" Kere asked, a hint of nervousness in her voice.

"Always. Besides, I've missed the chaos of the human world." Balor grinned.

"Don't cause any." Kere laughed at him as she watched his eyes dance with mischief.

"I'm hurt you would think I would." Balor grinned wider.

"Hurry back to me," Kere said to him.

"As fast as I can." Balor blew her a kiss and phased.

Balor phased in front of an old rundown gas station. On the outside, it looked abandoned. The gas pumps no longer held gas. The windows were tinted black; dust and cobwebs speckled the front of them. He let out a small yawn as he started towards the door. He knocked three times; the spacing between knocks was

delayed. Then he rang the bell twice. The door slowly creaked open.

"Business…or pleasure?" The voice asked through the small cracked space.

"I find pleasure in my business." Balor smirked and flashed his eyes at him.

"Welcome, Balor, I almost didn't recognize you." The fragile man said as he pulled the door open.

"It's been a while. I take no offense." Balor said as he stepped in.

The room instantly smelt of old cigars and whiskey. A u-shape bar was in the center, and walls were speckled with old signs. A set of pool tables lined one wall and slot machines the other. In the back, there was a red curtain that was left loosely open. Balor spotted the curtain and grinned. He knew exactly what went on back there. Old memories flooded his mind as he made his way back there.

"Well, I see something don't change." Balor announced as he made it over to the table.

"Some things do," grumbled a man who barely looked up at Balor.

"Hmm, same bar, same table, same game…same lower levels." Balor said his voice went frigid as he glared at the man.

"Low level." The man laughed and paused as he placed his card down and locked eyes with Balor.

"Better a lower level than a traitor to your own kind." The man said bitterly.

"Traitor is a bold statement from the likes of you." Balor cracked a smile.

"A demon's way is whatever is best for themselves. Always has been, always will be. Tell me that's not what being a demon is all about." Balor said as he placed his hand on the table and aggressively leaned across.

"Yes, but-" the man said; he could feel the power that radiated from Balor, and it took him back for a second. He just wasn't a powerful demon, his time away, he had somehow gained more power.

"So what I have done is good for me. Therefore, a demon's way. You are no one in any position of judgement. No one to judge me. You rot away in this filth thinking you're better. Fuck that shit. I would do what I did ten times over then to be considered by the likes of you." Balor said, his voice rattled the table.

"Balor-." The man began to protest, and as he said Balor's name the table flipped.

Balor crossed over the broken pieces of shattered glass and playing cards and snatched the man by his throat. He lifted him off his feet. His feet kicked as his air supply was being cut off. The man looked around at the people he thought were his friends, and no one even got up from their chairs.

"A demon's way is what's in their best interest for themselves. Saving you is not." Balor laughed and then dropped him.

"You have one chance to save your sorry ass, or you will be in the hall of judgement before you can blink. We all know where demons end up." Balor said as he pressed his foot into the man's chest and knocked him back.

"You think you are so powerful because you run around with Death and a goddess now." The man grunted from underneath Balor's boot.

"Now if you would have just brought up Silas, I might have let you pass. Death is honestly annoying. However." He pressed his foot down hard into his chest; a crack sounded as the man's ribs broke.

Balor placed his elbow on his knee as he looked down at the men as he struggled not to scream out in pain. A wick grin appeared across his face.

"You brought up my girl. No one talks about my girl." Balor's voice deepened and went cold as he spoke the words.

The man squinted up at him, unsure how to take the words. The pain searing through his chest was mind numbing. He heard a quick cling of metal, and a sharp, piercing feeling went through his chest. He let out a gasp as he looked down. A black demon blade was stabbed through his chest and punctured his heart. The man could barely blink before his body disintegrated into nothing but ash.

"See you in hell." Baylor announced as he stood up and held the blade in his hand as he turned around to the other men.

"So who would like to live and answer my questions and who would like to follow their friend?" Balor grinned, his voice cheerful as he twirled the demon blade.

"What, what questions?" A man stuttered out, his eyes locked on the demon blade.

"I'm looking for information about a demon, a demon who is stealing souls for itself." Balor asked his eyes scanned the room.

"Come now, don't speak all at once," Balor threatened.

"I mean, I could do this the hard way….it's been a while now since I killed anyone... oh well, not counting your friend there, but it was a good place to start." Balor laughed.

"There's been whispers." A small voice said from behind the man Balor was looking at.

"Whispers?" Balor asked as he moved closer.

"Yes." The man whimpered as Balor came close, blade in hand.

"What do the whispers say?" Balor said, getting annoyed.

The man shook his head, and Balor snapped. He was done. He plunged the demon dagger into the man beside the whimpering man. The man's eyes went wide as he quickly turned to ash.

"The whispers better speak quickly because my tolerant for drama I lost three years ago." Balor growled.

"Leo." The voice was sweet and feminine and came from the corner of the room.

"Maria." Balor smirked as he looked at her; she stepped out into the light, her long red hair wrapped around her as she sipped a longneck beer.

"Long time…aren't you forgetting something?" Maria grinned.

"Right." Balor nodded and turned and slammed the demon blade into the man who spoke of whispers.

"I've missed watching you work… Where have you been hiding?" Maria smiled sweetly as she walked to him.

"Another realm." Balor smiled.

"So it's true; you have found yourself with a goddess who was once a demon. Interesting." Maria said, her voice teasing.

"Maria, as I just explained to our dear deceased friend, I am no longer entertaining drama. What do you know?" Balor said shortly.

"Leo took a crossroad soul from me," Maria said bitterly.

"Leo as in-" Balor started to ask before he was interrupted.

"Yes, that Leo, old as hell Leo," Maria grumbled.

"Why would he want a crossroads soul?" Balor asked, his voice confused.

"Beats me; he's never gone for minor souls. He was adamant and dismissed me." Maria sneered.

"Who does Leo work with these days?" Balor said, trying to find a connection.

"Malcolm is his only …acquaintance. But the whispers our poor deceased friend was referring to is Pavel. Rumors say he wants Malcolm to come back to work." Maria said as she took a long sip of beer.

"Malcolm, he's been retired for decades if not longer. He paid off his debit and disappeared." Balor said, confused.

"Mmhmm, but Pavel thinks there's too much good in the world and wants the bring of wrath to return." Maria grinned.

Each powerful demon had his niche. Balor was chaos, and Malcolm was wrath; he brought wars and famines. Could turn brother against brother, families destroyed. Malcolm took to it quickly and easily. You think men get evil ideas from their own brain but demons laid the seeds. Malcolm was the seed planter of every known war and ones no one noticed. His soul intake was incredible, and once he had paid his debt, he left. Vanished.

"That would be an overload. Malcolm was allowed to retire because of the influx and the tipping of the scales so drastically. What is Pavel planning? Souls are missing." Balor said to Maria.

"Now that, I don't know anything about, but souls have always been the name of the game, Balor. Since the dawn of time." Maria said quietly as she set her beer down.

"It's a shame, really. We could have caused some havoc." Maria said as she stepped closer to him.

"Why are you helping me?" Balor asked, his eyes narrowed on her.

"Leo took one of my souls, and I've always liked watching you work," Maria whispered with a wink. Balor pressed the tip of the demon blade into her chest.

"Love the compliments, but as you said, I'm taken. I also think I have a few kills left in me to satisfy an old need… if you want to help me out." Balor whispered as he twisted the blade lightly.

"Easy, Balor, I meant no harm. You know how us cross road demons are. We love to play games." Maria said as she threw her hands up and stepped back.

"Keep your games at the crossroads." Balor said as his eyes glowed, preparing for his phase.

"Balor, this is between us; I don't need any heat from Pavel," Maria warned, but her voice had a hint of fear.

"You helped me. I won't speak a word about this. Cross me, and you will find out who you should be scared of," Balor threatened.

Chapter Twenty One

Leo

    Leo phased back to the crossroad intersection, and he found Evan still trying to figure out what this all meant and how it all worked. He would never succeed in this if he didn't get help. He needed Pavel to go back to leaving him alone.

    "Well, this is pathetic." Leo announced as he stepped out of the dark.

    "Fuck you." Evan muttered angrily.

    "You're not really my type." Leo sighed as he folded his arms across his chest.

    "I should hurt you." Evan threatened as he bowed up to Leo.

    "You would be dumb to even attempt it. But maybe you are dumb? Maybe you are pathetic? Look at you; everything you wanted has been taken from you. What real man would let anyone take what's his? I'll tell you what kind. A weak, pathetic, worthless, and dumb one." Leo said as he made sure to hit all of his weak points, all of his insecurities.

    Rage rushed through Evan, and his body began to shake. Hatred blinded him. The anger was worse now in this form than it ever had been when he was human. He locked eyes with Leo and wanted to rip him to pieces.

    "Perfect. You are rage. Now hold on to the anger and think of what you want. Think of where it is. Then, let your body go. Feel yourself drift while holding that fire to where you want to be," Leo instructed him.

Evan flickered for a second, his rage fluttered and he looked confused. Leo let out a low, annoyed growl.

"Come on, you fucking worthless piece of shit. I couldn't have been any clear on what you needed to do. No wonder she ran from your stupid ass." Leo snapped.

Evan felt like his veins burned with fire. He felt his body tremble and shake as he tried to fight through the pain.

"Let it fucking go." Leo yelled at him.

Evan shut his eyes and thought of what he wanted. He held on to the anger and then felt his body go light; he pushed the shaking to the side and imagined drifting in a breeze. Then everything snapped, and he was standing in front of Leo with his hand on his throat.

"Perfect! Took you long enough!" Leo laughed and grabbed hold of Evan's wrist and pulled it off of his throat.

"Now go on. Go get your girl." Leo winked at him and started to walk away.

Evan blinked and then realized how it all worked. He grinned, and his eyes went dark with hate as he phased once more in front of Leo and were gone.

"About fucking time." Leo rolled his eyes as he looked up at the sky, dawn was breaking.

Evan's feet hit the concrete ground as he phased. His body wobbled as he tried to gain his strength. As everything came back into focus, he saw the bar. He was supposed to phase Josephine. He gritted his teeth. Maybe if he did not know where she was, he couldn't do it. He clenched his hands into fists

as he tried to suppress the anger. A door shut loudly, and it caught his attention. He watched Danny carry a backpack out of the bar and to his car. His eyes narrowed at the backpack. He instantly recognized it. It was Josephine's. Danny had to bring it to her. Now he could know where she was, and he could go to her.

Jo

The smell of sweets drifted into the room. She pictured pancakes with a clump of buttered drizzled with syrup. She inhaled deeper as she opened her eyes. Malcolm smirked as he saw her smile and then her eyes widened as they looked at the plate he set down on the nightstand next to her. She let out a small yawn as she sat up. She was in his bed, curled up under the soft gray covers. He must have carried her in when she nodded off. She looked down at the overly large t-shirt and couldn't help but pull it up to her nose and inhale. It smelt like him. He must have put her in his clothes once she was asleep. Her eyes flickered back to the nightstand as she tried to avoid the warmth that flooded her face. He must have seen her smell his shirt. The sight of the pancakes saved her as her stomach growled as she looked at them. Blueberries and strawberries had toppled off the side of the stack.

"Did you go to the store?" Jo asked, as she remembered the kitchen was bare.

"Demon…I can go pretty much anywhere I want in a matter of seconds." Malcolm smiled as he set down a cup of coffee and a glass of orange juice.

"I couldn't decide if you were a coffee or juice person." Malcolm explained as he sat on the bed next to her.

"You didn't have to do all this for me." She whispered, taking the juice.

"You need food. If you're going to stay, then it's necessary." Malcolm explained as he grabbed the coffee.

"Yeah, but-" Jo went to say, and Malcolm held up his hand as if he stopped the words that were about to come out of her mouth.

"Ok then." Jo laughed and took the knife and sliced through the pancakes.

She picked up a small section of the buttery, syrup drenched pancakes and put it in her mouth. She made a mmm noise as soon as they hit her taste buds. They were the best pancakes she had ever had.

"Do you make these?" Jo asked, her eyes big with surprise, and her hand covered her mouth as she spoke so he couldn't see any pancake.

"Yes." Malcolm laughed as he watched her.

"I'm impressed." Jo said as she took another bite.

"Of pancakes?" Malcolm said as her eyes flickered with amusement.

"Mmm. They're so good," Jo said as she moved the pancake around to get more syrup.

"So you thought I couldn't cook," Malcolm said with a raised eyebrow.

"Well…Maybe." Jo giggled as she looked at him from the pancakes.

"Ouch." Malcolm laughed as he rested his arm on the countertop.

"You still owe me a song." Jo laughed as she finished the pancake.

A drop of syrup dangled on her lip. Malcolm smiled softly and reached over his hand, bracing the side of her face gently, and he ran his thumb up and caught the drop. Jo's cheeks flushed with embarrassment as she realized what he was doing.

"Gosh, I'm a mess sometimes." She said as she tried to play it off.

Malcolm's eyes darkened as he brought the drop of syrup to his mouth and sucked it off his thumb. Jo felt her body flush, but not from embarrassment this time. Her thoughts wandered to his mouth and how it made her feel the night before.

"So…um, do you just play piano?" Jo asked, knowing the answer, but she needed to divert the thoughts in her head.

"No, I can play almost all of them. Piano is my favorite." Malcolm smiled, seeing her reaction.

"Almost?" Jo smirked curiously as she looked up at him.

"I don't care much for the flute." Malcolm said a small grin on his face.

"The flute, really." Jo said as she stood up need some air between them.

She carried her plate over to the sink and placed the plate on it. Even a few feet away, she could feel her body pulling and calling to Malcolm. The way his eyes traced her every movement, the slightest brush of his

skin against hers, it all sent shivers and chill through her body.

She went to turn around, but he was behind her; he reached for a paper towel above the sink. She felt her breath catch in her throat.

"Malcolm," Jo whispered as she found her eyes glued to his lips.

"Yes?" Malcolm said; he dropped his hand from the paper towel and placed it on her waist.

"This…these feelings I get from you…Do you feel them too? It's more than want or lust. I don't know how to explain it. Or is it because you used your blood to save me?" Jo asked reluctantly.

She swore it felt like electricity that coursed through. It hit deep within, and she felt this tug. As if he was meant to be hers, like her soul recognized him. She would be crushed if he did not feel the same.
"I've been feeling this." He whispered as he picked up her hand and entwined his fingers through hers.

She shivered and leaned into his touch. Her fingers locked around his, like her hand had always meant to hold his.

"Since the moment I saw you. It is not the bond or the blood, for that matter. It's like we're connected." Malcolm said quietly.

"Like my everything-

"Needs you." Jo said, finishing his sentences.

Something flickered in his eyes; Jo couldn't tell if it was joy or concern. She tilted her head and went to ask him when a loud thud came from the front of the house. A repeated thud came in a pattern form. It took

her a second to realize it was someone knocking at the door.

"Company?" Jo asked as she looked to where the front door would be.

"No," Malcolm said, his voice short and his eyes narrowed as he stood up.

"Stay here." He said as he began walking out of the room.

"Wait for me." Jo said as she stumbled out of bed.

"No. Stay." Malcom said as he opened the door and stepped out into the hall.

"Excuse you, I am not a dog. I won't stay." She said sharply as she stepped into the hall as well.

He was standing at the top step ready to descend the stairs. He tilted his head up towards the ceiling and let out a sigh.

"Fine, just stay back and out of sight until I know who it is," Malcolm said as he started down the stairs.

Jo felt her heart tug and her chest tighten. Did he not want anyone to know she was there with him? Was he embarrassed or hiding something?

"No. I can feel your panic. I just want to keep you safe," Malcolm answered her rushing thoughts.

She felt relieved as she crept down the stairs behind him. Malcolm motioned for her to stay on the stairs as he made it to the door. He tried to peer through the frosted glass window of the door, but all he could make out was a shadow. He pulled the door open and let out a low grumble.

"Morning." Danny's voice came through the door.

"Danny?" Jo asked and hurried down the stairs; before Malcolm could say anything else, Jo was by his side looking at Danny.

"Morning." Danny repeated this time cheerfully.

"Hey! Is everything ok?" Jo asked as she looked behind Danny; there was something on the ground behind him.

"Yeah, actually I just figured you might need some of your stuff…like clothes." Danny said as he looked down at the oversized shirt that hung loosely around her.

"Oh, thanks!" Jo smiled and stepped out onto the steps.

"Here you go," Danny said as he pulled the backpack from behind him and handed it to her.

"Iris, are you sure you're ok?" Danny asked, his eyes glanced at Malcolm, whose face was stiff and held back anger.

"I'm actually really good. How's Violet? Is she mad at me?" Iris asked quietly.

"No, no. She's worried, like we all are, but she's not mad," Danny said as he stepped towards her. Danny's hand went to brush her arm lightly as a notion of comfort.

Malcolm grunted a little, but Jo smiled a bit and still focused on Danny.

"I promise, this is the first time in a long time I've felt safe. I'll come by the bar in a few days. See if maybe I can pick up a shift or two as long as I'm not alone." Jo laughed lightly.

"So you're not heading out like you originally planned?" Danny asked with a raised eyebrow.

"No, I think I'm gonna stay around a while," Jo said as she subconsciously reached back and grabbed Malcolm's hand.

Malcolm felt his heart stutter as she spoke, and then he couldn't help the small smile that came to his lips when she grabbed his hand. She was staying because of him.

"I'm glad you are," Danny said, as he ignored the sentimental moment between Jo and Malcolm.

"Yeah, so I'm still gonna need a job and friends." Jo said as she smiled softly at Danny.

"When do you think you'll be up? Violet misses you." Danny mumbled.

"Do you think I could grab a shift on Saturday? Work with her?" Jo asked.

"I'm sure it won't be a problem. We are hiring a bouncer so nothing like that will ever happen again. We're a small town, so it's never been a problem. Random tiffs and bar fights but nothing like that," Danny said, a tinge of bitterness in his voice as he spoke about the incident.

"It's ok. I'm ok. So see you Saturday?" Jo asked him as she pulled the back up onto her shoulder.

"Yeah, see you Saturday," Danny said with a small smile on his face.

"Saturday." Jo nodded as she watched him step down the stairs, Malcom's hand went to her waist and pulled her against him.

"Iris…call me if you need anything." Danny said as he stepped off the stairs.

"I will, Danny. I promise." Jo smiled with a nod.

Jo watched Danny reluctantly walk to his car and then slowly roll out of the driveway.

"Garden?" Malcolm said softly in her ear.

"That sounds nice. Then you're playing a song for me on the piano and I am sitting very far on the other side of the room." Jo laughed as she poked him in his stomach.

"Fine, said," Malcolm said with a smile curled at the corners of his lips.

The sunlight warmed her skin, and she found herself sitting on the bench next to the sunflowers. Sunflowers were her favorite. They followed the sun, moving with it, always searching for the light. She always reminded herself that's what she needed to do. When it was dark, the sunflowers looked at each other. Even in her darkest days, she needed to sort out light, for hope. She let out a small sigh as she looked at them. Malcolm came outside with some tea. He handed her a glass and sat down beside her.

"What are you thinking, Sunflower?" Malcolm asked her.

"That this is a little crazy." Jo laughed as she looked around.

"It's alot." Malcolm nodded, thinking she was talking about the existence of demons.

"I would have never thought that-" Jo started to say.

"I know demons exist. You hear about it in books and religious materials. Horror movies, but most humans never actually think they are real," Malcolm said, thinking he was finishing her sentence.

"No… not all that." She laughed as she shook her head.

"What then?" Malcolm asked her confused.

"That I would be… free. It feels like a dream; your house is gorgeous. There's a garden with my favorite flowers. You are …" Jo started to say but couldn't find the words.

"A demon?" Malcolm asked again, confused.

"Impossible. No, you are kind, different … and … and safe." Jo said finally finding the words.

"I haven't felt safe in so long. It's nice." Jo chuckled.

"Tell me," Malcolm said as he sat down next to her; he wanted to be angry, and there was anger in the pit of his stomach just burning, but he kept his voice soft.

"He…" Jo said quietly as she closed her eyes as if it was hard to form words.

Malcolm was quiet; he knew whom she met. He already knew his name; he had found it out before he appeared at the inn. He didn't want to interrupt her and gave her the time she needed.
"Evan…his name is Evan. It was sweet at the beginning. You know, opening the door for me, dates, holding hands — very textbook." Jo laughed as she shook her head.

"I was living in a crappy apartment with a water leak the slumlord wouldn't fix. So one day, complaining to Evan, I moved in, and the first two months were really sweet and nice. Then things got bad. It started off slow, and he didn't want me to go out on my own and said it was for my protection. He threw out all my clothes one

215

day and got me all new ones. Said he was treating me like a princess. I thought it was so sweet. Now I realized he just didn't want me wearing anything he thought was too sexy. He had me quit my job because he said it was too stressful for me. That he was getting promoted, and he would be traveling. He needed me to come with him. The first time he hit me, I couldn't believe it was real. It happened so quickly, and he acted like nothing had happened. I couldn't even process how I felt. He made me need him so much that I had no way out. When I was brave enough, I tried, and that's when he made the blue room." Jo said quietly, her voice shook as she tried to hold back the overwhelming feeling of sadness and embarrassment.

"The blue room?" Malcolm asked his body tense, his stomach burned with rage.

"It was an open room with no windows and one door. He painted the room blue to bring out the blue in my eyes. The room had a mattress on the floor with no bedding, a wooden chair, and a bucket. Depending on how mad he was, the bed would or would not be there." Jo said her voice had dropped so low it was just above a whisper.

Malcolm's mind snapped to the memory of her first night here and how she begged him to leave the window open. His stomach twisted inside him.

"The scars?" Malcolm said, his jaw clenched shut.

"Malcolm…the short answer is yes, but I don't want to think about it anymore. I want to let him go, let all of it go. I want to think about tomorrow and the future." Jo said softly and reached out to hold his hand.

"I'm sorry." Malcolm whispered, his voice just as quietly as hers.

"For?" Jo asked, confused.

"When you first came here, I...I locked you in the room." Malcolm said quietly, his voice full of shame.

"It's ok...it's something I need to work on." Jo said with a smile.

"Sunflower," Malcolm said as he turned her towards him.

Jo's finger pressed against his lips as she shook her head.

"I don't want to hear it. I just want to be here. With you. In the garden where you play me a song..." Jo grinned.

"Well, the piano is all the way upstairs, and unfortunately it's not exactly easy to take up and down the stairs." Malcolm smiled.

"I'll settle for....your second favorite instrument." Jo grinned back.

"Fine. I'll be right back." Malcolm laughed and then pressed his lips to her forehead.

Jo smiled big as she watched Malcolm not waste any time and chose to phase rather than just run inside. She shook her head. Imagine anywhere you wanted to go or be, just thinking of it and poof, you're there. The sunflowers shimmering in the sunlight caught her eye and walked over to them. She watched them shift in the sky. She titled her head up to the sky and let out a small breath. There was a sudden flash, and then there was movement. She turned, and her heart sank as she locked eyes with him.

"Josephine."

His voice reached into her chest and strangled her heart. Her chest tightened, and she couldn't find her voice. Her hand went to her chest as she backed away slowly as she stared at him in disbelief. Something was wrong; his eyes were black, and his skin looked pale. He stepped towards her, and she didn't take a second look. Her stomach dropped in panic as she turned and began to run towards the house.

"You can't run." His voice laughed behind her.

Jo slammed right into his chest full force as she ran from him. His hands captured her upper arms as he laughed.

"Josephine. You will never be able to escape me again." Evan laughed.

"Evan, let go of me," Jo said as she pulled back, still not sure what was happening.

"Never. You are never going away from me again. I have power now and abilities. Wherever you go, whatever you do, there is no escape." Evan laughed.

"What did you do?" Jo asked as she struggled in his arms.

"I made myself better." Evan laughed.

"Let her go." Malcolm's voice rang out behind her with such anger that Jo swore the ground vibrated. The violin he held dropped out of his hand as he became rigid.

Evan locked eyes with Malcolm and spun Jo against his chest. Evan locked his eyes with Malcolm.

"Malcolm," Jo said as she watched him tense up and take a step towards them.

"Don't say his fucking name." Evan snapped, and then suddenly something metal was against her throat.

Malcolm froze in place seeing the demon blade pressed to her throat. His eyes narrowed at the black blade.

"Don't touch her." Malcolm growled but still stayed back.

"I'll touch her anyway I want. She's mine." Evan growled and then leaned forward and ran his tongue over her cheek.

Jo flinched but kept her eyes on Malcolm. She watched him try to figure out the right move. Jo closed her eyes trying to get herself to think. She knew Evan and knew how he thought. She let out a small breath.

"Evan," Jo whispered.

"Josephine." Evan chuckled, his mouth near her ear.

"Can we go home?" Jo whispered, making sure her voice stayed steady so he wouldn't think she was lying.

"What?" Evan asked, confused.

"I want to go home. I miss home." Jo said a little louder.

"I missed you. I don't know what I was thinking." Jo said she slowly raised her hand and touched his cheek.

Jo opened her eyes and locked with Malcolm, who wore a look of anger and confusion. His brows were narrowed, eyes squinted and jaw locked. His focus completely on Evan as if he was looking for a weak spot to take him out.

It's ok. Jo mouthed to Malcolm.

Evan leaned into her hand, the knife moving a little bit away from her throat.

"Josephine, that wasn't nice. I've been so worried and stressed. I haven't slept since you left," Evan said as he brushed his face against her hand.

"I didn't know how much I needed you." Jo said, continuing to lie and play the part.

Evan grinned and looked up at Malcom. His grin couldn't be any wider.

"Do you hear that? She wants me. To leave with me. To be with me," Evan said and then let the knife fall away from her throat.

"Tell him." Evan demanded as he tapped Jo with the hilt of the knife.

"Don't fucking touch her." Malcolm growled as he stepped forward.

"Malcolm…I want…I want." Jo tried to say the words, but she struggled as she looked at Malcolm.

"Josephine," Evan growled as he yanked on her arm.

She couldn't lie anymore. A tear slipped down her cheek, and she closed her eyes. She opened her eyes and looked at Malcolm.

"I'm sorry." She whispered.

"We know that, Josephine. I want you to tell him that you don't want him and that you chose me. Go on." Evan said as he squeezed her arm.

"Malcolm." Jo stated his name and then moved her foot forward.

"Malcolm, I want…you." Jo yelled and then slammed her head back into Evan's face.

The blow didn't faze him but shocked him
enough so Jo could start running towards Malcolm.
Evan was right behind her, reaching for her. The demon
blade in his hand ready to stab her. Malcolm shut his
eyes and phased. He reappeared between Evan and
Jo, his arms wrapped around Jo and pulled her to him.
Jo turned to see Malcolm and felt a rush of relief, but
then horror flashed across her face. Evan raised the
blade and went to plunge it into Malcolm's back. Jo
yelled and grabbed hold of Malcolm, spinning him
around. She took his place, and the blade pushed into
her back and through her chest.

"No!" Malcolm yelled as he saw the tip of the
black blade poke out of the front of her chest.

Evan pulled the blade out, and blood rushed out
of the large hole. The dark shirt she was wearing turned
wet with blood. Jo looked down as the wetness spread.
She inhaled sharply as pain rushed through her body.
She felt her legs go weak and cold.

"Malcolm," Jo said as she went to fall to her
knees.

Malcolm caught her. His hand went to her chest.
He pressed his hand into the wound to try to stop the
bleeding. His eyes searched her face. The warm
wetness on his hand caused his brain to scramble; he
needed to fix this. He needed to save her.

"Josephine, I..I.. Stupid girl. Why? Why did you
do that?" Evan asked, looking down over her.

"Stay with me, Sunflower. Hold on." Malcolm
said as blood steadily poured out of the hole in her
chest and around his hand.

The blood came out in a pumping motion, each rush of blood was to the beat of her heart. Malcolm felt his body go numb and realized her heart was pumping blood out of the hole; the blade had pierced her heart.

"Give me the blade." Malcolm demanded.

"No," Evan said as he backed up.

"She needs blood; give me the blade." Malcolm bellowed.

Evan backed away, shaking his head. Malcolm didn't have time. He grabbed a hold of his wrist and bit down hard. His teeth punctured his skin, and blood slowly dripped out. He put it to Jo's lips.

"Drink Sunflower." Malcolm ordered as her skin turned blue.

"It's cold." Jo whispered as a drop of blood fell into her mouth.

"It's ok. I'm gonna fix it. Drink," Malcolm said firmly.

"It doesn't hurt." Jo said quietly as she felt her body go numb.

"Thank you." Jo said as she looked up into Malcolm's eyes.

"No. No. No. Stay with me," Malcolm said as he watched as the light began to fade from her face.

"It's ok." Jo smiled weakly and shut her eyes.

Her body went limp, and blood pooled out around her. Malcolm felt wetness on his knees as he kneeled next to her. He dug his fingernails into the holes in his wrist trying to make them bigger, trying to make more blood flow out. The blood dropped onto her lips. He pressed his wrist into her mouth trying to get as much blood into her. Malcolm looked down at her body,

wanting her skin to warm and turn pink in color. He silently begged for her eyes to flutter, her chest to rise, but nothing happened. She was gone. He looked around for death. He was not there. She was a soul that was not meant to die. Where was he! He would demand that she stay.

When neither Death showed up and his blood didn't work, defeat rushed through him. He felt rage fill him and then nothing. He felt cold as darkness settled in. His eyes turned dark as he stood up and looked at Evan. His skin turned a pale blue color. Black vein-like lines began to swirl and wrap around his arms, up over his neck. The world was cruel and worthless. The world didn't deserve to exist. He didn't want to exist. He would burn this place down. It would all end. He stepped towards Evan; the grass dying as he walked.

"Hey, she stepped into it. She wasn't supposed to; that wasn't supposed to happen. You should have let her go." Evan yelled at him, Evan finger pointed at Malcolm as he yelled.

"Who turned you?" Malcolm asked, his voice chilling as he stepped towards him.

"What?" Evan asked, still pointing at Malcolm.

"Who turned you! Malcolm screamed.

"A crossroad demon." Evan yelled at him. Malcolm looked at him with no emotion.

He took his finger and placed it on Evan's fingertip. Black poured out of Malcolm and into Evan; it traveled up Evan's hand and arm, then invaded his throat and lastly his mind. Evan screamed and began to claw at his face. His fingernails ripped and tore at his

flesh. Evan held the demon blade in his hand still and then suddenly plunged it into his own heart.

"Coward. You should have suffered more." Malcolm said as he stepped over Evan's dead body.

As he stepped over Evan's body, the darkness he poured into Evan floated back into Malcolm.

Chapter Twenty Two
Balor

    His feet touch the ground of the In-between. He frowned deeply as he looked up at the sky, it was darker than usual, and it had a sense of doom to it. The tall grass swayed in the haunted breeze that rushed through the In-between. As Balor walked through the long grass, it brushed against his legs and caused them to itch. He quickened his pace through the field. He needed to find them quickly, to tell them what he knew and come up with a plan as to what to do next. Balor knew his next step would be to find Leo, but he needed Ryan, Silas, and even Kere on standby in case something happened. If he could get to Leo, he could get to who was behind this, and he could go home. Home the word hit his heart as thoughts of Kere fell into his head. God, he loved her. Home was no longer a place for him, not that he ever had a place to call home. Home was Kere.

    "Balor." Ryan smiled brightly as she turned to him.

    "Beauitful. It's been a while." Balor smiled as he met her on the dock.

    Silas shot him a glare as he called Ryan beautiful, he did it purposely to make him. He adored Ryan, but pissing Silas off made him happy.

    "Easy, sweetness I didn't miss you there." Balor grinned as he winked at Silas.

    "Balor, I'm glad you're here Silas was telling me something was happening on earth. That souls are missing." Ryan said worried as she caught Silas hand as he went to move towards Balor.

"Boys, we don't have time for a scuffle." Ryan warned them as she pulled Silas to her side.

"What do you know?" Silas said as he put his arm around Ryan, her touch calming him.

"A demon named Leo is working with Pavel. Pavel wants Malcolm to come out of retirement. I think Pavel is also behind the missing souls." Balor stated what he knew.

"Malcolm is destruction, it was a blessing when he retired. How would he get him to come back?" Silas asked, confused.

"There's nothing that would make him come back into the game," Balor said with a shrug.

Ryan wanted to say something but stumbled. Her legs felt weak, and she buckled into Silas. He quickly steadied her as she inhaled sharply. She could feel the In-Between shift, and it weakened her.

"Ryan! Ryan, what's going on?" Silas asked as he held her tightly, he tried to mask the panic in his voice.

"Something's wrong. Something happened. There's been a shift." Ryan said as she steadied herself against Silas.

"What do you mean?" Silas asked as he tried to feel what she was spoke about.

"He must have done it. He must have got Malcolm to come back." Balor said as he thought of the only thing that could have happened.

"How though?" Silas asked, his eyes still watched Ryan closely.

"Hello?" Jo's voice was small as she walked towards the gorgeous looking woman all dressed in white, the man all in black held her tightly.

"Hell- Who? How?" Balor asked quietly and looked to Silas.

"I'm Jo…Did you say Malcolm?" Jo asked as she reached the dock.

"Jo?" Ryan asked as she straightened up and moved from Silas, holding her hand out.

"Yes, I know Malcolm…is he here? He's well he can go wherever he wants if he thinks about it." Jo smiled softly as she looked at the woman's outstretched hand.

"You know Malcolm?" Balor asked suspiciously.

"Yes," Jo said as she looked at the three.

"I'm Ryan, this is Balor and Silas. You are in the In-between," Ryan explained slowly.

"In-between…I died. So is this like limbo?" Jo asked, confused.

"Sort of. It's a waiting place." Ryan smiled at her, still not giving up on Jo taking her hand.

"Waiting for?" Jo asked and then took Ryan's hand.

As she touched Ryan, Ryan felt a rush of power. A feeling of joy rushed through her and light. Ryan looked at Jo and realized.

"Silas…She's his light." Ryan whispered.

"What?" Balor asked, confused.

"Malcolm, she's his light." Ryan repeated and watched realization spread across Silas's face. Ryan was Silas' light. He would have ascended into darkness

and destroyed the In-between, no souls would have moved on. Ryan saved him.

"Everyone has a light, without light, there is only darkness.." Ryan whispered a small amount of fear in her voice.

"Is Malcolm ok? Can he come here?" Jo asked, panic starting to set in.

"I have to get to Earth, Silas, you need to come with me. Ryan, get in touch with Kere…She's a goddess now, there has to be something we can do." Balor said quickly as he now realized the Earth and everyone on it was doomed.

"What's going on? Is Malcolm ok." Jo said, her voice was firm.

"We need to get you to him." Ryan said as she squeezed her hand.

"Ryan, are you ok?" Silas asked, reluctant to leave her after the spell she went through.

"I am. I will look after Jo, go be a hero." Ryan winked at him and then leaned upwards to place a kiss on his cheek.

Silas moved his head and stole the kiss. Balor let out an annoyed side and snapped his fingers.

"Let's go, Romeo." Balor groaned.

"They're at Malcolm's house. My ex, he did something to himself and then he went to stab Malcolm, and I blocked it." Jo said as she placed a hand on the center of her chest, expecting a hole to still be there.

"Thank you." Balor said and quickly phased.

"I'll be back soon." Silas said quickly and kissed Ryan on the forehead.

"Kere!" He yelled to the In-between gray sky before he phased.

Ryan shook her head and looked back to Jo, who was confused and concerned. Ryan took a deep breath and looked up at the sky, waiting.

"We need to find a way to send you back," Ryan said quietly.

"To Malcolm." Jo nodded, she could feel it. This empty hole in her chest and it wasn't because a knife had stabbed through it. She felt like a part of her was missing, and she could feel herself slipping.

"Don't. I gave into the darkness once and lost myself. You need to stay. You have to, Malcolm needs you. That darkness you just touched. He is in it, and he will need you to bring him out of it. If not, then he will leave death and destruction wherever he goes until there is nothing left." Ryan explained to her.

Jo felt the weight of her words and shoved the feeling down deep into her gut. She would not let Malcolm be lost. She glanced around at where she was. How would she ever get back to him?

"I know he's a demon, but death…destruction. He was intimidating to others, but I can't see him causing that." Jo whispered.

"Malcolm has a dark past. He is responsible for lots of bad things. He burned fast, bright, and caused almost every tragedy the earth knew. Malcolm was admired by the under lords and threatened the ones above. As they were trying to decide what to do with him. He announced he paid his dues and was retiring. No one knew why, some were devastated, others grateful." Ryan said quietly.

She looked at the sky, and there was still no Kere. She shut her eyes and her face pointed upwards.

"Kere." She whispered.

"Who is Kere?" Jo asked, confused as to why they were waiting on her

A flash erupted in the In-between. It blinded Jo as she shielded her eyes from it. Within a few seconds, a woman stood where the light once was. She wore a deep indigo dress, and her hair was the color of the evening sky. Was everyone here so stunningly beautiful?

"I am Kere…Goddess of night." Kere smiled brightly.

"Kere, we need your help," Ryan said quietly with a small smile on her lips.

"Who's the girl?" Kere asked as she met Ryan on the dock.

"This is Jo…She's Malcolm's light. Malcolm has gone dark." Ryan said shortly.

"Malcolm, Malcolm," Kere said with a raised eyebrow.

"Yes, Balor and Silas have gone to intervene, but we need to get her back to Earth," Ryan said quickly.

"Ok…we need to figure out how we do this," Kere said as she thought out loud.

There was a noise behind them, and all three of them turned to see Charon, the farrier of souls, dock his boat. The River Styx began to turn violent as he tied his boat off and stepped up onto the dock.

"Charon, what brings you?" Ryan smiled sweetly but tucked Jo behind her.

"What always brings me, a soul." Charon said with a cross look.

"Well, you can't have this one." Kere said as she crossed her arms.

"Again with this?" Charon asked, his face stern but his voice held a smile to this.

"Charon, its-" Ryan started to explain, but his face cracked into a smile and he shook his head.

"I'm not here for that one, I'm here for him." Charon said and pointed behind them.

"Josephine!" His voice yelled out behind them, and Jo turned in disbelief.

"Evan? How?" Jo asked in a small voice.

"No. Even in death I can't get away from him." She said as she looked at him as he stumbled across the field.

"Do not be frightened. He has no power here." Ryan said firmly as she narrowed her eyes at him.

"I'm going to take this one to the hall of judgement. He has a date with an under lord. Then I want to know what's wrong with my river. It's angry, something has shifted." Charon said to them as he watched Evan stumble onto the dock.

"There's something going on in the human realm. We're trying to fix it." Kere told Charon as she straightened her stance.

"Josephine! I told you, you would never escape me." Evan laughed.

"You think you can run, you worthless bitch." Evan yelled as he started to come towards her.

Kere growled and slammed her elbow into his mouth as Evan went to pass her. Evan dropped to his knees.

"Someone really needs to teach you manners," Kere said in disgust.

Evan covered his mouth with his hands, pain surged through him. Even in death, there was pain. He was confused as he spat out a tooth and looked up at the woman.

"This does not concern you. She's mine. I traded my soul for her." Evan grumbled.

"Stupid boy, you cannot trade your soul for someone else." Ryan laughed.

"Forget the hall of judgement. If you want, darling, you can toss him into the river. He can float around for all eternity, lost and hopeless." Kere smiled.

"Up to you, you would save me a trip." Charon shrugged.

"It's up to you, Jo." Ryan smiled at her, and Evan went to get up. She grabbed a hold of the back of his neck and pinned him down.

Shock flashed across Evan's face as he was surprised by how strong Ryan was. He didn't comprehend what was happening.

"I'm a demon now! You can't do this to me!" Evan bellowed as he struggled in Ryan's grasp.

Ryan's face twisted in anger at his arrogance and dragged him over to the river. She dangled him above the water. The water splashed up into his face, and as it touched his skin, a feeling of dread set in him, fear he never felt before. He tried to pull back, but Ryan was too strong for him.

"You should dip him." Charon chuckled.

"You said he will be judged?" Jo asked as she watched Evan be weak for the first time in her life.

She had feared him for so long, and now, to watch him cower in front of her, she saw him for what he was. He was not some powerful, powerful person. He was weak, flawed,and pitiful.

"Jo…please help me." Evan called to her as he scrambled.

"He will be taken to the Hall of Judgement, where he will be judged. If you chose so. I for one, am a believer in an eye for an eye personally." Charon smiled.

Jo walked over to him and kneeled down,her eyes studied him. His eyes were wide and pleaded silently for her to have mercy.

"It is crazy that you are looking at me, how I have looked at you. Begging for you to stop, begging for you to not hurt me. To let me be free. Here you are, needing my help, my mercy, and the anger in me says to deny you. To hurt you, to make you suffer." Jo said quietly, she spoke of anger, but there was none in her voice.

"Jo, I'm sorry. I need help. I've always needed help. There's something wrong with me," Evan cried.

"Let him be judged. Let him be seen for who he is and receive what he must for it. It is not my place to decide." Jo said as she stood up and looked at Charon.

"As you wish." Charon nodded, a coin appeared in his hand, and he held it out to Ryan, who snatched it.

"She is a better person than most." Ryan whispered and shoved Evan down to the ground.

233

She dropped the gold coin in front of him, and he looked at it confused.

"Pay the ferryman to take you to your destination. If you linger, if you speak or even look at her. I will make sure you suffer until the end of time." Ryan said through her teeth as she stepped over him.

Evan grabbed the coin in his hand and stood up. He looked over at Jo, who stood between Ryan and Kere. Both Kere and Ryan narrowed their eyes at him as he choked back the words he wanted to say. He then turned silently and made his way to the boat. He handed the coin to Charon. Jo turned her back, she was not going to watch him go, he would not see her face one last time.

"All aboard." Charon laughed as he kicked Evan in his ass to make him move.
The boat began to move down the angry river, once the boat was out of sight, Kere touched Jo's shoulder.

"You're a good person." Kere smiled.

"No, I just know right from wrong." Jo smiled weakly.

"But you chose to do what's right even when it is so easy to do what's wrong. You would not have been faulted if you chose to hurt him. That's what makes you a good person." Kere explained.

"I was going to ask if you were sure we had the right person, but seeing that. Earth needs someone like her." Kere finished her statement as she looked at Ryan.

"Ok enough about him, how do I help?" Jo asked, trying to change topics.

"That we need to figure out." Ryan said as she looked up at the In-between's sky, which seemed to darken by the minute.

"That doesn't look good," Kere whispered. "It's not. If Earth is affected, it rolls over here. The In-between first, then above, and down below. All realms are connected. The gods may have abandoned us long ago, but the universe is seeking out its guardians. That's what I believe is happening. If Malcolm doesn't choose right, we will all be lost." Ryan said, her voice heavy.

"Balor and Silas will stop this. We will work on our part here." Kere said confidently.

"Hang on, boys." Ryan said thinking of Silas and Balor, dread was pitted deep within her, but she pushed it aside.

Chapter Twenty Three

Evan

The ferryboat creaked as it made its way down the rocky river. Evan looked nervously around, unsure of where they were headed. He looked to Charon, who had said nothing since he got into the boat.

"Where are you taking me?" Evan asked quietly as he looked out.

It looked like the river just ended; there was a dark blue sky almost like a wall and nothing after. Evan shifted to the side of the boat to see if he could see better.

"The Hall of Judgment." Charon said shortly.

"But the river." Evan said, his voice excited as he pointed to the end.

"The river is fine." Charon said, his voice full of annoyance.

"But," Evan started to say but stopped talking when Charon shot him a threatening look.

Silence fell over the boat as it neared the end of the river. Evan grabbed the side of the boat and braced himself for impact. A flash of bright light blinded him and he ducked his head. The water roared around him, and the boat shook. He knew with certainty that they were crashing. Everything went silent, and Evan prepared for the worst.

"Get out of my boat." Charon said sharply.

Evan opened his eyes, and the river flowed to a stop in front of a stone building. A man waited for him, and as Evan stepped out of the boat, he grabbed hold of him and drug him to the building. The man was so

strong he could not even try to resist. The doors to the building opened, and the man tossed Evan inside.

"Evan Matthews, you appear before the judges, Minos, Rhadamanthus, and Aeacus, to be judged on how you lived your life. Are you ready for judgment?" A loud voice boomed out over the room.

"Judgement for my life. No, you can't judge me," Evan said as he stood up.

"We can, and we will. We actually already decided before you got here." Minos grinned.

"What, how is there no trail?" Evan asked, looking around.

"Your trail was your life," Aeacus stated unimpressed.

"Evan Matthews, you are sentenced to your own personal hell. Your soul will rot out eternity and your very own blue room." Rhadamanthus sentenced.

"What no!" Evan screamed.

"Jax, show Evan to his room." Aeacus yelled.

"Enjoy your stay." Minos grinned.

A tall man with a board chest came in from the dark. His blond hair was cut short on the sides and left loose on top. He looked like a Viking. He walked over to Evan and grabbed him by his throat.

"No…Jax…right, Jax. Listen, we can work something out; I'm a demon." Evan said through coughs.

"I might enjoy seeing you suffer." Jax smiled as he pulled Evan into the dark.

<hr>

Malcom

      Evan wasn't turned into a demon on his own. Someone did it. That would be his second kill. He would make them suffer. If Evan hadn't been a demon, he would have never come back after her. His chest tightened as he thought of Jo. His hands and legs shook from the anger that coursed through him. He clenched his jaw as he made his way towards the front of his house. The hatred he had for everything fueled him. Without her, there was nothing. The world had been cruel to her. The world was a rotting corpse that needed to be purged. Evan's words floated around in his head, a crossroads demon turned him. His mind began to race, thinking of all the possibilities, and then he knew. Maria. He closed his eyes and pictured where she could possibly be. She loved the bar down the street from the main cross point just out of town.

      He barely had to do anything at all to phase. Before he could even finish his thought, he stood in the demon bar. He appeared quietly, but the small bar was aware of the change in presence. A hush fell over the bar, and the fellow demons pushed away from him.

      "Not another one." Someone muttered.

      Malcolm reached over and grabbed the back of the man's neck and flooded him with darkness. It ate at the man from the inside out, and in seconds he was ash. Malcolm absorbed the pain into himself as the darkness rushed up out of the ashes. He felt himself ignite even more. The flame that burned his hunger to destroy. He looked around the bar as everyone backed away.

      "Maria," Malcolm said to the room.

The men quickly shifted and revealed Maria; she sat at the bar quietly. She looked at him, her eyes wide and her mouth open just a little bit. The surprise of seeing him made her freeze.

"Malcolm." She whispered as he began to move towards her, she could feel the rage that poured out of him.

"Why?" he demanded as he stopped in front of her, his hands clenched in fist at his sides.

"Why?" Maria whispered; her voice shook from fear.

"Evan. You turned him into a demon, why?" Malcolm said as he slammed his own fist into his leg.

"I didn't." Maria said as she pressed back into the bar, as she tried to create space between them.

"Who?" Malcolm leaned forward and locked eyes with her as he asked.

"Leo. Leo wanted him." Maria trembled as so much darkness leaked out of Malcolm.

"Leo!" Malcolm roared.

Maria nodded as she shrunk into herself, on the verge of begging Malcolm to not hurt her. She raised her hands over her head as she felt him come closer. She closed her eyes and waited. Nothing happened. The room felt lighter. Like someone had opened a door and let the air back into the room. She uncovered her head and peeked around. He was gone as quickly as he had come.

Balor

Silas and Balor appeared outside Malcolm's home. It didn't take long to track down where he lived. Balor looked at Silas, not really sure what to expect.

239

"You think he's even here?" Balor asked as he looked around.

"Look," Silas said as he tapped Balor and pointed to the scorched marks in the ground.

"Those look familiar." Balor said as he shook his head.

"He's draining the life out of the planet." Silas said as he walked over to the first scorched mark and touched it.

"Yup, when you went dark, you did the same to the In-between," Balor said with a small shrug.

"We need to find him." Silas said as he stood.

"Follow the marks, genius." Balor sighed and walked past him.

"Balor, I swear to God, if my sister didn't love you, I would let him turn you to ash," Silas said to his back as he followed him.

"You say it's for your sister, but you would miss me too much, sweet cheeks." Balor smirked as he rounded the corner of the house and hit something hard.

"Move!" Silas yelled as he grabbed hold of Balor and yanked him back.

A loud yell erupted as Balor was snatched from Malcom's grasp. Balor stumbled back to the side of Silas and looked dumbfounded at Malcolm. His eyes had turned completely black; his veins peeked through his skin, dark as coal. The same tribal-like marks wrapped up his arms. He looked like a monster. Balor put his hands up as if to say they meant no harm.

"Hey…we come in peace." Balor said his hands were still up in the air.

"Malcolm, we mean you no harm. We're here to help." Silas said as he threw a glare at Balor.

"Peace… Help. There will be no peace or help. This place needs to be purged. The human race is just a disease. They destroy anything that is good," Malcolm snarled.

"Listen, I understand your pain-" Silas tried to say but was cut off.

"Understand, you understand. Death. You should understand the need to be rid of all of them." Malcolm yelled.

"No, there is good in the world, Malcolm. You know that. You saw that. You need to hold on to it," Silas said quietly.

"The only thing good in this world is gone," Malcolm growled.

Silas looked at Balor, and Balor shrugged. He was not sure what to do next. He almost agreed with Malcolm, but he didn't say that out loud. Balor kept his distance. He remembered when Silas went dark and just a simple touch from Silas would drain and turn the person into ash. They couldn't touch him. Silas gave Balor a look; it was a strong "it's gonna be ok" look, and it made Balor's stomach drop.

"Silas, don't you dare." Balor yelled and went to reach for him, but he was too quick.

Before Balor could stop him, he wrapped his arms around Malcolm and attempted to phase. If he could take him out of earth he could stop draining it. Malcolm looked down at Silas and gripped his arm. Darkness began to leak into Silas. He held on still trying to shift, ignoring the pain that was flooding his system.

"No." Balor yelled and then grabbed hold of Malcolm and tried to pull Malcolm from Silas.

Malcolm reached behind as he held on to Silas and pressed his hand to his face, as he began to pour darkness into Balor. Balor let out a yell but still held tight as he tried to pry Malcolm from Silas.

"Balor, stop." Silas said through clenched teeth; his mind went to Kere and that she could not lose both of them.

"Fuck off, Silas." Balor yelled as more pain poured into him.

"Malcolm, we are not the ones who hurt you." Silas said as he drew strength, thoughts of Ryan entered his head. He felt the light that she gave him and battled against the darkness Malcolm tried to send into him. He stood up straighter, tightening his grip on him.

Malcolm blinked at the words. He was right; they were not the ones who caused this. Leo. His eyes narrowed, and his grip loosened. As soon as his grip loosen Balor yanked backwards. Malcolm let go of Silas, and he stumbled backwards. Malcolm gripped Balor's arm and pulled forward. Balor tumbled over the front of Malcolm and landed on his back. Malcolm let out a growl and stepped over Balor.

"Leo." He muttered and shut his eyes as he went to phase.

"He's not there." Balor coughed as he reached out and grabbed Malcolm's ankle.

Malcolm kicked his hand away and looked down at him. His eyes filled with hate as his hand twitched.

"He's not at the bar," Balor said as if he knew where he was going.

"I will find him." Malcolm said as he closed his eyes.

Balor went to grab hold of his leg again to stop him from phasing. Malcolm grunted and delivered a sharp kick to Balor's face. Balor's teeth slammed into his lip and his head went backwards. Blood trickled out of his mouth. Silas went to grab hold of Malcolm, and Malcolm phased, Silas hand went through the air.

Chapter Twenty Four
Pavel

"Do you feel that? It's like there was a shift?" Pavel said out loud as he titled his head back and looked at the sky.

He inhaled deeply as the sky grew dark. There was electricity in the air as he stood just outside his hideaway. The stone building resembles an old castle. It was a factory many years ago, and now Pavel has been using it to run his operation out of. The deep dark cellar was where he kept his container of souls.

"You need more souls." The figure said, he was cloaked in darkness as he hid in the shadows. His face was covered by a mask, and only his red glowing eyes could be seen.

"Malcolm is back; I will have all the souls I need shortly." Pavel said to him.

"That's what Nyx thought, and looked where she ended up." He snapped.

"Why does this concern you? I am nothing like Nyx," Pavel growled at the comparison.

"The gods have forgotten Earth and allowed it to be what it is. Each realm has been on its own without guardians for a long time. Once Nyx was banished everyone took a vacation. The In-between only got by because the ones who dwell there followed the old rules. There was a respect to uphold the way things were. They all could have walked away. Nyx could have easily gotten out, but she faltered. Her failure has now caused a ripple effect, and each realm is now calling for guardians again. Ryan's death set things in motion.

244

Now, the In-between has Silas and Ryan. Kere was promoted to a goddess. The opportunity for us is becoming smaller and smaller. We need earth. If we lose Earth, all I am left with is Hell," he said bitterly.

"All you have left? What do you mean?" Pavel asked; he didn't understand.

"All you need to know is you better not fuck this up. If not, there will be no place in any realm for you to hide." He snarled.

"I'm not fucking it up. Malcolm is back, and that's all we need. World war, destruction, famine, new virus. It's all about to happen. We wait and snatch up the souls as the world perishes." Pavel said confidently; his hand went to the necklace around his neck.

"If you fail, I will make sure what's left of your soul ends up in the Field of Punishment. I did not trust my necklace and this job on you for nothing." He growled as he stepped towards Pavel; his eyes glowed bright red as he did.
Pavel closed his eyes and waited for a blow or hit, some type of pain. He stayed cowered for a moment, but when nothing happened, he opened his eyes. The man was gone, and he was alone.
Jo:

A sudden pain rushed through her. Jo grabbed her chest and doubled over. She looked at Ryan and Kere, her eyes wide, not sure what was happening. Ryan started walking towards her when suddenly she looked like she was in pain.

"Silas," Ryan whispered as she looked at Kere.

Kere felt it too, and she shut her eyes as she tried to use her abilities to scan the Earth. She needed to see where they were.

"Jo, what are you feeling?" Ryan asked as she took a deep breath and walked to her.

"It was painful and then cold, dark. It was like everything became empty." Jo said, not sure how she could describe it.

"Jo, did you share blood with Malcolm?" Kere asked as she opened her eyes, not being able to get a read on Balor or Silas.

"Yes. He used it to heal me." Jo said her tone was confused.

"Ryan, I can't find them. I don't know what happened," Kere said, as she tried to mask the worry in her voice.

"Why did you ask about the blood?" Jo asked her with a raised eyebrow.

"A demon rarely shares blood because they become bonded to the person. Jo, you can sense and feel Malcolm. Maybe-" Kere went to say but a loud noise behind her stopped her.

"Silas," Ryan said as she left Jo's side and rushed to Silas, who was on the ground.

Silas hand was stretched out as if he had held on to something. She knelt down next to him, and another noise followed, and Balor appeared next to him as Ryan got to his side.

"What happened?" Ryan asked as she touched Silas's face.

Silas blinked and looked up to see Ryan. He was relieved he could phase. His body hurt all over. His mind tried to understand where he was.

"Is he here?" Silas said as he tried to sit up.

"Who?" Ryan asked him softly.

"Balor." Silas groaned as he sat up and looked to his side. He spotted Balor and instantly relaxed.

"Good." Silas grumbled as he grabbed hold of his head; his skull throbbed.

Kere knelt down next to Balor, who was out cold. She touched his forehead as worry flooded her face.

"What happened?" Kere said, worried.

"Malcolm went dark. We tried to stop him, but when he touched me, I could feel him draining me. Balor grabbed hold of him. The stupid bastard thought he was going to save me. Malcolm drained him more than me. He then got away and phased. Balor collapsed seconds after we tried to go after him. Then the world started to go dark on me. I grabbed hold of him and thought of home." Silas said as the world spun.

Kere closed her eyes and kept her hand on Balor's head; her body glowed slightly and then flickered as she poured some light into Balor. Balor's eyes flickered open, and he stared up into Kere's bright green eyes.

"Hello, gorgeous." Balor smiled as he looked up at her.

"Hey yourself." Kere said as she bent down and kissed Balor.

"Are they ok?" Jo asked as she watched the scene in front of them.

"Yeah, they will be ok." Ryan nodded as she rubbed Silas back.

"For now. We don't even know where Malcolm has gone and have no way of knowing." Silas grumbled.

"We might have a way." Kere said quietly as Balor sat up slowly and she steadied him.

"A way?" Silas asked.

"Jo and Malcolm have exchanged blood. Malcolm used his blood to heal her. They are bound." Kere said quietly.

"Meaning?" Jo asked cautiously.

"You can sense where he is. Maybe guide us to him." Silas explained.

"We need to get her to him." Kere said with a frown.

"We will need her body." Balor said shortly.

"My body!" Jo shouted as she thought for the first time about her body back on Earth.

"We will need to bring her to it. Heal her body and then find a way to get her soul back in it." Ryan said as she processed out loud.

"Well, it's a good thing Death is on our side. He can touch souls." Balor said quietly.

"How are we going to heal her?" Silas asked, looking at them.

"If demon blood can heal, I wonder what an ex demon turned goddess can do." Kere said quietly.

"So we go to Malcolm's; my body is in the garden. Do we heal my body first and then get…me back into it? Or get me back into my body and then heal it." Jo said firmly, she needed the plan laid out. She needed to know exactly what had to be done.

"We can try both." Ryan breathed.

"Silas…" Ryan said quietly; her voice had some resistance to it.

"I know, Love, we will be ok. You stay here and guard this realm." Silas said and kissed her quickly. He knew the resistance was him going without her, and he knew she had to stay behind. If they lose Earth, they need a safe place to retreat to and regroup.

Ryan squeezed his hand tightly as he stepped back. He took a deep breath, and his head killed him. He looked at Balor and Kere and nodded. Kere grabbed hold of Balor's hand. They phased, leaving Jo, Silas, and Ryan behind.

"You can do this," Ryan said as she looked hopefully at Jo with a smile.

"He needs you, and you are strong enough." Ryan nodded to Jo as she let go of Silas's hand.

Silas grunted and did not let go of Ryan; he pulled her into him and kissed her quickly. He broke the kiss and then let her go.

"Hurry back." Ryan smiled at him.

"Always." He smiled and then held his hand out to Jo.

"Let's go get you back where you belong." Silas said, and Jo grabbed his hand.

Silas phased as he held on to Jo, taking her with him.

Malcolm

His feet touch the wood of an old rundown house. He knew Leo had some connection to it. He needed to find Leo. The wooden floor squeaked beneath his feet as he moved around the house. He had found Leo here one night a long time ago when he needed help. He was after a high value soul, and it was a two person job. Leo was in one of the rooms upstairs, staring at old, stained photos. Malcolm made the world feel cold as he walked through the house; the anger he poured into the room made the air feel thick.

"I knew you would come." Leo said as Malcolm stopped in the doorway of the small room.

Leo sat in a rocking chair, staring at the wall. Malcolm studied him. The flower wallpaper was peeling off the wall. The picture that hung was dangling sideways; it barely held on.

"So you've found me," Leo said as he didn't even bother to look towards Malcolm.

"You set me up," Malcolm said from the doorway in a voice with no emotion.

"Yup…I'm not even gonna try to argue. Just get it over with. I can feel the darkness in you begging to feed," Leo said, his eyes still locked on the picture.

Malcolm walked towards him, his hand twitched by his side. Darkness that swirled around inside him gnawed at him. The need to feed it, to give into it, caused him physical pain. The small dose of light he took from Balor and Silas was not enough. It craved more, and he knew once he started he was not going to stop. He gripped Leo's shoulder and let go.

250

Leo was flooded with a pain that burned. It felt as if someone had taken his body and raked it across hot coals. He kept his eyes on the photo as he blocked out the pain the best he could.

"Do you think demons get to see their loved ones before they pass?" He asked Malcolm as he gave completely into his fate.

"Do you think she'll be waiting for me before I go to hell?" Leo continued as Malcolm didn't answer. He felt his skin die as it began to turn black. He could feel himself start to fade.

"Malcolm, I had no choice in the girl." Leo said as he reached up and placed his hand on top of Malcolm's.

Malcolm paused and looked down at him. His eyes narrowed, and there was a flicker of emotion in them, rage, anger and hurt all combined.

"I don't regret it. I have no regrets in this existence other than her. If maybe I sold my soul earlier, became a demon earlier, I could have stopped the cancer that plagued her body. Then again, if she had not died, maybe I wouldn't have. Pavel is the one you want," Leo said as the skin of his face turned to an ash grey.

"She will see you soon. Even if it's just to tournament you in the afterlife." Malcolm said as he let go of Leo.

As Malcolm pulled away, Leo's body crumpled into ash. A power rushed through him, and he felt a rush of excitement. He felt revived and anew. Leo had very little light left in him, but here at the end, in his most vulnerable state, it boosted Malcolm's strength. Malcolm shut his eyes as the name Pavel roamed around his

mind. It was a name he was not familiar with, but the demon's names varied. He gritted his teeth in anger. He had to come up with a plan. Malcolm needed to find another demon that may be in debt to this Pavel. He needed to go to a place where demons were. He closed his eyes and phased.

Chapter Twenty Five

Jo squeezed her eyes tightly and clung to Silas hand as the odd sensation left her. She felt like she could breathe again, and a familiar smell entered her nose. Jo knew the floral smell before she could even register the flowers. She slowly opened her eyes and looked around as they stood in Malcolm's garden. Silas smirked as he raised an eyebrow at her.

"I know I'm Death and all, but it would be great to feel my hand." He laughed.

"Oh, sorry." Jo said as she let go.

"Oh, your poor delicate hand. Did the poor human soul hurt it?" Balor chuckled as he walked past Silas and shoved him.

"I swear I wish Malcolm would have turned you to ash," Silas growled.

"You-" Balor went to tease him, but Kere's hand caught his mouth.

"You too can express your love for each other when the work is done." Kere smiled softly at him.

Balor took her hand and pulled it down from his mouth. He then kissed her wrist softly while looking at her. His eyes burned into hers, and Kere felt her knees go weak.

"Anything for you, gorgeous." He grinned as he watched her response.

Silas sighed and then turned his attention to Jo who looked white. Her eyes were locked on her cold body. Blood stained the ground around her. The blood looked thick as it was old and coagulated. The dagger

was gone. Jo walked slowly over to it and kneeled down. She could see how pale she looked and when she touched her own forearm, it was cold. The overwhelming urge to vomit and cry at the same time rushed over her. She shut her eyes as she tried to calm down. She had always known that Evan would be the death of her. That's why she ran in the first place. She figured death might be peaceful. Now seeing it, she realized how much she missed and how badly she wanted to be alive.

"Hey, it's going to be all right." Silas said as he knelt down next to her.

"Will it though?" Jo asked as she let a long breath out before speaking.

Silas paused; he didn't know if it was going to be all right. He needed her to think it was going to be. He took a second to come up with a better response.

"Nothing has ever been all right. Everything I've tried to do has fallen apart. Even running from Evan, that got me dead. How is this fixable?" Jo said quietly as she shook her head.

"You have Death, a demon and an ex-demon goddess in your corner. Not only that, I see strength in you. You try to do the right thing no matter what. You were dealt a shitty hand. But just maybe you were dealt that so you could become something more." Silas said quietly.

"What? Being dealt a shitty hand just makes your life shit." Jo laughed as she swatted a tear away from her cheek.

"There's something happening in the world. In the realms. I can feel it. There's a pull, a calling, a shift

in balance. You have to feel it too. Ryan was dealt a shitty hand. It took her life away too but she was meant for more. The In-between needed light, needed a guardian." Silas said as he reached out and took her hand.

"What does that have to do with me? Everyone keeps talking about light and dark. I don't get it," Jo asked as she tore her eyes away from her lifeless body and looked at Silas.

"I'm not sure. But there's a light in you that is so bright. Our trauma does not define us. What we do to rise above it does. You are not what has happened to you. You are more. You are that strength that made you fight, that push to pull you through even when you didn't want to. Hold on to that now. Earth needs you; Malcolm needs you. I see that. Do not give up on yourself now." Silas said as he squeezed her hand.

"Whew…Ok. I'm with you." Jo said as she blinked away the tears Silas's speech caused to flood her eyes with.

"Well, that was epic! I feel like we could fight anything now just off that!" Balor said as he walked over.

"Does he have to be here?" Silas growled as he looked at Kere.

"Balor," Kere warned.

"What I really meant it. I say one nice thing and I'm still the bad guy." Balor grumbled.

Jo started to laugh as she looked at her group of heroes. She shook her head as she grabbed her stomach and laughed.

"Oh God, Earth has really picked winners to save it." Jo said through her laughter.

"Look, you broke it. Jo, darling, this is a serious moment. Um, we need to put you back inside your dead body...," Balor smirked at Silas before he pretended to be very serious as he spoke to Jo.

Jo laughed more and stumbled sideways into Silas, who tried to steady her. He looked at Kere, not sure what to do as Jo continued to laugh.

"You are not making this any better." Silas grumbled to Balor.

"I don't think that's why I'm really here." Balor winked, and Jo laughed so hard that no sound came out of her mouth.

"Ok, the fate of the world is hanging in the balance here, can we wrap this up? Please and thank you." Kere snapped, and Jo bit back a laugh.

"Ok...Ok, I'm good. It's a little stressful...What do we need to do?" Jo asked as she covered her mouth.

"Silas needs to put your soul back into your body, and I need to heal you. I just don't know if I should heal your body then put your soul back in. I don't know if your body will heal without a soul." Kere , but it was more to herself as she was working out scenarios.

"Ok..."Jo said as she waited for instructions.

"Silas with Ryan...was her soul ever out of her body?" Kere asked him.

"Ryan was a human when Silas fell in love with her, but she was fated to die. However, Silas kept interfering and saving her from...himself." Balor said, catching Jo up to speed, like he was some narrator.

"No. I never took her soul." Silas said through gritted teeth, his anger towards Balor, who was never serious about anything.

Balor shrugged his shoulders at Silas as if to say, what. Kere sighed deeply.

"So let's just get me back into my body and then you heal me…right?" Jo asked as she looked at the three of them; she was missing something.

"There's a risk." Kere said as she rubbed her forehead as she became stressed.

"Risk?" Jo asked; he still didn't understand what had Kere stressed.

"Your body won't heal without a soul. However, if we put your soul back into a lifeless body and it doesn't heal…you might be trapped." Kere said quietly.

"Trapped?" Jo asked, confused.

"The human body is just a shell to harbor your soul until it is time to move on. Once it's done its purpose and the soul is gone, there's no connection anymore. Your soul might get trapped in the body, never to be able to be reaped or taken to the afterlife. You will enter this place of nothing and be lost." Kere said with regret.

Jo took a deep breath in as she played what Kere said over in her mind. Kere looked at her, not really sure what to say. This was her choice.
"What if we just go to Malcolm with me like this? He could see me? Maybe snap him out of it." Jo said, her eyes fixated on her lifeless bodies.

"Souls don't do well on Earth. They are not meant for this realm. You will fade or worse. The longer you stay, the more you become angry. It starts with anger and then fades to rage. You forget who you are and will roam the Earth, lost and angry." Silas said quietly.

"So I'm screwed either way. Yay! Life…afterlife." Jo said sarcastically.

"No, if I can heal you, we will be fine." Kere said as she tried to sound optimistic.

"Do demons go to the afterlife?" Jo asked curiously as she stepped towards her body.

"Yes…" Kere said quietly, her eyes flickered to Balor, a hint of sadness in them.

"They go to hell," Balor said quietly.

"So Malcolm…"Jo said quietly; she didn't want to finish her sentence.

"Let's not get ahead of ourselves. As long as Malcolm is still on Earth, we don't have to worry about a search and rescue mission into hell. Now let's get you back into your body. Kere love, what if you start healing her body before Silas puts her back in?" Balor said confidently.

"That might work." Kere whispered; she didn't know why she had not thought of it.

"Jo…it's up to you. If you don't want to try it, I will need to get you back to the In-between so you can cross over before it's too late." Silas said as he tried not to push her into either option.

If she chose to cross over, he would help her cross. They then would have to kill Malcolm. The thought made his chest tightened. He did not know what that meant for Earth; everything moved too quickly right now.

"I'll do it." Jo said with a quick nod as she pulled her bottom lip into her mouth nervously.

"All right then, let's do this." Balor announced and waved his hands over the body, as if to say ta-da.

"Balor." Kere rolled her eyes as she said his name and knelt next to the body.

"I'll let you know when Silas." Kere said and then looked to Balor.

"I need a knife." She whispered as she opened her palm.

Balor took a small pocketknife out of his jeans and handed it to Kere. She took the white handle in her hand and opened it slowly. The blade shined in the little bit of light left before dark clouds rolled across the sky. Kere clenched her jaw together and ran the blade across her palm. A flicker of gold light flashed from the cut. Blood then began to seep out; she opened and closed her fist a few times as she tried to get as much blood from the cut before she took a deep breath and pressed her hand into the hole on Jo's chest. Kere's eyes flashed the same color gold that her hand did before she shut them and began to draw on her powers. Jo felt something warm in the center of her chest. It startled her, and she placed her hand quickly on it. She then looked at her body, surprised she could feel it. She looked to Silas for answers, but his eyes were focused on Kere and her body.

"Silas," Kere said quietly as she kept her eyes closed. She had to be completely focused on healing Jo's body just enough and not too quickly.

Silas held his hand out to Jo. Jo took a deep breath and nodded. Silas led her over. He looked at the body and then to her. Silas had never put a soul back before. He knelt down on the ground and could feel the urgency that came from Kere. This had to be quick. He

motioned for Jo to get down with him. She fell to her
knees still and gripped his hand tightly.

"Jo, place a hand on your body," Silas said as he
prayed that it would be that easy.

Jo bit her lower lip and then slowly extended her
that shook and placed it on her own forehead. She
waited, and nothing happened. Jo glanced at Silas,
confused. Silas then reached out with his free hand and
took Jo's body's hand into his. As his fingers touched
hers, he felt a force run through and a jolt. He looked to
Jo, who seemed to feel it too, and then in a second she
was gone.

"I think it worked. Her soul should be back." Silas
said and he hoped he was right.

Kere nodded as she started to feel weak, but
she needed to keep going. She squeezed her eyes shut
as forced all of her energy forward. Kere's body glowed
and then the amber light floated down from Kere and
wrapped around Jo's body. She buckled forward but
kept her mind focused; her strength started to fade.
Balor gritted his teeth, he walked over to Kere and
placed his hand on her shoulder. He shut his eyes and
focused on what it would feel like to phase but forced
the energy into Kere. Kere sat up straight as she felt this
new force of energy flow into her. The light that floated
around Jo brightened, it flashed bright, and blinded
them. As the light faded it drifted back into Kere. Kere
sat up straighter as she felt a weight behind her. She
looked over her shoulder and saw Balor hunch forward.

"Balor." Kere whispered as she watched him as
his body swayed.

"I got him." Silas said as he stepped up and caught Balor underneath his arms.

"Oh, my hero." Balor smirked as Silas held him up.

"Kere…Jo?" Silas asked as he ignored Balor.

Kere leaned down over Jo; the wound was healed. Her chest came to life with movement as she began to breathe once more. Kere placed a hand on her chest and could feel her heartbeat. A rush of relief came over Kere, and eyes now locked on her face. She just needed to wake up.

Chapter Twenty Six

 Jo

The world around her was gone. There was nothing but darkness. She tried to move but her body felt weak and heavy, like there was an invisible weight that held her to her spot. Jo stood in the darkness, not unsure of what to do or how to get out. She held her hands out in front of her as she tried to move around, but it was like she was in emptiness itself. She closed her eyes and tried to listen to see if she could hear anything. A feeling of dread filled her as she remembered what Kere had said. You will be lost. Was she lost? Her chest tightened, and she felt herself struggling to breathe as she began to panic. There was no way out. This was what Kere had spoken about. She then began to hear something. It sounded like a whisper. She could not make out what it murmured. She couldn't tell where it came from, but it floated around the room.

"Give up." It hissed as it circled around her head.

"Stay, you deserve this." It muttered again.

"Nobody cares that you're gone." It laughed.

Jo covered her ears and sank to her knees. She didn't want to hear. She didn't know what it was. Why was it hurting her?

"Go away!" Jo shouted as she pressed her hands into her ears more.

She couldn't deal with this. Jo squeezed her eyes so tightly she felt her ears throb from the pressure she applied. She needed to block out the words it muttered.

"Trapped again. Poor mouse, always trapped. If not in one world in the next. This time there won't be a way out." It hissed and snickered.

"Leave me alone!" Jo shouted so loud that spit droplets clung to the bottom of her lips.

"Poor Josephine." It laughed.

"Weak Josephine."

"Pathetic Josephine."

"Worthless-

"Shut up!!" Jo screamed, and her eyes opened.

"You are weak and pathetic. Hiding in the darkness. If you're everything I am not, show yourself." Jo demanded, her voice shook with anger as she squeezed her fist tightly.

"Oh, look at the bravery, look at the anger. If only you had that when you were alive…We wouldn't have spent all those days in the blue room." The voice said as it stepped forward, and a spotlight hit where the voice was coming from.

"You're me?" Jo whispered as she came face to face with herself.

"Yes. I am every angry, broken piece of you. Every part of us, you let him kill. That you gave up on." The figure yelled at her with such force Jo had to take a step back.

"You let your light die; you let me die." The spotlight turned to a soft glow, and it looked like it came from within.

"I… I didn't know what to do. I tried. I tried to get out. I tried to escape but-"

"It was too late." The voice now was sad, and the glow flickered more.

"It's too late." It whimpered.

The sadness from within erupted into the empty room, and Jo felt like her chest would collapse inward from the pressure. Her knees shook and her body trembled as tears rushed her eyes.

"We can't be trapped again." Jo barely whispered out.

"It's your fault again. You keep giving up. We were so close." The figure whispered back.

"So close?" Jo asked as she looked up.

"We were almost free." It said as it flickered like a candle about to go out.

"Almost," Jo said as the words stung in her heart.

Almost, the world circled around her brain over and over. Rage burned in the pit of her stomach. Almost! Almost! There is no almost. She was not giving up this time.

"No!" Jo screamed and stood up.

"We are not pathetic, weak or worthless." Jo said firmly.

She looked across at herself, who looked like she was faded and almost gone. Jo would not let her go. She walked over to her and grabbed her hand. Her hand passed through hers.

"I'm sorry. You're right. I let him have control of me. I let him do this. I should have left earlier. Should have said no. He was not in control of me. I am so sorry I hurt you. Hurt us…let him hurt me." Jo said quietly to herself.

She could feel something break inside of her. She felt her head slump forward, and she was about to give into it all. Her other self was right.

"I forgive you." She whispered and then reached out and placed a hand on Jo's shoulder; the hand did not go through like when Jo tried to touch her.

"I forgive us. You need to forgive yourself. We did not deserve any of this." She said firmly to Jo.

"I forgive us…I forgive…me." Jo whispered as a tear slipped out of the corner of her eye and rolled down her cheek.

As Jo forgave herself, the other merged into her body and they became one once more. Jo shut her eyes as the feeling of being whole and at peace flooded her system. She felt a strange power deep within herself. She felt it vibrate, and then she was pulled backwards.

"What happened? What went wrong?" She heard a male voice say with urgency.

"I don't know. It should have worked. Her body is healed. You put her soul back right. You didn't do anything else?" A feminine voice asked quickly.

"Yes. At least how I thought it should be done. I have never put one back." He said firmly.

She felt drowsy and like she had been drugged. Jo could feel her body, but she was numb. She could not see, but she could hear. It was the first thing that came back. She could tell they were right by her, but they sounded so far away.

"What do we do now?" Another voice asked with a hint of hopelessness.

"We are gonna have to stop Malcolm. Without a light, he won't come back. We're just going to have to find a way to kill him." The feminine voice said firmly.

"We need a demon blade, a plan and a distraction." The second male voice said.

The words Malcolm and kill punctured her heart. No, they can't hurt him. No, she was here. Jo needed her body to listen. She focused on her fingertips and tried everything to move them. She could feel her pinky rub against her ring finger. It was working. Please don't hurt him. Wake up, she yelled at herself. The fog began to settle, and she remembered their names. The voices belonged to Kere, Silas, and Balor. They needed to know she was here. She could feel her eyelashes flutter against her cheek as she tried to move her hand. She wanted to reach out and grab one of them.

"He is a demon. We could summon him." Balor said with a shrug.

"If we summon him back here and he sees her body again, it might delay him." Silas said bitterly.

"Long enough to pierce his heart with a demon blade?" Kere asked.

The word no shouted in her mind as she gathered all of her strength and pictured her hand grabbing hold of Kere's and with one last burst of energy Jo's hand flopped over and grabbed Kere's hand.

"Ahh!" Kere let out a yell and looked down at her hand.

"Jo!" Kere said as Jo squeezed her hand in response.

"Holy shit." Balor whispered as he looked at Kere's shocked face and then down at Jo's hand.

"She's in there. She's alive." Silas said, his very serious face broke into a small smile.

"Shit took her long enough." Balor said as he let out a half laugh.

Jo's eyes fluttered open, and the world was blurry but she slowly began to move. She wondered if people who came back to life felt like this or was something wrong.

"Jo, it's ok, just relax, let everything come back to you slowly." Silas said as he hunched over her.

"It can take a few minutes. You're doing great." Silas coached her through it.

Her vision slowly came back to normal, and she could feel all of her limbs once more. She went to sit up slowly, and Kere braced her, her arm around her back, and helped her sit up.

"That..that...I don't ever want to do that again." Jo half laughed.

"Usually you don't get to do it." Kere laughed.

"Unless you're a zombie." Balor shrugged.

"Zombies?" Jo asked him with narrowed eyebrows.

"Kidding, love...I don't think zombies are a thing...Are zombies a thing?" Balor asked, now he confused himself and looked to Silas.

"Oh, shut up." Silas grumbled.

"You two are worse than siblings or old bickering lovers." Jo mumbled as she put her head into her hands.

"Siblings." Silas scoffed.

"Oh, like old bickering lovers better do ya?" Balor laughed and waggled his eyes brows at him.

"Kere." Silas growled.

"What do we do now?" Jo asked.

"We find Malcolm." Kere said as she ignored the boys.

"How?" Jo whispered.

"Actually, Balor wasn't half crazy. He is a demon, and we can summon him." Kere said quietly.

"Like a salt circle and a sacrifice?" Jo asked, saying only things she had seen in horror movies.

"No…maybe. We'll have to see." Kere chuckled.

"See about what? We honestly don't have any time. I heard two seconds ago you all were plotting to kill him." Jo said her voice was harsh and inpatient.

"If Malcolm weren't who he was. It would be easy. A simple demon is as easy as drawing a circle and summoning it. Malcolm is a high level demon; it takes something special to summon them, and each one is different." Balor explained and then paused at the end.

"Killing him might be easier than summoning him." Balor shook his head.

"We are not killing him!" Jo shouted and shoved Balor.

"Ouch…Fine, he can live…we all might die, but sure he can live. Fuck it." Balor grumbled as he rubbed his arm.

"Nice." Silas chuckled at Balor as he acted like a baby over the small shove.

"Anyway Jo, you're connected to Malcolm, we might just need you to summon him." Silas said, not hiding the grin he was wearing.

"How?" Jo asked, as she looked from Silas to Kere.

"We will just act like we are summoning any demon and see if you being in the circle will draw Malcolm to you." Kere shrugged.

"We have to do something." Kere said after Jo looked at her skeptically.

"Fine, let's do it." Jo muttered.

"I'll go get the goat." Balor smirked.

"Goat?" Jo asked in surprise.

"You know, for the sacrifice." Balor grinned while Silas shook his head.

"What?" Jo asked, concerned.

"Kidding, but seriously, unless you got salt in your back pocket, then I need to go get some." Balor laughed.

"Oh ok." Jo looked at him, her face still confused about the goat comment.

"See you soon, gorgeous." He said as he pecked Kere on the head and phased.

Chapter Twenty Seven
Malcolm

Think smoke filled the air; Malcolm had now gained their attention.

"What are you?" A man asked as he hid behind the bar.

"I am revenge." Malcolm said in a deep and dark voice.

The words hung in the air and the big biker demon stood up from the bar. He turned and saw Malcolm a confident grin on his face. He stepped towards Malcolm and smiled.

"If you think you can then come on." The biker grinned as he popped his knuckles.

Malcolm did say two words and matched grins. The biker demon walked over and cocked his arm back as he reached Malcolm he landed a blow across his face. Malcolm's head didn't even move. It was like the man didn't even hit him. The man's hand was pressed against Malcolm's cheek but nothing happened. Malcolm felt the pain ripple through him and it fed his inner need. In the pit of him there was this energy that growled, like a hunger pain. It wanted to be fed anger, hurt, pain. It craved it and with each demon he took gave it strength. He knew once he was strong enough the pain would crave the light left in the world. He knew he should stop but he didn't care.

The biker blinked, he stared at his hand, he did not understand what just happened. Malcolm's hand wrapped around his wrist and he turned to look at him. The white's of Malcolm's eyes went completely black as

he drained the biker. The biker attempted to struggle against Malcolm. He desperately tried to pull away, to do anything to get away from the pain that coursed through. He felt weak in the matter of seconds and couldn't help but give in. He reached out to touch Malcolm, his hand hung just in front of his face when he turned to ash. Malcolm brushed off his hands and looked around the room. Everyone shifted away from him.

"Now that I've gotten everyone's attention I am looking for a demon named Pavel. You give me information you make it out of here. You don't then you join your …co-workers." Malcolm sneered.

"We're not telling you-" A man said as he bowed up and before he could finish his sentence Malcolm had phased and appeared behind him. His hand wrapped around the back of his neck and in seconds the demon was no more.

Another demon moved out of the corner of his eye, and Malcolm snatched him up as well. He drained him before he could even make a noise. The more he drained them, the quicker he could turn them to ash.

"It doesn't matter to me; this feels great." Malcolm shrugged as he kicked the last demon's ashes.

"Pavel…he moves in the shadows. Likes dark places. He's power hungry. No one really knows where his hideaway is." The next demon blurted out as he ducked his head.

Malcolm walked over to him and leaned on the bar next to him. He looked at him; Malcolm's eyes studied him. The demon stopped hiding behind his hands and looked at Malcolm confused. Malcolm made

a small face and shook his head. He then pressed his finger to the demon's forehead, and he crumbled into ash.

"Enough." A voice rang out from behind him; Malcolm didn't even bother to look up, his eyes locked on his next victim.

"You are supposed to be collecting souls, not going on a demon killing spree. You're supposed to be tipping the scales too dark, not taking out dark players." He said, annoyed as he stepped through a pile of ash.

"Pavel?" Malcolm asked as he turned.

"The one and only." Pavel grinned as he held his hands to side.

"Leo…" Malcolm growled the name as he stood up and squared off with Pavel.

"Right, Lazaros, how is he?" Pavel smirked as he shook his head.

"Ash." Malcolm sneered.

"Pitty, he actually was very good at being a demon. Slow to collect, but there's a bunch of souls pledged for my box." Pavel chuckled.

"Box." Malcolm repeated; he did not understand what he meant.

"Well, since we're going to be on the same side, I'll let you know. I am collecting souls; they are not going to the afterlife. I have a container that is holding them. When we get enough, we can harness them and bring darkness to the world. Tip the scales permanently." Pavel grinned as he said his plan out loud.

"Leo was working with you?" Malcolm asked as he stepped forward.

"Well, kind of the goal was you." Pavel grinned.

"I needed the famous Malcolm. Someone at your level to gather souls in a quicker, more abundant way. Your work has always been…impressive." Pavel grinned.

"No one except death can touch souls." Malcom growled.

"No, but with this." Pavel tapped his necklace before he continued.

"This necklace is made from crystals forged in the depths of hell, and holds the blood of a reaper. It draws the souls out of the body for me." Pavel grinned as he dangled the black chained necklace with a ruby stone.

"I don't care about you, your necklace or anything else. She's gone because of you," Malcolm said as rage rushed through him; the darkness loved it, and he felt the power beg to be unleashed.

"Who?" Pavel looked confused as he stepped back away from Malcolm.

Malcolm didn't answer but closed the gap between them. Pavel put his hands up as if to say he didn't want trouble.

"Malcolm, think about what I am offering. Just wait a second and think." Pavel said as he stepped back.

Malcolm went to move forward but couldn't; something was holding him in place. He narrowed his eyes and focused on his legs, but they wouldn't move. No matter how much he commanded his feet to go forward, they wouldn't budge.

"Malcom?" Pavel asked, confused as he watched Malcolm's face change from anger to concerned.

"what's going on?" Pavel asked as he looked around the room.

Mal'akh.

His name was whispered in his ear, a small soft command, and his body reacted and he phased.

Jo

Jo watched Balor carefully pour the salt in a circle. He made sure not to step into it. Jo watched him, confused at why he acted like the salt would explode. She raised an eyebrow at him as he caught her stare.

"Salt circles trap demons. Speaking of which, why is the demon doing this?" Balor asked as he looked at Silas.

"You're being useful." Silas smirked.

"Well, I'm not getting in it so someone else needs to draw the star." Balor said, holding out the container of salt.

"You should have drawn the star first." Silas lectured.

"Give it here." Jo laughed and held her hand out for the salt.

"My hero." Balor smirked and held the salt out to her.

"Just a regular star?" Jo asked as she stepped into the circle.

"Mhmm." Balor nodded.

Jo walked in the circle and watched the white salt pour out. She walked diagonally across to make one of the points and then back across the way. After she finished, she closed the top of the salt. She looked at Balor and chucked the container to him. He caught and gave her a goofy smile.

"Ok, so now what?" Jo asked from inside the circle.

"I'm gonna go grab the goat." Balor smirked as he acted like he was going to phase.

"Shut up, stupid." Jo laughed.

"Ouch," Balor said, as he put his hand to his heart.

"Call him." Silas said quietly, his tone and demeanor serious.

"Call him? Say his name? There's no special wording, nothing needed?"Jo asked, confused.

"Balor is right; there needs to be a blood payment." Kere said quietly.

She pulled a hairpin out of her hair, revealing a dagger. She chucked it to Jo and watched as she caught it.

"Blood? How much blood?" Jo asked, unsure.

"Not much; cut your palm and squeeze some into the center of the star and say Malcolm's name. We can hope the right Malcolm comes. It would be better if we knew his true name." Silas said quietly.

Jo nodded. She knew she was not supposed to tell anyone Malcolm's true name. He was serious about it; she didn't want to use it, but what if they summoned

the wrong demon; things could go bad very quickly. She needed to make sure it was him.

"I need you all to move away." Jo said firmly.

"What?" Silas asked, confused.

"I know his true name, but I will not be sharing it. I want you to move away so you do not hear it." Jo said as she locked eyes with each of them.

"Jo-" Silas started to say, but Jo cut him with her hand held up.

Balor shrugged; he looked at Kere and nodded towards the house. He then phased. Kere nodded to Jo and phased as well. Silas grudgingly moved his foot. If they knew his name, they could force him to stop doing everything. Put a halt on the end of the world right then and there.

"Silas, I will not tell you his name." Jo vowed as she stared at him.

"Jo, we could stop everything by just using it." Silas said, frustrated.

"If it comes down to that, I will, but I am not allowing others to use it against him. I am going to try everything possible to get him back before that. I am the only one who will be willing to give him a chance. I heard you all planning to kill him when you thought I was gone. I am not giving you ammo to use against him. Go, or I will not summon him." Jo snapped as she folded her arms across his chest.

"The world ends, it's on you. Not only will this world end, but there will be spillage over into the other realms. I will not let Malcolm or you chance causing harm to the In-between or hurt anyone I love. This better work." Silas threatened back as he phased.

Once she was alone, Jo shut her eyes and ran the blade across the palm of her hand. The quick string sensation fluttered up her arm, and she felt a wetness in her palm. She made a fist and turned her hand over. She opened her eyes and watched several red blood droplets fall down into the center of the star.

"Mal'akh." She whispered as the center of the salt turned polka-dotted with red.

A bright light erupted from the center of the star, and Jo was thrown back out of the circle. Her body hit the ground, and she skittered across the way. As she was thrown, her head hit the side of the concrete bench, and everything went dark.

Chapter Twenty Nine
Malcolm

As the light cleared, he found himself in the center of a salt circle. He gritted his teeth; someone had summoned him. Malcolm looked around, and he did not see anyone. He sighed and tried to move his feet. As long as the salt was intact, he was stuck. Who would summon a demon and then disappear? He was growing angry the longer he stood there. Suddenly they appeared one by one, and Malcolm let out a long sigh.

"I am going to have to kill you now," Malcolm grumbled.

"Malcolm, we just need to talk," Silas stated, but his eyes were not on Malcolm but he scanned the area.

"What?" Malcolm snapped annoyed, Silas did not even pay attention to him.

Silas's eyes found her first, and he tapped Kere and nodded to Jo was underneath the cement bench. Kere nodded and went to her.

"You need to stop this. You're killing this realm. The scale is supposed to be balanced, and when you go around-" Silas started to say.

"Do not tell me about tipping the scale. I am well aware of what you did. Death saving a human girl over and over again. Then going to burn the In-between down when you lost her. It's not different. The only thing different here is I will. I won't fail." Malcolm bellowed.

"Malcolm, she's not gone." Balor said as he watched Silas bite his tongue.

"I watched her die. Don't feed me bullshit. She might be in the afterlife, but I will never see her again.

278

She is gone. Demons go to hell, and she already experienced hell, so we know she's not there," Malcolm snapped.

"No Malcolm, she's not gone -" Balor tried to explain again.

"I am killing you first," Malcolm threatened first.

"Are you stuck?" A voice came from behind him, and he felt his nostrils flare.

"Pavel," Malcolm said as he turned slightly in the circle.

"I couldn't have just given you all that information and not followed you." Pavel smiled.

"What are you doing here?" Balor growled from the other side of the circle.

"Depends on Malcolm." Pavel grinned.

"Malcolm, he's a lowlife demon you don't want to team up with him." Silas said as he looked at Pavel in disgust.

"You will all die," Malcolm promised.

"I'll let you out," Pavel whispered.

"Let me help you." Pavel smirked as he watched Malcolm slowly decide to let Pavel help.

Balor raced around the other side of the circle with Silas close behind. Just as they reached Pavel, he kicked his foot and the salt ring was broken. Pavel phased to the opposite side of the circle as Malcolm stepped out. Malcom instantly grabbed a hold of Balor.

"No!" Kere's voice rang out, but Malcolm tuned the noise out.

"You will die this time, annoying demon." Malcolm promised as he started to try to drain him.

Silas grabbed hold of Balor; he knew from the last time that if he touched Malcolm, he would start draining him as well. Balor's skin began to change to gray. Silas had to act fast. He closed his eyes and phased as he clung onto Balor. It broke Malcolm's grip, and they phased reappeared on the other side of the circle.

Balor began to cough, and his color slowly crept back. Silas locked eyes with Malcolm, ready for him this time. As long as Malcolm didn't get hold of him, he could wait him out.

"Kere, get Jo up." Silas said quickly as he watched Malcolm move towards them.

"Jo?" Pavel heard the name and his eyes followed to where Kere was.

"No…It can't be. She's supposed to be dead." Pavel whispered.

Malcolm's head snapped to Pavel, and he changed direction. Pavel began to move away from Malcolm with his hands up as he tried to think of something to say.

"What do you mean?" Malcolm demanded as he cornered Pavel.

"Just um I uh…" Pavel stuttered as Malcolm grabbed a hold of him.

Malcolm closed his eyes and focused on draining Pavel. Pavel's skin cracked and turned gray. The color spread up his arm and traveled through him as Malcolm stole his energy. Pavel struggled fiercely in his grip. Each thrash from Pavel fueled Malcolm's rage. "Malcolm." Her voice made him pause; he stopped.

He looked away from Pavel; the voice caught his attention. Malcolm glanced over and saw Jo standing there. He dropped Pavel to the ground and turned. His stomach turned inside him. He felt his heart sped up in chest. As he looked at her, not sure this was real. Jo slowly walked towards him, a soft smile on her face. Malcolm didn't have time to tell his feet to move; he rushed to her but paused just out of reach of her.
"You're here?" Malcolm whispered to her.
Jo nodded and held her hand out to him. She looked at him confused.

"I'm here." She said quietly and grabbed hold of his hand.

As soon as she touched him, he pulled her into him and wrapped his arms around her. He felt the darkness starting to fade away. The whole inside of him, the ache was gone as soon as she was in his arms again.

"How?" he whispered to the top of her head.

"Kere, Balor and Silas. They found a way." Jo said as she buried her face in his chest.

Malcolm pulled her back, and his hand went to her face; his thumb stroked the side of her cheek as he stared at her in disbelief.

"I'm here." Jo smiled at him as she placed her hand on top of his.

He looked at her, all doubt left him. She was here. She was in his arms once more, and any bit of darkness that still lingered in him was pushed completely back. He watched her face, praying it was not a sick trick. Jo smiled at him, then her eyes got wide.

"Malcolm!" Jo yelled as she saw Pavel coming up behind him with a demon blade.

Pavel raised the blade up and rushed towards Malcolm. If he was not going to help him get souls, then he was going to make sure he was gone completely. Malcolm turned slightly as he tucked Jo behind him protectively. Pavel went to plunge the blade into his chest. Malcolm tried to block the blade, but it pierced his arm. Malcolm ignored the pain as he gritted his teeth. The only thought he had was to keep Jo safe. Pavel pulled the blade from Malcolm's arm, and he let out a small grunt. Jo tried to pull Malcolm back, but he kept her behind him. Pavel went to slam the blade into the center of Malcolm's chest. Malcolm reached forward to block the blow, while he used his other hand to keep Jo tucked behind him. Pavel suddenly stopped short. Pavel's mouth dropped open, and he fell to his knees. Silas was standing behind him with a demon blade that pierced Pavel's chest.

"You think killing me will solve everything." Pavel said as he coughed up some blood.

"He will take Hell if he can't have Earth, and then it will trickle over into Earth and the In-between, and then there'll be nothing left. He's probably already taken the souls I have collected. This world is doomed. All worlds are doomed." Pavel laughed, as he fell to his back.

"Who…who is he?" Silas asked as he dropped down with him.

"Good luck finding him." Pavel laughed as his eyes rolled back.

"You son of bitch." Silas said as he grabbed his shirt and shook him, but Pavel turned to dust in his hand.

The black chain necklace fell onto the ground without Silas and Malcolm noticing.

"What the hell did that mean?" Silas muttered as he looked up to Malcolm.

Silas got to his feet and moved slightly away from where Pavel turned to ash. He was trying to make sense of it all as he stared at Malcolm.

"I'm not sure." Malcolm muttered.

"Kere, go see what you can find out." Balor said that quietly as he nodded to her.

"I will be back." She nodded to Balor; he grinned and blew her a kiss before she phased.

Balor still had a smile on his face when he turned to look across the way to Silas. As he did, his chest tightened. A shadow formed behind Silas. It brushed the grass, picking up something before it turned to Silas. The cloak figure began to move towards Silas with something in his hand. The shadow raised his hand, and Balor saw a blade. He didn't even think before he felt himself phase. He reappeared just in time to shove Silas out of the way, and the blade pierced his chest instead of Silas.

"Balor!" Jo screamed as she watched the shadow step back and fade away.

Silas turned around and watched Balor touch his chest. He looked down at his hand covered in blood, and he looked to Silas. Silas went numb with shock as he stared at Balor in disbelief. Balor wobbled, and Silas stepped into him and braced his side.

"This is what I get for doing hero shit." He half
laughs as Silas gets to his side.

"What did you do?" Silas said as he steadied
him.

"You can't let her go dark. Silas you can't." Balor
coughs as blood begins to drip out of his mouth.

Balor felt himself go weak, and his leg gave out.
Silas caught him and helped him to the ground.

"Silas. Promise me." Balor grabbed hold of
Silas's shirt and ordered him.

"You're gonna be fine. I won't have to." Silas
says, but he made sure to nod to his statement.

"It's a demon blade, I'll be ash soon... You're
lucky your good looks make up for your lack of smarts."
Balor cracks a weak smirk.

"You gotta make sure, Silas. Don't let her." Balor
said as he let go of his shirt and referred to Kere once
more.

The energy shifted, and Balor knew before he
heard her voice. The world always felt better whenever
she was near.

"Balor!" Keres' voice screamed as she phased
into the field. She knew something was wrong before
she ever got her. She felt something inside of her break
and shatter. Her feet pounded on the grass as she
rushed to his side. She dropped to her knees; her heart
broke into pieces in her chest as she felt like she
couldn't breathe.

"No, no. No. No. Balor. No. Please. Silas, you
can't take his soul. We need to fix him." Kere rambled
on as she placed her hand on the side of Balor's face.

"Hey gorgeous." Balor smiled at her and leaned his face into her hand.

"Shh, listen, you're going to be fine. It's ok." Balor reassured her.

"Silas, you can't." Kere's eyes flicker from Balor to Silas.

"He doesn't. I'm a demon. My fate is sealed. I'm not confused about it either. The hellhounds will be here soon. Gorgeous, listen to me. You do not go dark. You have done too much, and this world needs you." Balor said as he got weaker.

"Balor, I can't…you're my light. I… I can't.. don't leave me. We will do something." Kere said as a gust of wind and a hollow rose up around them.

The hollowing swirled around them like a tornado. They circled them. Silas had seen hellhounds come for demons. Only those who they came for could see them. There was always wind and a strange hollow. The demons were always terrified and fought to go. Balor didn't even look away from Kere's face. You wouldn't even know they had come for him.

"You have made my entire existence worth it. You don't need a light. You are your own light. It's so bright. It's deep within you. I love you." Balor said as he pulled her face down to his and placed a kiss on her lips.

A small sob escaped Kere as she pressed her lips back to his. They turned cold at her touch. She took a small breath and felt every part of her break as she leaned her forehead against his. She stayed completely still for several seconds. When Kere pulled back, the hollowing was gone, and so was Balor.

"Silas! Silas! Help me." Kere screamed as she pulled Balor into her lap and shook him.

"Kere, he's gone." Silas said as he went to her side.

"No. No, he can't. I can't." She cried and buried her face into Balor's chest.

"Silas, I can't do this. I can't be without him." Kere screamed, and then the world went dark around them. The clouds in the sky darken and the world seemed to be without light.

"Kere stop! Look at me, push it down." Silas grabbed her by her shoulders.

She couldn't go dark. He couldn't let her. If she went dark at goddess status, there would be no point and even tried to fight her. He had to think of something quickly to fix this.

"We will go to hell. We will get him. Don't go dark. Don't do it. We will get him. I will bring him back." Silas said as he cupped her face to get her to look at him.

"Hell?" Kere asked, her eyes flickered.

"We keep his body safe. We do what we did with Jo, with Ryan. We get his soul from hell and put it back." Silas said to her firmly.

"Ok... Ok." Kere's voice cracked as she said the word.

"You go dark and he's lost. I can't do it alone." Silas said as he watched her eyes fade back to their green color.

"Kere, you here, you with me?" Silas said as his chest stopped tightening.

"I'm here.. I won't go dark. We need to hurry."
Kere said and went to pull the demon blade.

"No stop." Silas said as he grabbed her wrist.

"What? A demon blade would be good to have,"
Kere said quickly.

"He hasn't turned to ash. I think it's because the
demon blades are still inside him. We take his body to
Ryan, let her keep him safe in the In-between times.
Time stands still there. It will slow things down, and we
go after his soul." Silas explained.

"We're coming too." Jo's voice came from behind
them.

"I owe you for giving me Jo back," Malcolm said
with a nod.

"Jo... I don't want to put you in any more danger.
Malcolm, I could use a demon of your level on this,"
Silas said, his other hand squeezed Keres as he tried to
make sure she was still with him.

"I'm going regardless," Jo said firmly.

"Jo." Silas started to say, and she frowned at him
and went to argue.

Suddenly she threw her head back, and a light
floated down from the dark sky. It trickled over her skin
and began to glow. Malcolm held tightly on to her,
wondering what was happening. The light flashed
brightly and then faded inwards inside of Jo.

Jo felt like she had a new energy inside of her.
She felt like she was in touch with everything around
her. She looked over to Kere with a confused look.

"It happened to Ryan and me. You're a guardian
now of this realm." Kere smiled at her.

"So I'm coming." Jo said as she looked at Silas.

"Alright, let's get moving." Silas said he did not
want to argue; the longer they took, the longer Balor's
soul sits in Hell, the harder it will be to get.

"Wait," Malcolm said quietly as he remembered
something vague.

"Pavel, when I was dark, said something about a
necklace. It's fuzzy right now, something about souls
and a necklace." Malcolm muttered.

Jo moved to the grass where Pavel had died and
looked through the grass. They watched her, and she
frowned and shook her head.

"We have to move. We don't have time right
now. Malcolm, if you remember anything else, we will
deal with it then." Silas said.

Jo walked over to Kere and grabbed her hand,
Malcolm on the side of her. Silas bent down and
grabbed Balor. He phased first as he transported Balor's
body to the In-between. Kere took Jo and Malcolm with
her.

Chapter Thirty
Ryan

She felt the shift immediately. Something had happened. She could feel the anxiety coming from Silas. It made her stomach uneasy; he was never anxious. Something horrible had happened. She found herself holding her aching chest and waiting. She didn't know why, but she knew they were coming here. Silas phased into the In-between; Balor was limp in his arms. Ryan started to move towards them, and her heart sank when she saw the demon blade that stuck out of her chest. She covered her mouth with her hand as she walked to him quickly.

"What happened? Is he?" Ryan asked; she couldn't bear to finish the rest of her sentence.

Jo, Malcolm, and Kere appeared behind Silas. Ryan noted the shimmer of light that seemed to radiate from Jo, and she knew the transition had happened. Her eyes looked to Silas, who was masked by his own pain.

"What happened?" Ryan asked as she walked over to Silas.

"Balor saved my life. I was caught up with Pavel dying when a shadow figure tried to kill me. Balor took the blow." Silas said through gritted teeth as he lowered Balor's body to the ground.

"He's gone." Ryan whispered, and her eyes went to Kere; the hurt and pain in Kere's eyes made Ryan's stomach turn.

"We're going to Hell to get him back." Silas said quietly.

"He...Silas. I..." Ryan said as fear rushed through her, but then she looked to Kere, and she knew if Silas was in Hell, she wouldn't have to ask Kere twice to go with her.

"What do you need from me?" Ryan asked, and the way Silas said we, it did not include her. She was ready to argue that she was going.

"His body hasn't turned to ash, and I think it's because the demon blade is still in him. We need you to look after his body. To keep it safe until we can get his soul back to it." Silas explained as he stood up and took Ryan's hand in his.

"I also need someone on the outside to make sure if anything happens-" Silas began to explain, but Ryan put her hand over his mouth. She did not want to think about anything happening to him, to any of them. It was not acceptable. It would not happen.

"Kere, I promise I will protect his body. We will get him back." Ryan vowed as she looked at Kere.

"Thank you." Kere said, her voice cracked a little, and she looked down to hold back her emotions.

"Silas, how are we getting to Hell exactly?" Malcolm asked as he cleared his throat..

"I have a friend." Silas nodded to the dock as the ferry pulled up.

"Charon." Ryan smiled.

The group slowly moved to the wooden dock as Charon stepped out of the boat with a smile on his face.

"I heard y'all are in need of a ride?" Charon smiled.

Silas grinned and walked over and clapped Charon on the back. Charon grinned back but then

frowned as his eyes landed on Balor's body not too far from the dock.

"You sure about this Silas, this is dangerous. Hell isn't for souls not condemned. You all could be lost." Charon warned.

"We're sure." Silas said firmly.

"Well, if I can't change your mind, you just need to pay the toll." Charon said as he held out his hand and moved aside.

Silas dropped four coins in his hand and nodded for Kere, Jo and Malcolm to get in.

Silas looked at the boat and then at Ryan and walked to her. His hand went to the back of her neck, and his mouth met hers. He kissed her fiercely and deeply before he broke the kiss.

"Silas, don't you dare be kissing me goodbye?" Ryan warned breathlessly.

"I'll be back before you even miss me." Silas smiled and kissed the top of her head.

"You better." Ryan whispered, if they don't come back, she would be going after them, and no one would get in her way, although she is the light piece to her and Silas. She remembered what it felt like to go dark, and she would go dark to save him and her friends. Without another word, he turned and got onto the ferry.

"Ms. Ryan staying behind?... That's good y'all might need someone to come rescue you." Charon laughed as he tipped his head to Ryan, got in the boat and pushed away from the dock.

The water was rocky as the ferry continued down the river. The waves splashed up over the boat. They were angrier than Silas remembered. There was

something more going on, and the In-between felt it. They crept along the invisible wall. It looked as if the world just ended. Silas saw Jo grab Malcolm's hand and brace herself. The boat sailed through, and in the next instant they heard scraping of rocks. Silas looked at the charcoal rocks that covered the landing, and Charon nodded. Silas followed the rocks to a large iron gate.

"You went around the hall of judgement?" Silas asked quietly.

"You do not need to be judged. So, I simply took you to one of the less used gates of Hell. Hopefully, you can slip in unnoticed." Charon said as he grabbed hold of Silas's shoulder and squeezed.

"Thank you, my friend." Silas nodded as he stepped onto the rocks.

"Stay safe and come back." Charon said as the rest piled out.

Charon pushed the ferryboat away from the rocky beach and drifted off towards the wall. He vanished as his ferry touched it. Silas looked up at the iron entrance to Hell and took a deep breath in.

"Ready," Silas said over his shoulder.

"Yes," Kere said and began to walk towards the gate; nothing was keeping Balor from her.

"I guess we will find out." Jo smiled and grabbed hold of Malcolm's hand as she started to the gate. Silas followed after them, not knowing what was ahead for them, but he knew that they would get through this together.

The Figure

He grinned as he touched the container of souls. He had made it out of Earth with it, and now he needed to hide it some place so deep in the underworld no one would find it. He had successfully killed one thorn in his side. He had hated Balor since the dawn of their existence. He was grateful when he left hell and did not return. Killing him was perfect. If Balor was truly the light to Kere, if she went dark, then it would be better then Malcolm going dark. He could simply follow behind her and collect forgotten souls. He may have lost Earth and the In-between but he would not lose Hell. He would take souls from down here and harness their power. Devour them, place them inside of himself and use them as a power source. Once he was more powerful than anyone in any realm, he would rule them all. Plus, Hell has an army he could take with him. He should have started here and not with Nyx. He was stupid to think she would have been the one to help him. Pavel was easy because he had already been plotting his own takeover. Now he would start by recruiting some low class demons to his army and move quickly from there. This was not over yet.

S.E Dymek's Other works:

The Alpha's War Series:

Between the Alpha's War
Breaking the Alpha Council
The Beta's Betrayal

The Star Saga:

The Morning Star
The Evening Star
The North Star

Coming Soon:

Saving Hell Book Three in the Trilogy of Light and Dark:

"CJ, you have repeatedly lived each life in the worst possible way. You have committed all seven of the deadly sins."

"For some reason, up until now, someone has been making exceptions for you. Someone wanted to see you succeed; this council doesn't believe very much in reincarnation, and now you are here. We belleve you reap what you sow. CJ, you have done nothing for the world, and you are sentenced to Hades, to hell."

"Jax...take her away"

CJ has never made it past the age of twenty-nine in any life. She has made sure she has gone down the worst possible path each time. This time there was no going back for another try. She finds herself in Hell, trapped in a cell with her own personal

294

tormentor, Jax. Jax one second in command to the king of Hell himself, has dropped down through the ranks and now is a lowly tormentor. He's done well at his new job and has goals of climbing back up the ranks to the top, that was until he stepped foot into her cell. His eyes locked with hers, and he felt something click inside of him. He could not be her tormentor, never mind leaving her to rot in Hell. Is he willing to throw it all away for her? Can she be the key to Saving Hell from the corruption that is now taking over?